TROUBLED QUEEN

The Marwood Family Saga
Book Two

Amy Licence

SAPERE
BOOKS

TROUBLED QUEEN

Published by Sapere Books.

24 Trafalgar Road, Ilkley, LS29 8HH

saperebooks.com

ISBN: 978-1-80055-723-9

To Rufus and Robin

With serving still
This I have won,
For my goodwill
To be undone.

And for redress
Of all my pain,
Disdainfulness
I have again.

And for reward
Of all my smart,
Lo, thus unheard,
I must depart.

Wherefore all ye
That after shall
By fortune be,
As I am, thrall,

Example take
What I have won,
Thus for her sake
To be undone.

Thomas Wyatt

ONE

The sun fell warmly upon Thomasin Marwood's back. She paused on the path, curving her lips into a smile, feeling those welcome rays blossom through the dark silk of her bodice. Spring was coming. Glorious, green, warm spring. It had to arrive eventually, but how long it had taken. How good it felt now, how hopeful, like the first spring ever.

It was four months since Thomasin's arrival at Windsor. At the age of seventeen, she had been accepted into the household of Queen Catherine of Aragon, to help wait upon the lady who had shown her family such kindness.

It was certainly a change from what she was used to. The ancient grey castle was a stark contrast to the rolling green fields and orchards of Suffolk, where she had spent almost all her youth. The rest of her family had returned there, after a brief visit to court last November, when her sister's intended marriage had failed.

Sometimes Thomasin envied them, sitting before the fire in the great hall or seeing the snow lightly dust the roof and chimneys of her beloved Eastwell Hall. Their letters were frequent, and had brought her great comfort. Her mother Elizabeth's health was improving and her father Richard had been newly elected as a Justice of the Peace, and was busy presiding over the local courts. The younger children were thriving and her elder sister Cecilia, Mother wrote, was healing her broken heart by taking long walks and plying her needle in embroidery. Thomasin had smiled at that. It hardly sounded like the Cecilia she had known, but the last few months had changed them all.

Thomasin turned to face the sun. It was a harsh, unforgiving sort of light. She screwed up her brown eyes, lifted her pert little chin. Queen Catherine had once described her beauty as earthy, like that of a milkmaid, brown as a nut or berry. Thomasin did not object to such backhanded compliments. It was pleasant to be noticed by the queen, and such words were often accompanied by a request to come and play cards, or to sing, or brush out Catherine's long hair, to help the long days pass.

Shadows moved before Thomasin's eyes, making her blink with the sudden contrast. Dark then light, dazzlingly so. She shaded her eyes with her hand, looking up to see her cousin, Ellen.

"Look, look here." Ellen was holding out a tiny flower, its creamy yellow petals crumpled between her fingers. "The first primrose!"

Thomasin smiled, but despite the sunshine, she shivered.

Windsor could hardly be described as warm. Or exciting. Neither she nor Ellen had known what it was going to be like when they accepted the placement with such enthusiasm. All they had in comparison was the king's court, the glittering, heady, intoxicating whirl of life that centred around Henry VIII and his beloved, the controversial Anne Boleyn.

Thomasin could not deny that she had felt at her most alive in those weeks, dressed in gold, dancing by candlelight, with Sir Henry Norris's arm around her waist. Yet there had been things said and done, such cruelty and games played, that the thought of them turned her stomach. There had been too many secrets, too much heartbreak, and such painful revelations, which stung her to the core. By the end of the

Marwoods' stay in London in October, Thomasin had been questioning everything: her family, her past, her very self, her nature.

Catherine's court was a world away from Anne Boleyn's. Quiet, modest, dignified. Yet sometimes, it was a little lifeless, barren even, although Thomasin would never dare voice such a thought.

During the long winter months, they had been cooped up inside the castle like cattle, stifling at the fireside or shivering in the corridor, the sun rising late and slinking away before the afternoon had taken hold. Huddled in their furs, they had played cards, read aloud together, sung songs of happier times. They'd hurried across the courtyard into the chapel at early morning or evensong, the darkness lit by tapers.

The season had bitten deep. Snow had piled in drifts against the walls and icicles hung off the castle stones. Ponds and puddles froze solid. But now, at last, there was a sweetness in the air. Even in this little half-moon garden, in the lea of the Round Tower, the warm light spilled over the clipped hedges, paths and flowerbeds.

"This way," called Ellen. "They're here."

Thomasin seized her blue velvet and tawny silk skirts and picked her way along the path towards her cousin. She passed between the topiary birds, looking rather threadbare now, and turned sharp right to hug the inside of the castle wall, which offered a little shelter from the wind.

Ellen was pointing down at the ground. Following her gaze, Thomasin saw the shy faces of primroses starting to unfold, making pale yellow stars against the soil. The newly gravelled path was hard under her soft-soled shoes; shoes which had been new when she'd arrived at court last autumn, and were now worn down by stone steps and wooden boards, with barely any outside use. The silk dress had been new too, a gift from Queen Catherine, and far better quality than any she had owned before. The hint of warm orange-brown tawny was welcome, although Catherine generally liked her ladies to wear sombre tones.

"Ah, the primroses are about to open."

"Look, there, see their little faces." Ellen pointed to the soil, with something like a smile.

It lifted Thomasin's heart, knowing the heaviness her cousin carried in her breast. Poor young Ellen, with her round, innocent face, had been so enchanted with court life, with the king and queen, ribbons and weddings. She had been five years married to Thomasin's cousin, Barnaby Russell, with a considerable estate outside Buxton, but last November, her world had come crashing down. Now Barnaby had returned north in disgrace, while Ellen's own sister, Dorothy, was set to deliver his child.

Thomasin placed a gentle hand upon her arm. "You found them. Spring is almost here and then the queen will travel. We shall have such adventures, meet new people."

"I hope you are right," Ellen whispered, managing a brief smile. "I need new company, new friends."

"You know I am right," replied Thomasin, with optimism. "We are all in need of new company." And they came again: the deep, rich, brown eyes with their tapering lashes. She quickly shrugged off the memory. It was no good thinking of Rafe Danvers, the man who had captivated her last autumn. He was gone now. Gone for good.

Ellen laced her arm through Thomasin's. "Come, let's walk."

Small birds rose up from the bushes ahead, flying to safety on top of the thick surrounding walls. Sparrows, perhaps, or dunnocks, maybe a pair of wrens. Thomasin wished she had some crumbs to throw to them. Instead, her eye lighted on a patch of colour.

"Oh, look there, under the vine, is that a bluebell?"

They hurried forward together. The small, shy bells with curling edges were just braving the air.

"Yes, bluebells!" Thomasin smiled to see her old favourites again. They would be lining the paths at Eastwell right now, their delicate shapes swaying in the soft Suffolk air.

"The vines will be in bud again within weeks," Ellen noted, following the sturdy trunk upwards with her eyes.

The branches had been pollarded, trimmed close and trained along ropes, so they grew in straight lines out from the centre. Tiny green shoots had begun to appear between the bark, promising the green flowers that led to grapes. By the summer, they would be thick with leaves and fruit. It had felt strange to think of summer in the depths of winter, or even at the start of spring, as if such a concept was always just out of reach.

"Look, Thomasin." Ellen turned to her cousin, but Thomasin was looking back down the path that led to the castle, along which two figures were slowly approaching, deep in conversation. First came the short, stout figure of Queen Catherine and then the round, equally short outline of the Imperial ambassador, Bishop Mendoza, marking her like a shadow. The sun fell upon the diamonds and pearls about the queen's forehead and throat, and upon the sparkling stones on the bishop's fingers.

At once, Thomasin and Ellen bowed their heads and curtseyed low.

Catherine of Aragon approached, dressed in an orange and gold gown, embroidered with pomegranates and roses. The gold laces were tight about her waist, and Spanish embroidery ringed her wrists, plump after years of the best food the court could offer, and the worst personal heartbreaks. She had borne six children, yet only one of them had survived beyond the first few weeks. And that one was a girl. A talented, smart, precocious girl, as many observed the Princess Mary to be, but a girl nevertheless, and girls could not rule kingdoms. It was this cruel hand of fortune that underpinned all the queen's present troubles.

Catherine's youthful beauty was still visible in the soft, round face framed by the gold gable bonnet. Her bright blue eyes and red-gold hair, with its grey streaks tucked away, betrayed her Plantagenet heritage, several generations back.

As the pair drew near, Catherine beckoned to the waiting women. "Ladies, please remove my fur collar, the sun proves warmer than I thought." She turned her back and stood still while Thomasin and Ellen hurried to lift the veil on the back of her headdress and locate the ties that kept the fur in place.

Waiting beside her, Bishop Mendoza continued their conversation as if no one else were present. "Dear Lady, I have told you so many times. You are not to blame for this situation; it came about through no fault of your own. You have ever been a virtuous, dutiful, obedient wife, and you have weathered the storms it has pleased God to send you."

The faltering marriage between King Henry and Queen Catherine was no longer a secret at court. After nineteen years together, the king had questioned its legality, recalling her marriage to his elder brother Arthur. The young prince Arthur had died, not yet reaching his sixteenth summer, and Catherine had always maintained that they had never shared a bed as man and wife. That she was a maid, pure and untouched, when she married Henry, eight years later. He had always believed her, until recently. Until he'd realised she would not give him a son.

Now Henry had turned to his ministers: the shrewd Cardinal Wolsey and his secretary, the slippery Thomas Cromwell, to find some precedent in canon law that could dissolve the union. Despite the court that had been convened at York Place last year, no resolution had been reached, the Pope had proved unwilling, and Catherine had refused to enter a nunnery. So the matter rumbled on, Catherine at Windsor, Henry and Anne at Westminster.

"But if I had followed my husband's wishes more?" replied Catherine, shaking her head, so that Thomasin lost hold of the lace she was untying. "Perhaps I allied myself too closely with the emperor's cause, made my interest in the Spanish match too clear, when I knew that the king favoured an alliance with the French?"

"It was natural for you to do so," said Mendoza. "The emperor is your nephew, the son of your sister, and you have cared for him with something like the feelings of a mother."

"I have done so. I have defended him as I would a son."

"Even when he broke off his betrothal to the Princess Mary."

"Yes," she said sadly, "even then. And even when he married the Portuguese Princess. But if I had supported the king's plans instead of speaking against the French, perhaps Henry would not be displeased with me. Perhaps if I wrote to him now…"

The bishop paused and wheezed. "No, no, no, My Lady, none of this is your doing. It is entirely a matter that has arisen in the mind of the king. You have nothing to reproach yourself for. Turn to God, ask for his forgiveness and help; it will be given to you."

Thomasin finished untying her side of the laces and gently lifted the fur collar from around Catherine's shoulders. She folded it towards Ellen, who placed it over her arm.

Catherine rolled her shoulders in relief and cast a quick look behind her.

"Keep close, in case I have need of it again."

Thomasin and Ellen fell in step a little way behind the glittering pair, but still within earshot.

"Your connection with the emperor was worth strengthening," continued Mendoza, "because he now has the Pope in his custody, and can command him as he needs, so the annulment will not be pronounced, no matter how many messengers the king might send."

They turned the corner, by the primroses, which went unnoticed, heading back towards the Tower.

"I have heard," said Catherine, looking up at the vast, round edifice that lay at the heart of the complex, "that Wolsey has applied for a commission to hold a papal trial in London."

"He can apply, but the Pope is not in a position to grant it. Clement will procrastinate and make excuses in the hope that Henry will come to his senses."

"That will only enrage Henry more. I fear for my daughter and her future."

Mendoza leaned in, confidentially. "You know the Spanish will never allow harm to come to her. There would be an army of thousands, six or seven, ready to land on the south coast if the princess is put aside, and more would rise in England. You and Princess Mary are beloved of the people. Surely her father, who dotes on her, knows this? Surely he would never do so?"

Catherine was less convinced. "Once I would have agreed with you, but these days, I find I know him less and less. I had thought to write to my nephew again. He understands it is my calling to be Queen of England. God made this my destiny. I cannot turn away from his will, and I fear for my husband's eternal soul if he persists in this course."

"Now that England and France have declared war upon the emperor, you must not write. It would be considered treason to write to the king's enemy, and you do not wish to give your enemies that excuse."

Catherine thought hard. "Unless some secret way can be devised. A new cipher, a different messenger?"

"I do believe, My Lady, that the risk would be too great."

She sighed and drew herself up to her full height. Although she was not a tall woman, Catherine was still regal in her bearing. "Then I will continue in my prayers, asking that my husband be removed from temptation."

"From the lady Anne?" Mendoza raised his straggling eyebrows. "I will add that to my prayers."

They were nearing the gate, where the carved arch bore the royal arms. A short walk took them across the Upper Ward towards the privy steps that led up to the queen's watching chamber.

A page in the queen's livery hurried out and bowed low.

"What is it?" asked Catherine, always impatient for news.

"Please, My Lady, the Venetian ambassadors have confirmed their visit."

"When?"

"Tomorrow. They will arrive between ten and noon."

Catherine turned to the bishop with a look of triumph. "There. Ambassador. I am not quite forgotten. I am queen yet."

He inclined his head with a smile. "As ever, My Lady."

TWO

Footsteps and voices in the corridor outside roused Thomasin from her dreams. The waking hour was approaching at Windsor, and the early servants were bringing coal and wood to rekindle the fires. The light in the chamber was dim, and the air hung heavy with sleep and smoke.

Thomasin had been on duty at Catherine's bedside. Once a week the women took turns to pass the night in the painted chamber, with its silver and gold drapes and the piles of embroidered cushions. They helped Catherine undress, prayed with her, and read to her from *The Lives of the Saints*, before sleeping on one of the low truckle beds that were hidden away during daylight hours.

Catherine had only woken twice, through discomfort, complaining of the aches in her bones and wanting her legs rubbed with salve. That smell of mint and thyme, that oily balm, belonged in Thomasin's mind to the darkest midnight hours. But now that the daylight was streaming in, there was no time to notice her own stiff limbs, or the cold, or her thirst, as the maids brought in a bowl of water, soap and towels, and Catherine was calling for assistance to rise.

"Quickly," she urged, "quick fingers today. We have much to do before the ambassadors arrive."

Thomasin grappled with the material, arranging the skirts, smoothing out the hem, while her head still reeled with sleep.

Catherine was impatient. Although she stood perfectly still, statuesque, Thomasin could feel the tension in her body, the nervous desire to be active, to proceed with the day, with fate, with the future. "Come, come," she urged, "I must away, to chapel, to chapel, to God."

All around them, Windsor was waking. Thomasin and Ellen followed Catherine through the corridors, past great windows and paintings, grey in the morning light. Ahead of them, candles and tapers were lit, budding into life with welcome flames. They passed open doors where the workers dressed the castle's chambers in their gaudy best: carpets were dusted and draped across tables, patterned with exotic designs; cushions were beaten until the dust rose out of them in clouds; carved chairs were positioned.

Dozens of hands unrolled and shook out the hangings of gold and silver; feet climbed ladders against wooden panelling and careful fingers hung the drapes from unseen hooks. Fabric billowed like sails, glinting in the dim light, descending in soft waves. Catherine's coat of arms, embroidered upon red tissue, were given the central position behind the chair of estate. Passing through, Thomasin saw the special touches being made for the Venetians and felt a mounting sense of excitement.

It was necessary to cross the courtyard to reach the chapel. The wind was harsh and Thomasin shivered under her thin cloak. It was a hard climb up the steep steps, while sleep still clung about her, before they reached the cool mustiness of St George's. Here, the bones of the king's forebears lay in repose, and the air carried a sense of expectation.

Thomasin and Ellen joined the other waiting women kneeling in a semi-circle behind the queen, as Catherine prostrated herself before the altar. Candles flickered as she lay her forehead upon the cool stones. Thomasin had been surprised when she had first seen Catherine do this, but she had quickly learned it was her way. Catherine took her faith seriously, not merely as a virtue, but as an example of piety to be modelled for her people. It was her very core, her true devotion, that made her pray like this, for hours each day. She denied plates of food when she was fasting, and refused to sleep when she was keeping a vigil.

Thomasin knelt in the centre of the women, their heads respectfully bowed. Over the winter months, she had come to know the companions of her long hours at Catherine's side; she shared with them her duties, her meals and her leisure hours. Beside Ellen, there was the dark-haired Gertrude, with her melancholy eyes and the stout, smiling Mary, who had advice for them all.

To her left knelt the Spanish Maria Willoughby, neé Salinas, who spoke in a rapid, lilting tongue, and whose English was still thick and stilted. Often, in the evening, Catherine slipped into her native Spanish, and their talk would race away into the past, before Catherine would remember herself, smile at her English companions and steer the conversation back. Finally, beside Thomasin herself was Maria's young daughter, the nine-year-old Catherine, tiny and delicate like a little bird, whom Thomasin had met in Catherine's rooms last year.

"Let me take your arm," said Catherine to Thomasin, as she rose from prayer. "I feel unsteady; it is time to break my fast."

They emerged from the chapel's gloom. The sky had changed from a pale grey to broken clouds, static as they hung above. Descending in pairs, Thomasin noticed a figure in a dark, furred cloak, waiting at the bottom of the steps. The queen's chamberlain, William Blount, Lord Mountjoy, was approaching his fifties, a man of gentle gravity and much learning whom Thomasin had found kind and fair to all. She had noted his friendship with Thomas More, on the handful of occasions when the scholar had visited Catherine's court, riding over from Chelsea.

"My Lady." The chamberlain bowed low.

"What is it, Mountjoy, that cannot wait?"

"I thought you would wish to know, My Lady, that the ambassadors have been sighted on the road."

Catherine lost no composure. "I go to break my fast. Let them have wine and pastries in my watching chamber."

"Very good, My Lady."

And Catherine swept across the courtyard, like a galleon in sail, moments before the horsemen thundered up to the outer gate.

The great hall was decked with gold and silver. Flames roared in the hearth. Minstrels in the gallery played a lively, upbeat tune, with the sounds of the trumpets and rebec reaching up to the rafters.

Catherine sat in her chair of state, resplendent in red and gold with the arms of England, Aragon and Castile behind her. Chains and jewels hung in great ropes about her neck, and the folds of her black and white skirts had been carefully arranged by Maria and Ellen. Her back was straight, her head held high, her Spanish bonnet tidy, her tiny hands clasped over the chair's carved arms. The very picture of a queen.

Catherine's waiting women were ranged about her in absolute stillness. Either side of the throne, they were fixed in position, like a living tableau, each pair of eyes upon the doors ahead. They understood their strict instructions; the code of rules by which they lived, although such visitations were rare. It was a long time since outsiders had come to visit Catherine, let alone foreign ambassadors.

Thomasin stood beside Gertrude, on Catherine's left, with Ellen over to the right. Still and straight, her only motion was her breath, in and out, rhythmic, loud in her ears. She held her limbs utterly motionless, as Catherine had instructed, no matter how strong the urge to fidget and twitch. For they were not women right now; the only woman in the room was Catherine, the others were furniture. Like a picture, they waited, poised as if the artist's brush was flickering across a canvas before them, capturing them in paint. The minutes ticked by. The waiting was agony.

To the side, Bishop Mendoza in his full costume and the Spanish scholar Juan Luis Vives, with other learned gentlemen, sat posed upon stuffed chairs. The musical notes washed over them: the taut plucking of strings and the breathy flights of recorder and pipe. Catherine had a small circle of gentlemen who preferred her court to that of the king, and those who came were fiercely loyal to her.

"Chins lifted, stand straight," Catherine whispered, so only her ladies could hear. "Show dignity, eyes above them."

The hall waited. The doors at the far end did not move. Thomasin's shoulders ached from the strain.

From the other side of the dais came a snuffling noise, midway between a sniff and a sneeze.

"Hush!" hissed Catherine. "Silence."

Again, they waited, waited, waited as the moments ticked away.

Finally, they heard the approaching feet of a number of people. In the stillness, the sound echoed along the corridor leading towards the watching chamber, growing louder and louder as Thomasin held her breath in anticipation. At the far end, the double doors flung open. Noise burst in upon the women.

Lord Mountjoy came first, striding forward in his confident way. Behind him, he conjured a party of twelve gaudy gentlemen, quite a caravan of colour and exoticism, that prompted the women to take a collective breath. For a moment both sides looked at each other, as if they were the dancers at the start of a masque. Then the men came forward, each a dazzling star amid this new constellation, dressed in riding habits and boots over soft leather and taffeta, but each had a little personal addition somewhere — a feather, an earring — and touches of gold, giving them the air of importance. Perhaps in their own country, they were princes, dukes or noblemen of vast estates, with vineyards dripping down green hillsides, or the owners of merchant ships returning from the spice trail. Their leader wore a wide-brimmed, green hat, which he pulled off with a flourish as he bowed low. He was a lean, tanned man of middling height, whose elongated features certainly did not look English.

Mountjoy signalled upwards. The music abruptly halted and the trumpeters blew a final rapport. "The Ambassador to the Doge and Signoria of Venice, Signore Marco Antonio Vernier and his company."

The Venetians advanced a step, before removing their hats in the same manner as their leader and bowing low. Moving in perfect unison, they made an impressive sight.

Catherine beckoned for them to rise. "Gentlemen, you are welcome at Windsor."

Vernier remained on one knee. "Most gracious Lady. We could not be visiting your esteemed country without making a detour here to pay our respects to Your most excellent Majesty, of whom we have heard such wonderful praise, of your learning, your piety, your dignity." His voice was stilted, with long vowels, but rich.

Thomasin sensed that Catherine was pleased. It was a most flattering address, and the ambassador was an elegant gentleman, perhaps in his late thirties. When he spoke, his face had an animation about it, which, added to the timbre of his voice, was attractive. *Attractive for a foreigner*, Thomasin thought, surprised at herself.

Vernier rose to his full height and threw back his cloak, giving them an opportunity to admire the expensive clothes beneath. His doublet was embroidered with cherry coloured thread and sewn with tiny pearls and gold laces.

"It is our great honour to present you with these humble gifts," he said, gesturing his men forwards. "For Your Majesty, we have rolls of the best coloured silks, metres of our famous golden lace, bottled orange preserves and our fortified wines, brewed with local spices, sweet yet not too strong; perfect for a queen's dining table."

One by one, the men laid their bundles at the queen's feet. Catherine sat aloof and watched them accrue.

"And for your ladies-in-waiting," Vernier continued, smiling along the line, "such pleasant, welcoming, beautiful ladies, I bring dates, almonds, comfits, the purest white writing paper for their letters, and silken ribbons."

Catherine eyed the spread, making her guests wait for approval. Thomasin could not help but turn her gaze upon the colourful display.

"These are most generous gifts." Catherine paused again, looking at them each in turn. The Venetians were poised, erect, holding themselves still before her approval. Her face softened a little. "I thank you, and bid you welcome. How was your journey?"

Vernier grinned and relaxed. "Most troublesome, My Lady, and we are grateful to have arrived safely. We came by land —

taking the shortest route through Switzerland, Germany and the Low Countries, keeping to the north of the border with France — but we ran into trouble, as French troops tried to detain us more than once."

"Of course," mused Catherine, "the Italian states are at war with the French again. However, Signore, since my husband declared for Francis, that should, in theory, make you England's enemy too."

This observation did not deter the smooth Vernier. "My Lady, we are aware that your husband has chosen to side with France, which is why we did not take him so many gifts." He paused to appreciate the ladies' smiles. "But we know that Your Majesty's vision is wider; with your Spanish heritage and blood ties to the Empire, you see a larger Europe. You are a stateswoman in your own right, who is no enemy of Venice."

"You are the consummate courtier, Signore Vernier. I wonder that the ladies of Venice allowed you to leave. Tell me, are you as honest as you are flattering?"

The ambassador inclined his head. "Why, My Lady, of course, you have my word."

"You have been first to visit my husband at Westminster?"

"Yes, My Lady, as protocol dictates."

"And how fares he there? Is he merry?"

"As merry as he can be, My Lady, without yourself at his side."

Catherine gave a wry smile. "Come now, Signore, you can do better than that. You are not at all in ignorance about the state of my private affairs. It is a secret that has been leaked across Europe."

"My Lady…"

"So tell me, truly, is he merry?"

"It is true that such sad news had, indeed, reached us in Venice." Vernier looked about, trying to catch Mountjoy's eye for affirmation, but the baron kept up a very English, stoic detachment. "If I may speak plainly, Your Majesty, and within these walls only, I would say that I do not believe the king to be in his right senses while he entertains thoughts of separation from your good self. It is my opinion, My Lady, that the king cannot be truly merry, even when he thinks himself so, while he fails to value such a jewel as yourself."

Catherine was not so easily won. "But he does believe himself to be, does he not? Did he dance? Make merry with his friends? He always seems to be merry these days."

"Yes," admitted Vernier, unfazed. "I saw him making merry. But it was a false jollity, a forced gaiety, a distraction for his uneasy mind."

"You believe his mind to be troubled?"

"He strikes me, My Lady, as a huntsman chasing an elusive hart, which he can never reach."

"He can never reach?" asked Catherine, with greater interest.

"Of course not, My Lady. What he seeks is unattainable. He is temporarily misguided, under unwholesome influences, chasing dreams. The Pope will never grant his wishes and his temporary infatuation will fade."

There was a pause. Vernier had directly voiced what had been whispered for so long.

Thomasin wondered if Catherine would ask about Anne Boleyn, or liken her to the elusive hart, pursued by the king. But if Catherine considered clarifying the metaphor, she decided not to voice such a thought.

"Sir, you are bold to speak thus," she said slowly, watching Vernier to judge the effect of her words. The Venetian's face did not flicker. "But your boldness is welcome in a place where most people are too cowed to speak. Perhaps it is your foreignness that makes you so."

"Perhaps," he smiled, revealing a line of even white teeth, "or perhaps it is just that I say what I see."

"You have no fear of speaking the truth?"

"No man should fear the truth," Vernier flashed back. "And no woman, either."

Catherine rose to her feet. "Thank you for your gifts." She indicated for her women to collect them, and Thomasin hurried forward with the others to sweep up bundles of silk ribbons and laces.

Catherine offered Vernier her arm. "If you will accompany me to my chambers, a banquet awaits us."

Thomasin watched them lead the way, then followed on with the other ladies, carrying the gifts into the antechamber before rejoining Catherine in her painted rooms. Catherine was deep in conversation with Vernier and two others of the Venetian gentlemen, as the rest partook of the delights of the table. Maria Willoughby was conversing with one in Spanish and Gertrude's dark beauty had attracted admirers, each offering her different sweetmeats on gold plates.

Thomasin resumed her place with the queen.

"Do not worry," whispered Mary, Countess of Essex, sidling up, "we've been given permission to eat. Serve yourself, before it all goes."

Thomasin smiled, needing no more encouragement. The table stretched before her with its colourful display of pasties, pies, larks, flans, meats, gingerbreads and marchpane.

"Might I tempt you with these, sweet lady?"

One of the Venetians had approached her, bearing a plate of spiced apples. He was a heavy-set man with a wide face and prominent eyes, which were fixed upon her.

Usually Thomasin liked apples, but something about his manner made her reluctant to accept one. The thought struck her that she would have preferred to take them with her own hand.

"I thank you, sir, but they are not to my taste."

He would not be deterred, but cast his gaze across the table. "In which case, is there anything else I might offer you? Something sweeter, perhaps?"

"Thank you, but I am quite able to help myself. That is the custom here."

He put down the plate at once.

"I have no doubt you are," he smiled broadly, and came even closer. "What would you recommend?"

She sighed but recalled her manners. "Whatever your good self desires. The wafers are especially fine."

To her dismay, he scooped up the plate, taking one of the delicacies and holding it up to his face. Yet he did not eat as she had expected, but inhaled.

"Ah, cinnamon, that sweetest of spices, and nutmeg, I believe. Almond too. A true wedding of flavours."

And with that, he finally took a bite, showing exaggerated appreciation on his face.

Thomasin turned away to conceal her smile at the theatricality of his performance.

Once he had finished, he inched even closer. "I wonder what good English name was bestowed upon such a fair lady by her honourable parents?"

So far, nothing in Thomasin's training for the queen's household had quite prepared her for this, but after four months, she understood Catherine's expectations.

"I am Lady Thomasin Marwood, my Lord."

"Thomasin Marwood," he repeated slowly, dwelling on the vowels like a caress. "Tho-ma-sin Maaar-wood. Such a melodious name."

Protocol dictated her reply. "And you are?"

He stood up straight, thrust out his chest. "I am Signore Matteo Vitruvio of Venice."

Thomasin bowed her head in acknowledgement, refusing to dissect his name as he had done to hers.

"Might I, dear lady Thomasin, ask a question of you?"

"Yes, you may, Signore."

"Did you like the gifts we brought your mistress? The silks and orange preserves?"

Thomasin reminded herself of the formalities. They were playing hosts to the Venetians, and gifts were never just gifts; they came with expectations, and there were clear diplomatic answers which the situation required her to offer. She retreated into them now. "They are very splendid gifts; you honour us by bringing them."

"Would you like to earn some of those yourself? An allowance of silks, or golden lace, or a small payment, now and again?"

"Earn?"

"Yes, earn a little, in the service of your mistress."

Thomasin looked over to where Vernier had picked up a lute to strum a tune for Catherine. "How do you propose I do that?"

The Venetian looked about cautiously. "I am sure you write the most beautiful letters. Perhaps you might be willing to write them to me, once a month, when I have returned to Venice, to give me news of how you do."

"News of how I do?"

"How you fare. I would like to have a lady to write to, to improve my English."

"It seems to me that your English is quite good enough."

He smiled, a wide, predatory gesture. "There is always room for improvement, is there not?"

"I suppose there is."

"And, when you write to me, perhaps you might mention how your mistress fares, just by way of subject matter. Tell me about yourself, but also who she sees and how her case is unfolding? For a good price and many gifts, of course. Silks and oranges and wine."

"And I suppose you would not wish me to tell the queen about this correspondence?"

He smiled again, with bulging eyes, and spread his hands wide. "There would be no need to trouble her with it, as she already has so much on her mind."

"I am sure it would be no bother to Her Majesty at all. I will ask her after the banquet."

"Oh, no, no, there is no need. Let it be a little arrangement between ourselves, Mistress."

Thomasin inclined her head. "If you will excuse me, I have much to do."

"Of course, dear Lady, of course. Please think on it. Remember, my name is Matteo, Matteo Vitruvio of Venice. Remember it."

Pondering his suspicious request, Thomasin returned to the table, but as she picked out the delicacies before her, she watched the ambassadors with new eyes. Vernier kept his attention wholly for the queen, but she soon noticed that his gentlemen had scattered and each, alone, had singled out one Catherine's ladies. There was an earnestness about them, a particular drive in their friendliness that went beyond mere diplomacy. It was, perhaps, more of a concerted policy being put into action, a pattern of attack. She looked back at Vernier, with his slick manner and knowledgeable dark eyes. Watching him in action, she felt sure that his elegant show towards the queen was a veneer to conceal something else.

"They are very attentive," said Ellen, appearing at her side.

"Too much so," Thomasin whispered back. "I do not quite trust it."

"And very keen to give away gifts. The tall one offered me silks and laces."

Thomasin turned to her. "Oh, really? Did he ask you to do anything in return?"

"He asked me to write a few letters, about…"

"The queen and court? Where she goes? Who she sees?"

Ellen's pretty eyes widened. "Why, yes! You too?"

"I had the same."

"Mine was named Enrico."

"Mine was Matteo."

They both looked towards Catherine, listening intently as Vernier recounted a story.

"There is something more to this visit," Thomasin went on, nodding towards them. "More than I can see. We just do not know what it is yet."

"You think there is something sinister, pertaining to the queen?"

"We cannot say yet. It may be entirely innocent, but we must be watchful."

"Indeed." Ellen fixed her dark eyes upon Vernier. "Watchful. Let watchful be the watchword."

THREE

Windsor's upper courtyard had been transformed. Red and gold pavilions formed a rippling semi-circle, ready to shelter the queen and her guests against the wind. Their bright embroidery featured the royal arms, with lions and fleur-de-lys, unicorns and dragons, while lines of colourful flags strung between them fluttered in the breeze. Braziers burned around the outside, filling the gloomy day with bright flames and the spicy tang of the perfumed pastilles that had been placed amid the hot coals.

Catherine paused on the castle steps and clasped her jewelled hands together. "Oh, that scent in the air!" She turned to Vernier at her side. "You smell it? Cedar wood and musk."

The Venetian paused and turned his face to the wind. He made an elaborate gesture of breathing in through his long nose, slow and deep. "Ah, it comes back to me. As if I was sitting in St Mark's Square. The scent of home."

"The same for me, like walking through the Alhambra, the scent of home. Shall we?"

He offered his gloved hand, and she took it.

Thomasin followed Catherine as she processed across the grass, the ladies in a tight-knit train behind their mistress. Their skirts made a colourful line, with different shades of blues, greens and browns, each displaying touches of white at the sleeves or wrists, tawny or yellow details and a string of pearls or a jewelled pendant about their throats.

Even from far back in the line, Thomasin could see Vernier walking at the front, still engaging Catherine in conversation, with his sharp, witty quips that made her smile. The other

Venetians strutted along behind him, a snake of silver and gold that ran alongside the ladies. They were a tall, proud company, slick and elegant, and used to receiving attention. Among them, Thomasin spotted the wide-eyed Matteo, who had attempted to win her over before with his proposition. Even now, as her face was turned his way, he tried to catch her eye again and flashed her a smile, but she only inclined her head politely and looked away.

Chairs and cushions awaited them under the canopies. Thomasin and Ellen were seated to the left of Catherine and Vernier — close, but not close enough to hear any of their conversation.

Thomasin looked over to where the rest of the queen's household were turning out to view the entertainment. They came out of the bowels of the castle, the middling employees from the laundry and wardrobe, cellars and antechambers, summoned by anticipation, leaving behind their work and empty corridors. The only people left inside were toiling over the boiling pots and roasting spits, or sweeping the straw out of corners or swilling the soiled pots.

The castle ran on a strict system where everyone knew their place and none were foolish enough to step outside it. Now those middle servants took seats on wooden benches or leaning against the wall, surprised by the sudden holiday. Thomasin knew them by their faces and roles: the girl who lit the fire, the man who brought the water or the fresh linen. The little red-haired seamstress who had mended Thomasin's hem returned her look with a smile. It was a revelation to see just how many people were involved in the complicated machinery of the court, especially as this was only the queen's court.

Thomasin's eyes were drawn back to the green. Four tall stands, or posts, were being prepared for action, where the keeper of the queen's birds was tending to the falcons. The birds sat patiently on these, each on their own little platform, hooded and tied by the foot, awaiting their orders, and Thomasin could not help but feel that in some way, their situation echoed hers.

It wasn't that she disliked her position with the queen; serving Catherine was a quiet, busy and sober task, in her chamber and chapel, and although she frequently proved to be a generous, kindly mistress, Thomasin sometimes paused, took a breath and found the days merging together. There was a restlessness inside her now, a sense of unease that had grown, day by day, through the long, dark months.

They'd been stuck at Windsor for so long, through the entombed winter, that she longed to see a different view. Her feet itched to walk down paths outside the castle walls, and even their rides into the forest now felt familiar. If only she could glimpse London or Suffolk, or anywhere in between, any place new would do. She looked across the ward, which was filling up with members of the queen's household. If nothing else, the ambassadors' visit was a splash of colour amid the routine.

Lord Mountjoy approached Catherine and bowed low. "My Lady, Thomas More has arrived." His face betrayed his pleasure; the pair had been friends since their youth.

"More? It has been a while. Send him across to join us."

Thomasin looked up at the name. Last autumn, she had been fortunate enough to speak with More and his eldest daughter, Margaret, on a few occasions, so that she felt bold enough to call them friends. They were an intelligent, cultured family, and she had enjoyed the time she spent with them. More's thoughts about an ideal society, outlined in his book *Utopia*, had taken hold of her mind, although she'd not have the chance to explore them further due to her duties at Windsor. Instead, it hovered at the edges of her world like a new landscape, visible and waiting to be discovered.

More's tall, lean figure was instantly recognisable as he headed across the grass, wrapped in brown furs and wearing his habitual expression of interest. His dark eyes were intent, almost fierce. Yet he was looking older and more tired, and Thomasin wondered how much the king had been calling upon his services lately. His knowledge of canon law was second to none, and Henry's marital dilemma demanded that no stone be left unturned. No doubt More had been burning the candles late into the night at Westminster.

Behind him came the familiar face of Margaret Roper, with her beautiful dark eyes and long, sharp nose, and her husband, the constant, steady William. With them were a small party of gentlemen and women, among whom Thomasin recognised the strong features of John Dudley, son of her father's old ally. The thrill of seeing friends for the first time in months seized her, so that she longed to jump up and wave as they were conducted down to the seating by the braziers. But there would be time afterwards, Thomasin told herself, time to smile and talk, and to renew the acquaintance. She would ask More what he was writing, and Margaret what she was reading. John's wife Jane had borne a little boy last year, who must be almost four months old now.

"Thomas!" beamed Catherine as he approached. More and his companions bowed low. "It is a pleasure to see you at Windsor. What brings you here today?"

"We come from Hampton Court, where we have been guests of the cardinal this past week."

The changes in Catherine's face were barely perceptible at the mention of Cardinal Wolsey, but her personal dislike of the man was well-known.

"And is the cardinal well?" she asked pointedly.

"We left him in good health," admitted More, moving closer so that his voice did not travel so far. Thomasin strained to hear him. "But not in such good spirits. Like all of us, he is troubled by this business and longs for its resolution."

"I expect he is," replied Catherine, "but I doubt the resolution he seeks bears any resemblance to that which I desire. Tell me, does he still hope for a French princess for the king?"

"He has quite given up that scheme now, I believe. His eyes have been entirely opened to the king's true intentions concerning Mistress Boleyn, and she is no friend to him, no matter how much he courts her favour."

"No, I think she is not. There is bad blood between them, at least on her side."

Anne Boleyn had never forgiven Wolsey for breaking her engagement to Henry Percy when she had first come to court, years ago. They had been betrothed in secret, but Wolsey had intervened to prevent the match. What had seemed a mere trifle to the cardinal then, now returned to bite him.

Catherine inclined her head. "We will speak of this at greater length after the display. You must join me for the dancing. Come, take your seats. The falcons are ready to fly."

The falconers had taken their positions at either end of the ward. One sent his bird up with the long, practised throw of his arm, so that it soared overhead on wide, powerful wings. Thomasin watched its graceful path as it fought against the currents of air, high overhead. How different the scene must look from up above, with all the people, and even the castle appearing small and insignificant below. What a big world it must seem to a bird and yet, how accessible, how traversable, how free.

A shrill whistle brought the falcon back down, swooping quickly, as if closing in upon its prey. It was a streak of feathers behind the curved talons, bracing itself as it shot down, fastening onto the keeper's glove. After the motion, there was stillness.

Then the cry came. "Fly!"

A second bird rose into the air, followed by the third, circling together in a majestic dance. They followed the vagaries of the wind, rising and falling, coming together, then breaking apart, before being summoned again by their keepers and returning to the gloves.

"They are beautiful, are they not?"

One of the Venetians had stolen up behind Thomasin. She understood at once that he had singled her out, slipping into her shadow and speaking to her softly. It was not the tall, wide-eyed Matteo, to whom she had spoken earlier, but a slight, slender man, about her own height. As soon as she was aware of him, she caught his scent: a sharp, musky perfume that carried her away from the ward for a moment.

Thomasin allowed herself to glance at him briefly, but it was long enough to see the exotic, deep golden eyes and arched brows above them. She had never seen eyes that colour before, but they made her think of frankincense or myrrh, or something equally rare and precious.

He noticed her attention. And her silence. "It has been made into such an art form in England."

It took her a moment to realise he was speaking about the display. "You don't fly falcons in Venice?"

"Oh yes, we do, but not with such ritual and skill. It is quite magnificent to see."

She nodded and turned her eyes back to the field, where the birds were rising again and responding to their masters' calls. The eyes of the crowd were upon them, the courtiers and servants alike enthralled by the creatures' rhythmic circling motions. Two, three, then four in the sky. Then, with a quick whistle, they turned at the same moment, diving down, and tucked back into the earth in breath-taking unison. He was right, Thomasin thought, it was art. An art they took seriously.

"You attend the queen?"

His voice was softer, that lilting accent sweeter and more lyrical than that of the other Venetians, and she wondered at the difference, but she had no frames of reference. Perhaps he was educated, or from a noble family, or had been sent to be educated in one of the other Italian states, or somewhere else entirely.

"Yes, I am one of her ladies."

"I see she is fortunate in her ladies."

Thomasin kept her eyes on the falcons, feeling no obligation to reply to his compliment.

"I have found you English women to be something of an enigma," he added, with a little playful note.

She turned her head slightly, so he could not see her smile.

"But I think you are kept on a tight leash, like songbirds in a cage."

Thomasin's feathers were ruffled by this comment. She stared ahead.

"Do you ever get to fly free?" he asked.

Again, she watched the birds.

"To be your own mistress? Do you know how that feels?"

She turned her head with a little rush of irritation, but he was already backing away into the crowd.

"I am still watchful of the Venetians," whispered Ellen, as she linked arms with Thomasin in the dance. "And I think them as slippery as eels."

The queen's party had exchanged the falcons in the lower ward for flights of their own in the hall. A striking tune was playing as they took up their partners, Ellen with one of the gentlemen ushers and Thomasin with John Dudley.

"And how does your little son fare, John? What is his name?" Thomasin asked her friend as they came back together, alongside the other pair. The dance required them to work in a four, back and forth, with swift steps in a circle.

"He is John," Dudley laughed, "named after me, but finally sleeping much better than I ever do, and growing good and hearty."

"And Jane? Is she well? I hope to see her properly ere long."

"I am certain that you will. She tires of the country and longs for court life."

"Will she come to court?"

"Soon enough."

"Here, or to the king's court?"

Dudley smiled. "I think she hopes to escape that conundrum by waiting until the king and queen are in the same place again."

Thomasin nodded, passing by his side. "Your wife is a very wise woman."

"I would not have married her otherwise, although, to be fair, she did accept my proposal."

He turned to face her, smiling at his jest and joining the line of male dancers. Thomasin was aware of the Venetians in the next group, with their flamboyant moves and the light catching their bright clothing. Vernier had partnered Maria Willoughby and was dancing close to the dais where Catherine sat. It was rare these days that Catherine participated in any kind of formal dancing, preferring to watch her younger ladies perform.

At the side, More and the Ropers were conversing with Blount and Vives. Thomasin wished she could be among them, listening to their talk, their faces intent upon ideas and their laughter arising at the jokes and wordplay she imagined flying between them. Margaret Roper was looking particularly well, in a bodice laced with silver and with her dark hair pulled back under a green and cream bonnet.

The closing steps of the dance were being played. Verniers had left his Spanish partner already, as the others made their bows, and had moved swiftly onto bended knee before Catherine. He seemed to be making some impassioned speech, quite unsuitable for the occasion and the company. Thomasin caught Ellen's eye again as they completed the formalities of the dance, and an understanding passed between them. As soon as they could get away, both women hurried forward to Catherine.

"My Lady," offered Ellen, interrupting Vernier mid-flow. "Is there anything we can do for you?"

Catherine looked up, slightly bemused. "Yes, take this gentleman away and dance with him."

Verniers looked reluctant. "But, My Lady…"

"Now, Signore, you have just proved to me that you dance so well. You cannot deprive me of that sight again. We can finish our conversation another time."

"As you wish, My Lady," he said with disappointment. He then turned and offered his hand to Ellen. At the same moment, the slender figure with the golden eyes appeared beside him, deftly slipping his fingers through Thomasin's.

A gasp escaped her, and she felt obliged to follow it with a frown.

His face split into a smile and those eyes glowed. "Shall we?"

She allowed him to lead her into position, with Gertrude at her side. The two women eyed their exotic companions with suspicion as the men bowed low before them.

The first chord took them close, almost face to face, chest to chest. Thomasin averted her gaze, but she could not avoid his sweet, spicy scent. They retreated momentarily, opening up the space between them, but then the dance called for them to close in again. Thomasin could not put her finger on what made her uneasy, but something did. Something unsettled her, in his manner or movements; there was an air about this man that reminded her of Rafe Danvers.

It seemed a long time since she had thought of Rafe. The truth was, he might not have been uppermost in her mind, but he was often present just below the surface. She had only known him briefly, as a ward to Anne Boleyn's father, but the impression he had made upon her was profound. He had seized her innocent heart, consuming her with a fire that she had felt unable to control, and which she feared. Those dark looks: the blue-black hair, the eyes like deep pools, had caught her attention at once, when she'd first seen him in the rose garden at court.

She did not doubt there had been a genuine attraction between them, his ardent kisses told her as much, but in painful steps, she had understood that there was more to their connection. He was an instrument of the Boleyns, sent to do their bidding, to win her over to Anne's cause. She had not seen him since the day she'd ridden out of the city, no doubt for the best, as those haunting eyes still returned to her dreams once in a while, so that she woke unsettled and filled with longing.

Now, this golden-eyed Venetian made her feel on edge, just as Rafe had. He moved with grace, with finely shaped limbs, and an effortless sense of style. It was something raw, even animal, and it called to a hidden chamber of her heart she had not known existed. Rafe had been the one to first kindle it to life, and she better understood her own vulnerability because of it. But this man, with his seductive ways and golden eyes, was merely passing through. He and his fellows would be gone tomorrow. There was no danger that he could pose which she might not resist in that short time.

"You seem cross," he said in his soft lilt as he passed her by.

The comment took her by surprise. "Cross?"

"Such a pretty face to spoil with a frown."

She ignored him, turning away with a swish of her skirts. He passed her, returned and stood, facing her again. A new chord struck and they were forced together.

"Will you not tell me your name?"

He offered his hand and she placed hers in it, just as Ellen was doing with Vernier.

"What can you possibly want with my name?"

He smiled, pulling her close towards him. "To roll it round my tongue."

His audacity surprised her, but she recovered quickly. "A dangerous place to be."

He laughed, short and high. Briefly, she swapped places with her cousin and came face to face with Vernier.

"Madam," he smiled, leading her through the moves. "So many beautiful women in the queen's household."

Thomasin's eyes were drawn to More and his circle again, as she passed close by their corner. This time Margaret Roper was watching the dance, and waved to her friend as she passed by. The final steps seemed drawn out. She was returned to her original partner, with his laughing golden eyes, but every time it seemed that the song was drawing to a close, fresh chords struck. Eventually, they were bowing low, although he still held her by the fingertips.

"May I see you later, this evening?" he urged suddenly. "Outside the queen's chamber?"

"The queen will have need of me," Thomasin replied pertly, extracting her hand and heading across the floor.

"Thomasin!" smiled Margaret, rising. "I thought it was you."

"Mistress Marwood," More smiled, extending his hand to her, "what a welcome sight you are."

FOUR

In pleasant company, the time flew by quickly. Soon Thomasin was bidding goodnight to her friends, wrapped in their fur-lined cloaks as the carriages waited in the outer courtyard. Fortunately, the clouds that day meant that the night was milder than of late. It smelled cold and clean, as spring nights sometimes did in Suffolk.

"You will not stay?" Thomasin asked again. "The queen was happy to offer you a chamber, and we have truckle beds enough for all."

"Thank you, kindly," More replied, "but we have secured lodgings in the town."

"At much trouble," added Dudley. "I had no idea Windsor would be so busy at this time of year."

"You must come to our house in Chelsea," said Margaret Roper, enclosing Thomasin in her arm. "And see our books, and let me take you round our garden. We had our friend, Herr Holbein stay with us last year; he is an artist, visiting from Germany, and he painted a portrait of us all. It would interest you greatly to see it."

"He is quite a master, our Holbein," smiled More. "He captures people, just so. I saw the portrait he made of Tom Elyot, and it was such a likeness it was as if you could reach out and touch him. Those dour cheeks he has, and the hair, just like Tom."

"Dr Elyot?" asked Thomasin, recalling the man who had attended her mother during her illness last autumn. He had also been the one to make her the gift of a little scent bag, filled with mixed flowers and herbs, to wear beneath her clothes. She smiled to think of it now, believing that it might help her ensnare a wealthy husband.

"The same," nodded More, leaning upon his daughter. "Such a distinctive face, such meat for Holbein. I hear he is going for Archbishop Warham next, and that will be a challenge."

Thomasin had never seen the archbishop they mentioned, but their tone led her to believe he must be a character.

"He is quite ancient!" added More, by way of explanation. "Born before the conflicts of York and Lancaster, and almost eighty, so Hans will have to paint the whole of history in his face."

"We should depart," replied Margaret, "or else the whole of history will be apparent in my face on the morrow."

"Never," replied her husband, William. "You must rise fresh and new as a girl, because I cannot afford to summon Mister Holbein for another sitting."

The company laughed.

"And you have letters to write tomorrow," added More. "Now that the queen has agreed to write on our behalf, we cannot renege on our side of the bargain." He turned to Thomasin. "We are trying to encourage Erasmus to return to England, so we can benefit again from his wisdom. We are all writing our pleas to try and entice him to leave Freiburg and cross the sea again. My motives are purely selfish, of course. I long to debate with him on the topic of free will."

"Free will?"

"The ability of souls to make their own choices, but that will have to be for another occasion, I am afraid, as the hour advances and we must bid you goodnight."

"Yes, goodnight," smiled Thomasin, "it was a pleasure to see you all again," but the words resonated with her. Free will, the choice to direct your own life, was a subject she had given much thought to previously. A subject she found both exciting and dangerous.

"We hope you will visit, when the queen allows you," smiled Dudley from behind.

"Shh! You will get me into trouble. You must not even hint at any reluctance. I am lucky to be here."

More and the young people exchanged glances.

"The queen is a good mistress," More replied, "so long as you are content."

"I am," replied Thomasin, truthfully. Even though she sometimes felt constrained, she was not ready to leave Catherine's employment. "I know how fortunate I am to be here."

"You miss your family? They are well, I trust? Especially your mother?"

Thomasin nodded. "I do. I miss Suffolk too. This is the longest I have been away from them all, but my sister Cecilia writes that they are all well and that Mother's health improves daily."

"That is good news indeed," More smiled. "Please send them our fond love in your next letter."

"Thank you, I will do so."

"And more good news to come, I think," added Margaret, "when we hear of Giles's betrothal being announced."

The name gave Thomasin pause.

"Giles?"

"Yes, you remember Sir Giles Waterson? It is rumoured at court that he is soon to become betrothed in marriage. It only wants the bride's acceptance."

Of course Thomasin remembered her friend, with his easy laugh and the kindness and attention he had shown her and her family last autumn. She remembered the meals when she had sat beside him and they'd fired their wit against each other, and their walk in the garden at Monk's Place, when he had confided in her about his sad past, the loss of his wife in childbed. It had been Sir Giles who helped them when Cecilia's marriage fell through, after her liaison with Will Hatton was exposed, and Giles who rode with Thomasin to Windsor, bidding her farewell in the great hall, on a dark November day. And suddenly, she felt a pang of loss for his chatter.

"Yes," she replied softly, "I remember him. Who is his chosen bride?"

"That's the secret," Margaret said, raising her eyebrows. "He will neither confirm nor deny the rumours, so the whole court is guessing. He is currently in the north, attending to business there for the king."

Thomasin realised she had not seen Giles lately. He had attended the queen's court at Christmas, and once after that, to dine in the hall, but otherwise he had kept away. She hadn't even thought about it, assuming him to be busy. It seemed there was another reason.

"Come then," said Dudley, "we are starting to shiver and must proceed to our lodgings. We really must bid you farewell and hope to see you soon."

As they were climbing into the carriage, Margaret first, helped up by her doting Will, More beckoned Thomasin closer.

"Good Lady Thomasin, I was unsure whether I should speak to you on this before I depart, but the moment has resolved that I must. I saw your father last week, at Westminster, in the company of Thomas Cromwell. He looked in good health. I am sure there is nothing amiss, but from our conversation this evening, I thought you may be unaware. Please forgive me if I have overstepped the mark."

The news sent Thomasin into confusion. "Father? At court? You are sure it was him?"

"I am. I passed him and he greeted me by name, as I did him. I saw that he wished to speak with me, but Cromwell required him. I am sorry for any confusion I have created."

"When was this?"

"Two weeks since, maybe more, but as I said, he was in good health."

"And good spirits?"

More shrugged. "He was with Cromwell. It is enough to make anyone sombre."

"Are you coming, sir?" Dudley called from the carriage.

More looked over his shoulder. "I must be going. I am sure your father will write to you, unless he visits you in person." He swiftly took up her hand and kissed it. "You are looking well, dear Thomasin. It is a pleasure to see you, as always. Dwell not upon my news; I am sure it means nothing. Throw yourself into the service of the queen, and we will speak before long."

Thomasin watched the carriage draw away. Thomas More's words resounded in her ears. Father, at court, with Cromwell? The thought sat uneasily with her. And Giles remarrying. It was right that he find happiness, after the loss of his first wife. She must push any lingering thoughts of him aside and wish him joy with his new wife. Undoubtedly, he would prove an excellent husband.

Ellen was standing in the doorway as Thomasin returned to the hall.

"The queen is tired. She has withdrawn; come quickly, we are to put her to bed."

They passed swiftly back through the hall, where the final dance was taking place and the empty plates were being carried out. At the far end, Catherine had deserted the chair of state. It stood empty, save for a pile of golden cushions, the red and yellow drapes behind embroidered with the arms of England, Aragon and Castile.

As she followed Ellen, heading towards the queen's private chambers, Thomasin noticed Vernier, standing a little to the side. He was staring intently at the chair, inching closer, and at once Thomasin sensed he was minded to sit in it, to try it out, in Catherine's absence.

He looked up and caught her eye. His gaze betrayed his intention, filling her with indignation at his audacity.

"Do not!" she said with quiet force. "Do not touch it. It is treason to do so."

The Venetian bowed low and slipped away, without meeting her eyes again.

FIVE

It was not yet midnight. Thomasin paused in Catherine's antechamber. Moonlight filtered through the carved screen. It fell in patterns across the velvet bed curtains, across the tiled floor and the smouldering grate. The last coals glowed orange, and the scent of snuffed candles still lingered in the air.

After bedding Catherine down, both Mary and Ellen were stretched out on truckle beds, lone ships mid-floor, as the hours of the night slipped by. Thomasin, Catherine and Gertrude had their beds in the adjoining room. They were not uncomfortable, with their wooden frames and knotted ropes, and horse hair mattresses on top, but neither were they soft, and the women often woke stiff and sore.

Sleep would not come. Thomasin found herself thirsty after the heady Spanish wine, her mouth dry, her mind racing on her father. Catherine's restlessness certainly didn't help. Through the partition, Catherine could be heard fidgeting and turning, muttering prayers and reliving memories. She had drunk her medicinal draughts, sat patiently as her ladies rubbed her with ointments and brushed out her greying hair, compliant as they unlaced her gown, but with melancholy in her eyes. Once, Catherine would have stayed up into the early hours, dancing and feasting, and it was hard to think of those past times, with a doting husband at her side. Seeing her faded face, hearing her mournful sigh, Thomasin could not help but think how cruel it was that time had slipped away unobserved. One minute a beloved wife, the next a burden, undesired, unsought.

For a while, Thomasin lay awake, listening to the sounds of the castle. Distant horse hoofs reached her, and men's voices, then the clatter of feet and the scrape of metal in the direction of the kitchen. Windsor was still not quiet, even though the queen was abed. She let thirst guide her and slipped out of the room.

The corridor outside was still. Four guards in livery were stationed here, standing still and alert, turning their eyes upon her.

"I'm thirsty," she explained.

Knowing her face, none of them challenged her; one nodded her on.

Thomasin was passing through the hall when she noticed a figure sitting in the corner. Bishop Mendoza was wrapped in a cloak, gazing out of the window.

Thomasin approached gingerly. "My Lord? Are you quite well?"

He turned, a little startled to see her, trying to read her face in the gloom.

"It's Thomasin Marwood, the queen's gentlewoman."

"Ah," he nodded, "yes."

"Can I bring you anything, my Lord?"

"Not unless you have a new pair of legs to swap for these old ones. I am a martyr to the gout."

Thomasin saw he had arranged himself on gold cushions.

"Are you not more comfortable in bed, my Lord?"

"I will be, shortly. It is getting there that is the problem."

"Shall I send for some assistance? Two of the men for you to lean upon?"

He put out a hand. "Perhaps, in a moment. This country will be the death of me. Some days I fear I will never get home to my native Castile, to feel the sun on my face again."

"I'm sorry to hear that."

"You know it is only my second winter here? I was imprisoned by the French and held under house arrest in London last year, with guards standing outside the front door, refusing to let me send or receive letters. It was only fear of the emperor that finally made the king order my release. Can you believe it?"

Thomasin fidgeted from one foot to the other. "I am truly sorry for it, my Lord."

"I grow too old and too tired for these troublesome politics. Now I hear that heretic Tyndale is being discussed at the English court, with his ungodly translation of the Bible, because he is favoured by the harlot."

Thomasin realised he was speaking of Anne Boleyn and blushed.

Mendoza shook his head. "I will write to the emperor and ask to be recalled."

"I shall fetch two gentlemen, my Lord, to assist you to your chamber, with as much haste as I can."

Thomasin headed towards the kitchen, which was the best place to find someone still awake to assist the bishop. Servants were running final errands, fetching wine and snuffing candles. Some of the stable lads were hanging about the kitchen door, begging for scraps and drinking ale, sitting on the steps. Thomasin recognised one or two she knew by name.

"Ned, Martin, Bishop Mendoza is in the hall, in need of assistance. He suffers from the gout and needs to be supported to his chamber. Can you go to him?"

Ned, a tall boy with long limbs, jumped up. "We'll go at once. In the hall, you say?"

"In the alcove, thank you."

The lads hurried away and Thomasin turned back to the kitchen. Odours from the meal still lingered in the air, but they were coupled with the clean freshness of soapy water and the night air.

Cook nodded when Thomasin asked for something to quench her thirst, handing over a cup of small beer, weak and sweet, but most welcome. She wiped her mouth and prepared to head back to the queen's chamber.

"My Lady?"

She recognised the soft voice. He had been standing with a group in the doorway but broke away from them now to join her in the corridor. Moonlight glinted on his golden laces and silver buttons.

He was a guest of the queen. Courtesy dictated that she stop. He came towards her, lithe yet strong, golden eyes fixed on her.

"You never told me your name, mistress."

Should she? He would be gone tomorrow. Did it matter?

"Otherwise to whom am I to send my gifts?"

"Your gifts?"

"When I return to Venice and dream of the beautiful lady at the English queen's court. To whom am I to send them?"

She was alert at once, recalling Matteo's approaches.

"My name is Thomasin, but you do not need to send me any gifts. I shall be writing no letters for you."

He held up his hands in mock surprise. "Letters? You had thought of writing letters to me? I am touched, I am encouraged, to think you might favour me so."

Thomasin smiled at his quickness but shook her head. "I must get back."

"Wait, please. Will you walk a little way with me?"

Her duty and common sense told her to refuse. Yet with the moonlight catching his face, he was one of the most handsome men she had ever seen.

"Just a little way. My name is Nico. Nico Amato. It means beloved."

Of course it did.

He saw her hesitate. "Would you show me the way, as I am the queen's guest here? I have only a few hours left."

Again, courtesy required her response, as he well knew. He was playing the game well. But some other impulse was acting in her too. She did not ask why, or enquire which destination he sought. She simply allowed herself to feel, not think, and fell into step beside him as he headed outside, down the path.

"It is a beautiful night, is it not?"

Thomasin looked up at the sky. The stars were barely visible behind the clouds, but there was a mildness in the air that was not unpleasant. "I suppose it is."

"You are used to it, maybe, living here all your life. Your England is still a new place to me. I only came here first three weeks ago, in the service of Signore Vernier."

"And what do you think of it?"

"A most intriguing country. I had heard it spoken of, many times before, by my visiting countrymen, who praised its beauty." He laughed, adding, "But you will not like this… They also warned me about the English women."

"Did they, indeed?"

"I heard that the women are the most beautiful in Europe and very free with their affections."

She laughed. He was so obvious. "Then I trust the reality has opened your eyes to that untruth."

"I have only found the English women to be among the most welcoming and kind I have encountered, and I could not wish for more."

"You do not think yourself a little forward, offering such an opinion?"

He professed himself hurt. "Forward? Whom have I offended? Yourself? I would not it were the case for anything." He tried to take up her hand, but she slipped it away quickly, their skin touching for the briefest of moments. "Do say I have not. No harm was intended, only a little light teasing."

She turned away, drawing out the moment, pretending to have taken offence.

"My Lady?"

They had reached the path that led to the gardens, which Thomasin knew were locked at dusk.

"We cannot go further, not at this time."

"I have offended you with my plain speech?"

"The gate is locked."

His face split in a smile. If he only knew how weak she was, how full of passion.

"That is all, Mistress Thomasin? A locked gate. A locked gate is like a poem, a riddle, a knot to be unpicked."

Again, the contradictory impulse. Part of her wanted to roll her eyes and send his platitudes away, but the moonlight in his golden eyes made the other half of her linger. She had only discovered this weakness in herself lately, when she'd come to court, and it was a source of shame for her. From having thought herself a resilient woman, who disliked nonsense, Rafe Danvers' saturnine good looks had taught her that she harboured this vulnerability when it came to beauty.

Nico's eyes were drawn into the garden. "Do roses grow in there?"

"Not at this time of year. Primroses, certainly, and bluebells."

"Are there no roses to be had, anywhere, for a price?"

"Not in the gardens here, I know for certain."

"That is a shame." He turned to her. "I would like to make you a gift."

"That is not necessary; you have already given us gifts."

"I meant you, and you alone, Mistress Thomasin."

"And I said it was unnecessary." She turned back to face the castle entrance.

"But I was hoping we might become friends."

"Friends? Of what duration?"

"I may be leaving Windsor tomorrow, but I hope to remain in England."

This was a new turn. "You do? To what end?"

"I could not say this openly before the others, but I seek a fresh start, a new country, perhaps a role at court."

Maybe he was genuine. Maybe he was not seeking out a spy among the court, or a flirtation, or a little fool for the evening. Maybe he was truly intending to stay in the country. "What would you do?"

"I was hoping to charm the king or queen into giving me a position, perhaps as a scribe or clerk. My French and Spanish are good too."

"The queen always values those who speak in her native tongue."

"Perhaps you might be so kind as to put in a good word for me?"

"I will consider it."

"Please do not take too long, dear lady, as I am due to depart on the morrow."

"What if you spoke to the queen yourself? If you had an introduction."

"If you think that possible."

"You might see her tomorrow, as she leaves chapel."

He reached for her hand, and this time, she allowed him to take hold of it. "Thank you, thank you for your kindness."

Then, unexpectedly, he pulled her towards him and placed a kiss full upon her lips. Taken by surprise, and conscious of the group of drinkers not too far away, Thomasin pushed him away.

"Signore, you should not have done that! I must return at once. I bid you goodnight."

Thomasin hurried past him before he could protest, along the side of the ward and in through the gate which led to the queen's quarters. Hopefully no one had seen. Such misconduct in public could lead to her losing her position.

The antechamber was dark, and the draughty truckle by the door was the only bed left. She climbed into it, her limbs still chilled but her lips warm from the pressure of Nico's mouth.

SIX

Lights, warmth. Flickering candles and laughter. The borrowed pearls roped about her neck made her feel charmed. Her chest rose and fell with excitement. Someone was taking her arm, bare to the elbow. She felt that charge, skin upon skin. The strains of music. The yearning, the longing, a pair of dark, dark eyes. The turn of his head, the caress of his voice. His hand, twining behind her head, so that her headdress was knocked to the floor and her long dark hair came tumbling out. And all the time, she was there, leading them. The woman in red, lithe, sinuous, playful, addictive…

"Awake! Awake, ladies! The king is on his way!"

Thomasin sat up, rubbing her eyes. Her dream faded, like sunbeams at the end of the day. Her mind tried to clutch at them, hold on to those memories: those feelings of last autumn, at Anne's court, in Rafe's arms, but they were already vanishing, leaving a sense of loss. She was back in the cold chamber, smelling rosemary, stone and cold ashes.

Dawn had barely taken hold. Weak spring light filtered through the carved screen and exposed the sleepy forms. The women stirred reluctantly, slowly, stretching their stiff limbs.

"The king?"

"Yes, the king! He has ordered a banquet to be prepared ahead of his arrival. He will be here by noon. Arise and make haste to the queen, to the queen! Spread the word."

Thomasin swung her legs from under her blanket and put her stockinged feet down on the bare floor.

"Hurry, hurry, the king is on his way!"

The candles kindled into light, one after the other. She hurried to light the fire.

Catherine's breath came short with impatience. Her round back with its ample flesh heaved up and down with a kind of creak inside. Thomasin's fingers fumbled with the laces at her waist, making a mess as she teased out the loops. Then, in haste, she pulled them too tight, making Catherine gasp.

"Sorry, My Lady." She picked them out of the holes to loosen them again, then tied the knot. "Sorry, My Lady, all done now." She anticipated a reproach, but Catherine's mind was elsewhere.

Ellen carried forward Catherine's doublet, stiff with embroidery in raised silver thread and spangles. Catherine raised her arms with a catch of pain. Behind her, they waited. Slowly, with caution, she eased her arms into it, one at a time, then Ellen settled it on her shoulders.

"I am stiff," Catherine said. "My shoulders ache, my arms are weak; I feel age creep upon me."

Thomasin and Ellen exchanged a look, but Maria Willoughby was there first, holding out Catherine's jewels.

"Oh, My Lady, you are but young still — no such talk, or else you shall age me!"

Thomasin stood back to let Maria's deft hands place the string of pearls and rubies about Catherine's broad neck. There was so much love and tenderness in the gesture between the two friends, who had come to England in their teens. Such an adventure it had been, then.

"My mirror?"

Ellen was there with the burnished glass. Its pale ellipse shone dully in the morning light. Catherine winced into it then turned away.

"No, no, the red one, the red one."

"You are sure?" asked Maria.

"As I said. Change me."

Ellen and Thomasin carefully lifted away the green doublet and Gertrude hurried forward with the deep red one, sewn with gold and pearls. Ellen's deft hands plucked it into place. Catherine nodded approvingly at the glass. "Yes, that is better."

Catherine was looking at herself with satisfaction as there was a knock on the door.

"Enter."

Baron Mountjoy appeared, his face the picture of composure. "Would My Lady check the list of dishes before they are sent out for the banquet? The king has requested it specially."

"What were his exact words?"

"He requested a banquet to be set in the little lodge, in the park."

"In the park? Not in the castle?"

"No, My Lady."

"But we expect him here afterwards?"

"His chambers are being prepared."

"At his instigation or yours? He gave no indication of visiting the castle?"

"I am told, My Lady, that he is taking an extended hunting trip. It was decided at the last moment."

"Is…" began Catherine, her mind clearly running on Anne Boleyn.

Mountjoy understood her pain. "His Highness is accompanied only by a small group of gentlemen."

Catherine sighed in relief. "Then convey to them that we expect them for dinner tonight. Make the necessary arrangements. I shall ride out to the lodge with a small group of my ladies when the hour strikes."

"Very well, My Lady."

Catherine turned away, then paused. "And the Venetians?"

"I believe they are departing, My Lady."

"They do not wish to take their leave of me?"

Mountjoy looked uncomfortable. "I believe they do not wish to be discovered here, attending Your Highness, when the king arrives."

A moment passed while Catherine let this sink in. A frown chased across her brows. "And why so? Is it a secret that they are here? Do they not wish the king to know of their visit?"

Mountjoy spread his hands in silence, unable to answer her questions.

Thomasin pondered this. If the untrustworthiness of the ambassadors had not already been a matter of understanding, it was confirmed now. For all their fine words, Vernier, Nico and the others had been pursuing some business of their own. So much for giving Nico an audience with the queen!

Catherine narrowed her eyes and lifted her chin. "They come to me with talk of honour, of friendship, and say they understand my situation. They want to ally with me against the French, but to keep the alliance a secret because the king is a friend of Francis! This is double-dealing."

She looked about in anger. "What a fool I have been. They would befriend me behind my husband's back, making secrets between us. Now I understand why Signore Vernier was so keen to speak to me of the emperor, my nephew. They would have my ear, try and make me influence him to support their cause. They would make me a vassal of Venice! Win the emperor through my friendship!"

She brought her fist down upon the table. "They would make use of me, me, a Queen of England! The daughter of Spain! Behind my husband's back! They would make me work against his will, make me a treasonous part of their cause, all dressed up in gifts and honeyed words."

"My Lady," spoke Thomasin, sensing the moment was right. Even the memory of Nico's kiss did not deter her. "We have further proof of their dealings."

Catherine fixed her pale eyes directly upon her. "Then speak up, girl, speak up at once."

"It was at the banquet held for their arrival. I was approached by one of them, a Matteo of Venice, who spoke cordially at first, but then he asked me to supply him with information about yourself and the court, by writing letters in exchange for gifts. He wanted to know who visits you, and what happens with your marriage. Another asked Ellen the same. We both refused, of course."

"I was asked too," said Mary from the corner, "by some slick gentleman half my age, and I laughed in his face."

"As was I," added Gertrude. "They promised me gold lace."

The fury rose in Catherine. "So this is their plan. All those sugared words and elaborate attention. Do they think we are so easily won? And what was their purpose? To whom are they to report this news?" She strode to the window and looked out across the forest. "What is it they want to know? Or their master, whoever pulls their strings. Who is it? Who is behind this? It is not of their doing alone, certainly. Who is behind this?" She turned back and looked around at the assembled faces in her chamber. Thomasin felt herself prickle uncomfortably.

"I am sure this business has its roots in their conflict with France," said Mountjoy reflectively. "They know about Wolsey's visit to Francis's court last year and they seek allies. I do believe they are testing the waters to see if Your Highness would back the emperor above your own king and husband."

"Yes, yes," she replied, impatiently. "But they are being encouraged by someone here. Someone who wishes me ill, and wants to see me led into trouble."

Mountjoy cleared his throat. "Perhaps the cardinal encouraged them to visit you here."

"Really? Can Wolsey be a part of it? He is no friend of mine, but would he stoop so low?"

"When I saw him at Westminster last, he was a man desperate to retain the king's favour. He sees himself being replaced in Henry's affections and he would do anything to win back his former influence."

Catherine was quiet. The parallel with her own situation was painfully obvious to all. "You think he would go so far? A man of the cloth? A cardinal?"

"If he could implicate you in an Imperial plot, My Lady, he would give the king ample cause to seek annulment of your marriage, in the hope that Henry would look kindly upon him again."

Catherine spoke slowly. "Such a thing would be treason on his part, but it would appear also to be on mine."

"Yes, My Lady, and that would put you in the gravest danger."

A chill settled on the room. The memories of dancing, feasting and the falcons in flight resolved into a clear and present danger.

"Unless…" added Mountjoy.

Catherine looked at him sharply. "What? Speak your mind."

"Unless the Venetians have been bought by others. By those who wish to know your business, My Lady."

"Whom do you have in mind?"

Mountjoy looked thoughtful. "Whence had they come? Westminster."

The implications of this were evident to all those present. Thomasin understood this was where the Boleyns currently awaited Henry's return from his hunting expedition.

"It might be Wolsey," Mountjoy drew out, slowly. "Or else it is the Boleyns themselves."

Catherine's face wore a storm. "Send word to Vernier. The Venetians do not have my permission to leave court. They must remain in their lodgings until they hear from me again. Until I return from the hunt. Go, at once."

Mountjoy bowed and retreated. They heard his feet echo in the corridor outside.

"Unless," Catherine whispered, "unless it is worse."

"What?" asked Maria at her side. "How could it be worse?"

"Unless it is the king himself, laying a trap for me to walk into…" Her voice trailed away.

"Oh, My Lady, I am sure he would not resort to such underhand methods, not the king himself," Maria replied. "He has the utmost respect and love for you and would not willingly deceive you."

"Unless he felt he must."

Thomasin caught Maria's eye and read the doubts there, seeming to contradict her words.

"But you have done nothing for which he can reproach you, My Lady," Thomasin added. "You, and we, have given the Venetians nothing but hospitality."

"And this." Catherine drew out of her sleeve a gold chain set with a carved ballas ruby. "This was Signore Vernier's special gift to me at the dance. I will return it to him in the morning. I cannot keep it for fear of it seeming a debt or a bribe."

"Then we shall return it to him on the morrow," said Maria.

Catherine's face was pensive but determined. "Suddenly that sweet Venetian wine tastes like ashes in my mouth."

SEVEN

A wide vista of green trees spread before them. Windsor forest had been completely still that morning, full of cool, dark spaces and the brightness of nature beginning its regrowth. Ahead, bathed in pale sunlight, the tall hunting lodge stood in a clearing overlooking the track as the women approached. Led by Mountjoy and Catherine, they rode up to the red brick building, with its open gallery overlooking the view. A handful of colourful figures came spilling out to bid them welcome.

Thomasin felt a constriction in her stomach as the king strode across the grass. Dressed in green and yellow velvet, Henry VIII was a magnificent man in his late thirties; tall, broad-shouldered, with his beard neatly trimmed, red hair blazing in the light. Every inch the king, he carried himself with an air of expectation, in the complete belief of his due, as the representative of God upon earth. When he walked, it was as if the forest itself stopped to listen and when he spoke, the very trees and creatures in their branches fell silent out of respect.

Yet Thomasin's feelings were mixed. Her eyes could barely rest upon him for questions. Besides the suspected plot with Wolsey, and the secret intentions of the Venetians, Thomasin had her own, personal reasons for doubting him. She could not forget the disturbing facts she had learned last year. That her mother, Elizabeth, had once shared Henry's bed, in a brief romance, and that there was the slimmest of chances that this gaudy, dazzling man before her was actually her own father. It was the first time she had seen him since those revelations. Her throat constricted.

"You are welcome, My Lady," Henry boomed, holding out his hand courteously to Catherine, as she dismounted.

The entire court was aware of his intention to procure a divorce and to marry the dark-haired beauty Anne Boleyn, yet in his treatment of his wife, he was still publicly attentive and went out of his way to show her every courtesy, as protocol demanded. He dared not snub or slight her in public for fear of offending the emperor. Thomasin found it hard to believe he would plot against her, using the Venetians.

Henry looked down the assembled line of women. He nodded first at Maria, whom he knew well, then Gertrude. "My Lady Willoughby, Lady Exeter." When he came to Thomasin and Ellen, he paused.

Catherine stepped into the breach. "My Lord, you know Mistresses Marwood and Russell, who have been with me since my arrival here at Windsor."

He eyed them with quiet caution, tempered by last autumn's events. "I do."

They waited, but no more came.

Catherine straightened her spine. "I trust you are well, My Lord?"

"Very well. I was seized by the desire to hunt in these good woodlands," Henry continued, brightening up and indicating the greenness behind him with the spread of his arm. "So we rode apace for the pleasure."

"We are most happy to welcome you to Windsor," replied Catherine, bowing low, speaking formally. "Your presence honours us. We have come to wish you a happy day's hunting and hope that you will accept our invitation to dine at the castle tonight. Your chambers are being prepared."

Henry inclined his head slightly, as if in agreement, but not speaking to confirm his intentions. "You are gracious and thoughtful, as ever."

Thomasin looked at the small company of men emerging from the lodge behind the king. She recognised his close companion, the slight, dark-haired William Compton, his Groom of the Stool, who best knew his secrets, and beside him, William Carey, married to Anne Boleyn's sister, tanned from being in the saddle. Next to emerge was Charles Brandon, Duke of Suffolk, the king's brother-in-law, an excellent rider and, after Henry himself, the best jouster in the field, always eager for action. Two other young men followed, unknown to Thomasin, but then she caught her breath at the sight of a third emerging: an easy-going, well-built man with a shock of very fair hair. She had not thought to see Sir William Hatton again so soon, and could have wished against such an encounter, had she the choice. His bright smile faded a little as he recognised her among the queen's ladies.

It was barely four months since it had happened. No, not even so many as that. The Marwood family had come up to London for the wedding of Cecilia, the eldest daughter, to Sir Henry Kytson, a worthy man with estates not too far from their own home of Eastwell, just over the Suffolk border. The match had been arranged by the mothers, in correspondence, and received the blessing of the king. The families had met in London, and Cecilia had found her worthy husband to be a little more plain than she had wished, but this would have been of no account, had her head not been turned by the charms of Hatton.

He had wooed the impressionable girl, won her, had his fun with her, all in the space of a mere two weeks, and then denied her, when she wished to elope with him. Cecilia had returned to her family, broken-hearted and resigned to the match with Kytson, but by that time, it was too late. The whispering tongues at court had done their worst. Kytson did not want a tainted bride. And so she'd returned to Suffolk with Lord and Lady Marwood, unmarried and disgraced, when she should have been starting her life as the wife of a worthy knight.

It had been a bitter episode for them all. And now here, amid the sunshine of the forest, returned to the king's side, was the author of their woes. Hatton grinned, running his hand through his hair, looking for all the world as if nothing ailed him.

Thomasin looked away, unable to bring herself to lay eyes upon him a moment longer.

"Will you walk inside?" invited Henry. "You may partake of the banquet and watch from the gallery as we hunt."

Thomasin followed Catherine, her stomach churning with fury. Hatton, here, so soon returned to favour while her sister's life lay in ruins. She had to pause and catch her breath halfway up the winding staircase.

"Are you well?" asked Ellen, who was behind her.

"You saw who it was?" Thomasin whispered back, clawing onto the stone step before her.

"I did. The cheek of him! But hold in your anger."

On the first floor, a table was spread with cakes and pastries, wafers and marchpane, oranges, apples and quinces, and dishes of comfits. Jugs of Hippocras wine stood waiting to be poured. But Catherine threw a cursory eye over it and went straight out onto the open gallery. From there, the view stretched away in glorious colour, with the castle turrets visible beyond the trees and, just below them, the men's horses were tethered, in their bright trappings.

"It is a good day for it," said Will Compton, squinting as he looked out, "a good, dry, bright day, with little wind. I hear the hunting is currently good in the park."

"The forest has not been disturbed for months," agreed Catherine. "There will be plenty of deer for you."

"And I trust Your Highness is in good health?" asked Compton.

Catherine shot him a look. Compton had been known in the past to facilitate the king's romances, although his question seemed genuine enough. "I am quite well, thank you."

William Hatton was heading for the banquet, his eyes greedy. Thomasin made a start towards him but Ellen's hand fell upon her arm.

"Do not say anything troublesome."

"I cannot say nothing."

"But choose your words with wisdom. He will get what he deserves in time."

Thomasin felt her hands shaking. She approached slowly and stood behind him as he picked at a dish of fruit. And those evenings came back to her, when he had sat at the table in her uncle Russell's house and eaten his food, making merry, smiling and drinking, whilst all the time he was a serpent in the garden.

He felt her eyes upon his broad back and turned. "Pardon me, Mistress, I did not see you there."

"I am surprised to see you at all, William Hatton. Surprised that you dare show your face here. You have not forgotten who I am; to whom I am related?"

He dropped his amicable air, and attempted to pass by her. "Of course I know you, Thomasin Marwood."

"And that is all you have to say to me? To my family? To my sister, whom you ruined?"

He turned back to face her, those bright blue eyes focused. "Is this the time for opening past wounds? While the king takes his pleasure?"

Thomasin cast her eyes about the room. Most of the others were on the balcony. Save for Ellen and Gertrude, they were alone. For a rare moment, she had the chance to speak freely. "You do not get to choose your time, given that you have already taken your pleasure."

His lip curled. "Your sister was a willing participant in all; she pursued me, she begged me to run away with her."

"But she never would have done so if you had not dallied with her. With a woman engaged to be married."

"Then she should have behaved like a woman engaged to be married!"

The words cut deep. Thomasin recalled Anne Boleyn's own comments on the day that was supposed to have been Cecilia's wedding; that she had brought this upon herself.

"So, was it just sport for you? We welcomed you as a guest and friend, we thought you an honourable man. Was it only a game for you?"

Hatton spread his arms in protest. "A game your sister willingly played. There is always a cost. She knew the risks and yet she still indulged."

"And what have the costs been to you, William Hatton? How have you suffered? A few weeks away from court and then back at the king's side?"

He picked up an apple and headed to the balcony, throwing a line back over his shoulder. "Some of us play better than others."

"Snake," she hissed after him. She was sure he had heard, but he did not turn.

Alone for a moment, Thomasin felt as if her blood was about to boil. She longed to launch herself upon him, claw at his hair, scratch his eyes out of his face, but that was the swiftest way to be removed from the queen's service. Her parents did not need another Marwood daughter returning home in disgrace.

"You do look angry."

Gertrude was by her side.

"I am angry. I am struggling not to let it show. That is the man who ruined my sister."

"Will Hatton?"

"You know him?"

"I know of him. His reputation precedes him. I am sorry to hear about your sister, but she is not the first woman to fall victim to his charms."

"Really?" Thomasin narrowed her eyes as Hatton strolled over to converse with the king.

"I heard of at least one case before. But the king always takes him back, brags about it in private, and the number of women whose hearts they have broken."

The two men suddenly burst out laughing, the king roaring from his belly at something Hatton had said. Thomasin reddened.

Gertrude put her hand upon her friend's arm. "Do not show your feelings. Such men will receive their just rewards."

"That's what Ellen said. If only I could believe it were true," Thomasin whispered, as the king clapped his hand upon Hatton's shoulder and the pair strolled out together, towards the gallery. It would only take one moment, one slip upon the wet wood, for Hatton to plunge over the edge. She could picture it now. Or else, if someone should come up behind him, unexpectedly, trip and clutch at him, a little too hard. A fall from the first floor might not kill him, but it would do enough damage. It would wipe that mocking smile clean off his face.

She stopped herself, grateful that her thoughts were private, as Catherine appeared in the doorway.

"What is this gossiping? Come, attend me in the gallery."

The edge to her voice made them hurry. Catherine went to join Henry, overlooking the scene, and they hurried to take their places behind her.

Below, in the clearing, William Carey and Charles Brandon were preparing the horses. Two other gentlemen were assisting them: a tall sturdy man with hair the colour of autumn and his short, lean companion in a jewelled cap, whose beard was greying.

"These other gentlemen?" Catherine asked, surveying them with critical eyes.

"Newly come to court from their business in the Low Countries, Charles Cotton and Sir Hugh Truegood. They have been entertaining me with tales of the emperor."

"They have seen the emperor?" Catherine asked in a quiet voice. "How does my nephew fare?"

"They did not see him in person except the once," Henry added swiftly, "at a formal gathering. They were present more to oversee shipping and tax arrangements; Truegood inherited a silk weaving business, which he has been winding up, to transfer to England."

"What is his parentage?"

"Noble," said Henry, "but a junior line."

The sun broke out from the clouds that moment and caught the red-headed man in full beam. His colour drew their eyes and stilled their talk. Thomasin felt herself unable to escape the sense of admiration for this merchant of the minor gentry.

"He will not stay at court for long," added Henry, "but he can tire out six horses in a day."

"And has he brought word for me from my nephew?"

"He was there on business," replied Henry, a little shortly, "not to bring personal messages."

Catherine's lips shut in a firm line.

A roar came up from the forest below. Henry looked down to see who it was.

"Come, Henry. Why do you dally?"

Charles Brandon, Duke of Suffolk, was shading his eyes from the sun, looking up at the king in the gallery. Only he, as Henry's brother-in-law, could get away with calling him by name. "The day proceeds apace and the deer will not catch themselves."

Henry laughed. "There would be little sport in that, indeed, and they will not dine upon themselves, either!"

The company politely laughed at his joke, but he was already fidgeting, itching to be underway.

"We shall take our leave for the moment, Madam." His tone to Catherine was most respectful. "I hope our valour in the hunt brings you pleasure."

For a moment, Thomasin glimpsed how things used to be, back in the days before Anne Boleyn had returned from France. Long, happy days that her parents had spoken about, when the king and queen had been young and in love. The removal of Anne from the picture almost made it seem as if she did not exist.

"God give you good speed and make your arrows fly true," replied Catherine, giving her best smile.

Thomasin watched the king depart, with Hatton at his heels. They thundered down the wooden staircase in their riding boots, then appeared on the ground outside, by the horses. Henry and Suffolk began inspecting their tack.

"I heard," whispered Catherine, as the women looked down on the men below, "that he has quarrelled with the woman."

Thomasin's ears focused on her words.

"Suffolk's man told me. They had a terrible row and he left her behind in London."

As if Henry could sense them talking about him, he turned and waved up to the gallery. Catherine waved graciously.

"I wonder what it can mean," she said softly. "He looks merry, does he not? Perhaps this awful business is over."

Neither of her waiting women dared answer. Instead they watched the king adjusting the reins and speaking softly to the horse.

"Bring Hippocras," Catherine instructed, concealing her pleasure. "I will take a glass."

Thomasin returned to the table and poured out the drink. When she brought it back to the gallery and handed it to Catherine, her attention was drawn outside. A manservant she recognised from Windsor had ridden up and dismounted, as if in a hurry. He knelt at Henry's feet and as they watched, distanced, the man delivered his news.

The women could not make out the words, but they could see the impact the message had upon the king. Henry's entire demeanour changed, as if clouds had eclipsed the sun. He took a step backwards, then his eyes went up to the gallery, his face ghastly with shock. The impact was so dramatic that Catherine rose from her chair.

"Mary and all the Saints, what can this be? Not our child?"

At the king's indication, the servant sped towards the door. They heard his feet on the stairs as they waited, hearts pounding.

The man hurtled down onto his knees before the standing queen.

"Speak, man, what is it?"

"My Lady, a case of the sweat, in the kitchens at Windsor."

"At Windsor?" asked Mountjoy, behind him.

"A maid, complaining of illness last night, was taken much worse this morning. The doctor has been with her and confirmed it as a case."

Catherine became very still, understanding Henry's response at once. It had been the dreaded sweating sickness which claimed his elder brother Arthur, Catherine's own first husband, who had been destined for the throne. Outbreaks of the illness were common in the summer months, but the king had always been careful to avoid it, making up medicines, fleeing to the countryside and limiting contact with his court. But this was early. It was merely spring. The dangerous heat of summer had not yet arrived.

Henry had given up all thoughts of hunting. Now he strode into the room, fast after the messenger. Thomasin was shocked by the change in him. He seemed as a man with the devil at his heels. His face was white as a sheet.

"You heard?" He did not wait for Catherine to answer but continued at once. "You cannot return to Windsor. No one can. The risk is too great. All there must be quarantined." He thought for a moment. "We are within easy ride of Hampton Court. Wolsey will shelter us. There is a straight road and we will be there before nightfall. Take these ladies, no one else, and have only necessary items sent on."

"At once?" asked Catherine.

"At once, without delay."

Catherine was very quiet.

"What is it?" he asked, agitated. "We must be on the road."

"Will the cardinal be ready for us?"

His brows knit. He was a huge figure, in comparison with the diminutive Catherine. "The cardinal will do whatever I command."

But Catherine would not relinquish her concern. "I fear that the cardinal is no friend of mine."

"The cardinal will do his duty. He has no business doing otherwise. He will show you every respect or else he will vacate his palace and I shall lower him as far as I have raised him. Now, make ready to depart at once."

Henry strode away and, as Catherine turned, Thomasin saw that her face was strangely content.

"My Lady?" The messenger had not yet delivered all his news.

"What is it?"

"The Venetians have left Windsor. They were told to remain, and wait for Your Highness's permission, but they departed in haste, as soon as they heard the news."

Nico's golden eyes flashed in Thomasin's mind again.

"So be it," Catherine replied. "At least they went away unsatisfied. They will not be admitted to my presence again."

"Very good, My Lady."

"Now, send word back to the castle. Pack up only my necessaries and let them be dispatched for Hampton with three or four men who are in good health. Mountjoy," she added, seeking her minister, "question them closely. Look into their eyes, feel their brows and the palms of their hands and see that their breath is sweet. Take no chances. And God be with you."

"As you request, My Lady. And also with you."

Below them, outside the gallery, they heard the horses whinnying and the clatter of hooves. Thomasin walked towards the viewing place, only to see the king and his men riding away.

EIGHT

Hampton Court. Even at a distance it was magnificent: red brick, turreted, sun gleaming in its rows of windows, glancing off its twisted chimney stacks. Small details on the rooftops were picked out in gold, and smoke streamed upwards from a dozen locations. A thread of burning wood reached them through the air.

Henry had ridden ahead with his men, their horses' hooves kicking up the dust. The queen's company followed at a slower pace, taking the path along the riverbank to avoid the villages. Despite the ribbons and bells that adorned the horses, the party made a dejected line of fears and doubts, consumed by the news of illness and this unexpected change to their plans. Thomasin struggled to believe that they would not be returning to Windsor as planned: what had started as a simple ride into the park, for a banquet in the hunting lodge, had resulted in this long, tiring journey. In an hour or so, the sun would be setting and Windsor was far away. She pictured it encircled by a miasma of illness, cloudy, opaque and penetrating.

Then, as she was lost in thought, Hampton Court had suddenly appeared on the opposite bank. Thomasin had never seen anything so entrancing, so like the ideal of her dreams, and found she could not tear her eyes away from it. Now she understood why people whispered behind their hands about Wolsey, repeating that little poem. The one written by the court poet John Skelton:

Why come ye not to court?
To which court?
To the king's court? Or Hampton Court!

Ellen was behind Thomasin, so they could not talk, but Thomasin managed to turn and catch her cousin's eye. The awe she saw written there matched her own. Before long, they had reached the wide, red brick entrance gates and turned into the long approach, drawing them straight down towards the front of the palace. It seemed even larger as they rode close, sprawling more like a small village than a palace, with the tiltyard towers, tennis courts and gardens that Gertrude had described on the way.

A deep moat spread along the front, crossed by a stone bridge guarded at each corner by carved heraldic beasts. Servants in Wolsey's livery were lined up in welcome as they entered, bowing their heads as the horses clattered upon the cobbles. Inside the vast courtyard, they dismounted, Thomasin and Ellen helping lift the tiny queen down onto her feet.

Mountjoy was looking around impatiently. "Where is Wolsey?"

It appeared that the castle owner, their host, was nowhere to be seen. Instead, to her annoyance, Thomasin saw the cardinal's man, Thomas Cromwell, approaching them with his decisive, neat walk.

He was wrapped in a fur cloak, gold chains about his neck. As he drew close, he bowed low, but brought himself up a little too quickly and surveyed the group with his small, scrupulous eyes. Thomasin had not forgotten the pressure he had attempted to exert upon her father last autumn, trying to recruit him to the Boleyns' cause, and the news that he had been with her father recently. She could not help but read the welcome in his red, pock-marked face as disingenuous.

"Most honourable lady," he addressed Catherine, "you are welcome at Hampton Court, as a haven from this terrible pestilence. The cardinal is currently meeting with the king but extends his welcome. If you would please follow me." He turned smartly on his heel and strode away towards the far gateway.

Catherine paused, aghast. Her face was white. "He did not greet me as queen. Honourable lady! As if I am nothing and nobody, and not the daughter of Spain and Aragon, nor queen of this realm in which this miserable wretch dwells!"

Mountjoy came to the rescue, stepping forward and offering Catherine his arm. "I will ensure his master hears of it and that the man is spoken to."

"Blacksmith's son," muttered Maria Willoughby behind them, in her Spanish tones, "upstart, blacksmith's son, rodent!"

Walking behind them, Thomasin also felt Catherine's pain. The queen could only walk slowly, tired by the exertions of the day, while Cromwell strode ahead, neglecting to look back and check upon her progress. They found him waiting under the archway ahead, with a look of something almost like impatience on his face.

"Thank you, Cromwell," snapped Mountjoy, barely able to contain his anger. "I know the way to the queen's chambers. I will take it from here."

"Oh, my sincere apologies, but you are not being housed in those chambers," the red-faced man replied. "They have not been fully cleaned, so could not be prepared in time. You are placed in those rooms usually reserved for the Duchess of Suffolk. This way, if you please."

"The Duchess of Suffolk's rooms?" asked Mountjoy. "Are they suitable for the queen?"

Cromwell turned, his eyes wide in feigned innocence. "Would you prefer unswept rooms, where the beds are not made?"

"Don't be absurd, man; we have been a good few hours on the road. Why have the beds not been made?"

"You may have been hours on the road, my Lord," Cromwell replied, "but your messenger only arrived this hour since, a little ahead of the king himself."

"See to it that the rooms are prepared for the morrow. The queen is tired and needs to rest. Take us to the prepared chambers at once."

"As I was, my Lord," replied Cromwell, determined to have the final say before he headed through into the second courtyard and up a flight of stairs.

Thomasin followed, quite sickened by the man's disrespectful tone.

They met their host at dinner. Wolsey was waiting at the top of a flight of steps to welcome Catherine and her party as they approached. The cardinal was in his mid-fifties and wore his full red robes around his corpulent body and the soft, four-cornered hat upon his grey hair. He had the air of a great statesman, wise beyond his years and birth. However, as he laced his fingers together, dazzling with gems, Thomasin suddenly saw that he was uncertain. At first, Henry had chosen not to confide in him about Anne. Wolsey had been one of the last to know, and that had shaken him.

"Most reverent lady." Wolsey bowed low and deep, in a far better show of deference than Cromwell had mustered.

Thomasin looked at the stitching on the top of his cap, wondering how long he would remain in that position.

Catherine released him. "Arise."

He did so slowly, with a hint of age and pain. "Most reverent lady, it is my pleasure to put my palace at your disposal. Please, make it your own. Whatever you wish, shall be my pleasure to provide."

Thomasin saw Catherine and Mountjoy exchange glances. So did Wolsey.

"Is there something, My Lady? May I be of service?"

"There appears to have been some confusion over our apartments," braved Mountjoy. "The queen has been lodged in the rooms of the Duchess of Suffolk. Quite insufficient for her needs and wholly unsuitable for her station. Also, we were met at the gates by your minion, Cromwell, whose manner of greeting was not appropriate for one of Her Majesty's rank. I am sure," he added, to make the point, "the king would be most displeased to hear it."

Mixed impulses struggled across Wolsey's face. He appeared to choose the path of least resistance, his features resolving into a smile. "My most profound apologies for any slight that was felt. I am sure it was not the intention. I will see to it that the royal apartments are made ready at once and that you are settled as soon as possible. Will you come in to dine? It is only such humble fare as could be found at short notice."

Catherine held up a hand. "Cardinal. Can you give me your assurance that all are heathy and wholesome in your employ? You have had no reported cases of illness, no fainting or sweating? I am most anxious to take no risks and I know the king, my husband, is also most anxious for the same."

She was admirable, thought Thomasin; regal, authoritative and yet considerate, even under such duress.

"My Lady, you have my word. All here is clean and wholesome; at the slightest murmur of any illness, you will be the first I inform."

She inclined her head gracefully, and they followed Wolsey into dinner.

The great hall was more elegant than that at Windsor or Westminster. Both were older buildings, designed with defence in mind, their inhabitants existing inside thick stone walls which the sunlight hardly penetrated. Hampton Court was a new creation, not yet twenty years old, drawn up from renaissance chateaux Wolsey had seen on the continent. The hall was spacious, and light streamed down from the lines of windows above. Below them hung tapestries depicting hunting scenes, all below a carved wooden hammerbeam ceiling. To the right of the dais ahead, a long oriel window was set back in a recess, flooding the top table with multicoloured light. Henry sat in the centre, while his men had placed themselves on one side of a lower trestle table.

The king rose when he saw Catherine approach. His gentlemen hurried to their feet and bowed in deference.

"We give thanks to the Lord that you have arrived safe and well. Come, sit and eat. You must be tired after the long journey. We will be safe here, until this pestilence passes."

Thomasin was surprised by the warmth of his welcome. Catherine also seemed to be appreciative of his words. The sweat always brought out his insecurities.

"Thank you, My Lord, my good husband, for your kind attentions."

If Henry noticed her inclusion of their relationship, he chose to ignore it and beckoned her forward to a seat on the dais. Thomasin, Ellen, Gertrude and Maria were faced by a table that already contained the king's closest friends: his games-master William Compton, Anne Boleyn's brother-in-law, William Carey, his own sister's husband, Charles Brandon and the disgraceful William Hatton, grinning under his mop of fair hair. Beside them, the new men: red-haired Hugh Truegood and the slight, soft-haired Charles Cotton.

Mountjoy urged them to be seated, but Ellen knew that Thomasin could not stomach being close to Hatton, so at the last minute she signalled to her cousin to wait, and they swapped places. Thomasin found herself to be opposite Brandon and Compton instead, and thanked Ellen with grateful eyes. Nor could she resist turning them briefly upon the king, still in his riding habit and jewelled cap. Henry's face was serious, unreadable.

The humble fare which Wolsey had described as having been found at short notice, proved to be a rich side of venison, jugged hare, stewed pork with prunes, chickens in saffron and beef patties. Suddenly, Thomasin found herself hungry. They had departed the hunting lodge without partaking of the banquet that had been prepared for them, so had eaten little but bread and wine on the road. Ellen, too, ate with appetite.

"It's almost like old times," said a voice opposite, softly.

Seated opposite, Brandon looked across at her and smiled.

She was disposed to like his broad, handsome face, but recalled the occasion of Cecilia's failed wedding, when he had swept past her without a word. Still, she reasoned, a dignified silence was better than the mockery they had received at the hands of Thomas Boleyn.

"Old times?" asked Compton beside him, with his laughing eyes.

Brandon nodded towards the top table. "King and queen, husband and wife, dining together in peace. As it was before that woman came along."

Thomasin was surprised, but knew she had to tread carefully. She bit her tongue.

Compton spoke instead, dismissively, between mouthfuls. "It is well known that you are no admirer of the Lady Anne, Charles."

Brandon turned his pale blue eyes towards them. Thomasin took in his lined, weather-beaten face with its thick, square beard, a veteran of many military campaigns. "All that men admire in her is mere glitter and masques. I was there when Queen Catherine arrived in England from Spain, a girl of fifteen. She and my Mary were close companions in the old king's court. I was there when she married Arthur, and when she returned to London as a widow. I was there when she married Henry and when we buried the children she bore him. What is more admirable than two decades of devotion?"

Thomasin was deeply impressed by his loyalty.

"Those are the things that matter," he continued, "not some young chit with her fancy ways from France. She has changed him. Put ideas into his head that Henry would never have dreamed up alone, not the old Henry, anyway."

"The king has changed?"

"The world has changed," said Brandon. "In the last decade. I rode beside Henry when he met King Francis at the Field of Cloth of Gold, when Catherine dined with Queen Claude, God rest her soul, and that pert Boleyn madam was a translator, working for the French to earn her bread."

Thomasin looked to the top table where Henry was passing a dish to Catherine, helping her most gently.

She dared to ask the question that was in her mind. "Do you think there is a chance for reconciliation?"

Brandon shrugged. "The king has had his head turned. But it is not the first time. What affects him most is the woman's presence. Keeping her constantly by his side causes the damage. If she was somehow prevented from attending court, he may forget her in time, and the queen could use her gentle good graces to remind him of happier times."

"You think that would work? Out of sight and out of mind?"

"So long as the king thinks the idea was his own. Some more amenable young woman could be found to slip into his bed and distract him. Remind him of his true calling."

"Is that all?"

Brandon looked at her sharply. "All? What do you mean?"

Thomasin floundered. "Is it that simple, keeping him from Anne? I mean, that will not give him a son."

"No," Brandon admitted. "You are right. It will not." The pale eyes were fixed upon her. "You are Marwood's daughter, aren't you?"

Thomasin felt her cheeks colour. "I am, sir."

"Not the one…"

"No," she jumped in at once. "The younger one."

"Ah," he grunted, biting into a haunch of venison. "Could you see yourself in the role?"

"Which role?" asked Thomasin, feeling uncomfortable.

"Why, in the king's bed, of course. Pretty thing like you."

Thomasin's throat contracted. It could be her father of whom they were speaking. "No, sir, absolutely not."

"You sound most certain."

"I have the most particular reasons for refusing."

He looked at her oddly. "Already taken, are you? That's no barrier, never has been. Even better if they're married."

She could not stop thoughts of her mother arising. "No, sir, I must be adamant."

"Taken a vow, have you?"

"Something like that."

"Well, never mind, plenty out there willing. Another woman would break the hold the Boleyn girl has on him."

"Have a care to whom you speak so freely," added Compton at Brandon's side, his expression serious for once. "You never know to which allegiance you speak."

"But it is a matter for all," Brandon asserted, "bigger than king and queen alone. The Boleyn woman and her friends speak of reforms to the faith that she saw in France. She encourages the king to overturn two centuries of allegiances to Spain and the Empire, and would have him imperil our very souls."

"Still," said Compton, eyeing the women.

"Please, do not hold back on my account," Thomasin said, with feigned innocence. "I am only a young girl newly come from the country; I am here merely to serve my mistress."

Brandon looked into her face for a moment, then roared with laughter. "A green girl, she claims, although her ruddy cheeks speak of quite the opposite colour. Mistress Marwood, you are sharper than you would have us believe. Come, let's drink to the health of king and queen, whatever our allegiances might be. God will decide all."

"Indeed he will," said Compton, raising his cup.

Thomasin blushed and followed suit.

NINE

A fire had been lit in the wide, stone hearth, filling the room with heat and light. The Duchess of Suffolk's apartments were pleasant enough, Thomasin thought, looking around her, with the gold embroidered curtains and the pleasant view over the gardens. It was getting dark outside, and the torches had been lit on the walls, glimmering in welcome.

Ellen helped Catherine into the chair closest to the flames. Catherine eased herself down slowly, suffering from her old complaint in her back and hips.

Gently, Thomasin knelt on the floor and pulled back the embroidered hem of Catherine's dress, sewn with pomegranates and roses, to reveal her red velvet shoes. The little button was easy to release from its hook and each shoe slid off in turn. Catherine sighed in relief. Ellen brought wine.

Mountjoy had followed them up from dinner. He came into the room and bowed low. "My Lady, I have spoken again with the cardinal, and he assures me that the queen's apartments will be ready tomorrow. They need to be fumigated and washed down in case of infection. I hope that will be sufficient."

"Thank you, William, that will suffice. We shall be comfortable here for one night."

"Is there anything else I can do for you, My Lady?"

"That is all. Except…"

"Yes, My Lady?"

Catherine sighed. "I do not trust the cardinal. I believe him behind the ambassadors' visit to Windsor. He wishes to learn my secrets, even to entrap me. We must be vigilant. Share nothing with him."

"Of course," Mountjoy nodded.

Catherine turned to her ladies. "That goes for all. Speak to no one but those you trust."

"Yes, my lady," said Thomasin, in chorus with Ellen, Gertrude and Maria.

"Good, that is understood. That is all."

Mountjoy bowed. "Then I shall bid you a goodnight. I go now to meet with Wolsey to discuss our needs over the coming weeks. I shall guard my tongue most carefully and keep my ears open."

His final words resonated in Thomasin's mind. Weeks? They could remain here at Hampton Court for weeks, shut away from the world, receiving no visitors due to fears about the pestilence. No ambassadors, no friends. Could this be worse than Windsor?

As Mountjoy was leaving the room, he passed the Duke of Suffolk entering. Brandon strode in boldly, his blue eyes glinting in his tanned face. "My Lady."

Catherine beckoned him forward. "Be seated," she invited him. "Drink some wine with me. Where is the king this evening?"

Brandon took the seat opposite her and accepted the glass that Ellen brought him. There was something in his manner, in his ease with his own body, in the air that he projected that spoke of great physical confidence. He was certainly dignified, powerful, even royal, although it did not run in his veins. He was a few years older than the king, in his mid-forties by now.

"The king is writing letters," he replied.

"Writing?" Catherine was surprised. "Not dictating as usual?"

The king's usual practice was to dictate his correspondence to a clerk, unless they were personal letters.

Brandon looked uncomfortable and tried to deflect her question. "He is about his letters, I believe."

Catherine looked thoughtful. She played with her wine glass. "I suppose his usual clerk is not here. And yet I wonder to whom he takes the time to write."

Brandon stared into the flames and pretended not to hear. "He awaits news from Rome, I know that much. Bishop Foxe is meeting with the Pope to discuss…"

"I know what they will discuss," replied Catherine, bitterly, "the legality of our marriage. My husband need not send the bishop to Rome, when he knows the answer in his heart."

"Hopefully Foxe will return with the answers you seek. And that might be an end of it."

"Foxe is not alone, though. Garrrdiner is with him." She rolled out the r sound in his name, like a dog growling.

Maria understood her at once. "A pox upon that man. How can a bishop be so ungodly?" She looked at Brandon. "You know I named my dog after him."

"Ha, did you indeed!" Brandon was genuinely amused.

"Come," Catherine called, nodding. "Remove my headdress."

Thomasin and Ellen stepped up behind her chair, and Catherine straightened her spine to help them. Working their deft fingers through her hair, they pulled out the pins and gently lifted the contraption from her head. Underneath, she wore a white cap, hugging close to her skull. The long red hair coiled beneath was tinged with grey. Thomasin had noted, only last week, as she'd brushed out those locks, just how thin and fine they were becoming, and how many hairs were shed upon the brush.

"Oh, I quite forgot." Brandon reached inside his doublet. "I bring you a letter from Mary."

"Mary?" Her eyes lit up at once, thinking of her daughter, far away in the Welsh Marches, in her establishment at Ludlow.

"Duchess Mary," he said softly, holding out the letter, meaning his wife. "She sends you her continuing love and loyalty."

Catherine took it between finger and thumb. "I am most grateful to receive it." She dandled the missive in her lap for a moment, her eyes distant. Then, in a low voice, she asked, "Is there any more news?"

"Nothing from court, My Lady. All is quiet at Westminster."

"And the king's intentions?"

"So far as I know, he has no intentions to leave Hampton in the coming weeks, until the pestilence has subsided."

Catherine nodded. "And the woman?"

"Still at Westminster, although there is talk of her going into Kent, where her family have an estate."

"Let God will it." She broke open the red seal and unfolded the paper. Her eyes ran across the neat, tight writing that filled the page. "Ah," she said at length. "Your dear wife is well. She writes that Frances and Eleanor are in good health, playing the virginals and reading their lessons."

Brandon smiled at the mention of his daughters.

"And little Henry has been put into his breeches already." She put down the letter. "That feels so soon. He is too young, surely?"

"Already past his fifth birthday."

"So soon! What a comfort," Catherine said softly. "You must cherish him."

"Indeed," nodded Brandon, mindful of the children she had lost. "We do indeed."

The evening was slipping by, and the wicks burned down slowly on the candles. Thomasin and Ellen had retired to an alcove, where they were seated on cushions, feeling the exertions of a long, unexpected day. As Catherine and Brandon talked, Thomasin let her mind wander back to Windsor, where the queen's chambers would be dark and cold, her kitchen depleted, her table bare. It felt strange to have escaped so suddenly, just when she was feeling closed in, like the hooded falcons. That pair of golden eyes briefly flitted through her mind, to her surprise. Where had the Venetians gone, she wondered? Had Nico ever really intended to pursue a career at the English court, or had it simply been more flattery, designed to entrap Catherine? And the kiss he had planted upon her lips? She shook away the memory. He would be forgotten in a seven night.

A knock at the door interrupted the peace in the chamber.

"Now, who can this be at this hour?" asked Catherine, her brow furrowed.

She had not had the chance to respond before the door swung open and King Henry strode in. He had taken off his doublet and walked towards them in his shirt sleeves, his collar open to show his thick, tanned throat. Even in that state of undress, he was magnificent but also terrifying. Thomasin turned her eyes away.

"My Lord!" Somehow Catherine made it out of her chair and down to her knees. Her ladies followed suit. "This is an unexpected pleasure."

"Arise, arise." Henry beckoned to servants behind him and gestured towards the empty table. With careful hands, they deposited three or four wooden platters. "I found oranges in the kitchens, and walnuts. I thought you might like them."

Thomasin could almost feel the warm glow spread over Catherine. The happiness brought by this small gesture, the memory of their former intimacy, the hope that it might be rekindled.

"Your Grace is so very thoughtful."

He offered her his hand, whereupon she rose and resumed her chair. Brandon, who had bowed, now stepped aside so the king could take his seat.

Henry looked around the rooms. "You will not be too uncomfortable here, I hope." Then, without waiting for her answer, he proceeded, "I had thought to ride out tomorrow, perhaps to have the archery butts set up, too. It is a shame to be stuck indoors, even if we must remain here. I have heard of no cases in the village, but will head in the opposite direction anyway, beyond the park to the south. Depending upon the weather being fine."

Catherine did not reply at once. Thomasin wondered if, like herself, the queen was unsure whether or not she was invited.

"It may well be another dry day like today," offered Brandon. "I am sure the air and exercise will do you good."

Henry nodded. "You think it safe?"

"Utterly. Keep on the cardinal's land and you will meet no one."

Henry drummed his fingers on the carved arm rests of his chair. Conflicting emotions chased across his face. "Perhaps I should send for my dogs from London; they could be here within a day or two, then I can hunt. The coming weeks will take us through spring and the best weather. I shall write to Westminster in the morning and have them dispatched. I have not heard of dogs carrying a risk of infection. And if I only ask for the one man to deliver them, he could stay outside the palace while Will Carey goes out to collect them. Is that wise?"

Thomasin was surprised at the insecurity that the fear of illness brought out in him.

"If Your Grace wishes it," spoke Catherine quietly, recognising his mood.

"I do wish it, but is it wise? I asked whether you thought it is wise?"

"I am sure my good Lord consults his best wisdom in every decision he makes."

"Hmm." Henry bounced up from the chair and paced the room. "This fresh outbreak of the disease … it's more than the danger. The situation itself, the waiting, the uncertainty, is enough to send a man into a state of fever."

Brandon and Catherine exchanged looks. For Henry to actually admit to weakness, even indirectly, was a rare occurrence.

"Your Grace should rest assured," said Brandon, pacifically, "that you have taken every sensible step to avoid the illness. Remaining here, at Hampton, will allow you the space and wholesome air, so that you might avoid the dangers of Windsor and the city."

"It really is the worst place to be, is it not?" asked Henry, stroking his beard. "The city? And Westminster hard upon it."

"My Lord, of course, you are best here, away from people."

"Away from people," Henry echoed.

And it was then that Thomasin realised the nature of Henry's concern. He was away from Anne. They had quarrelled and he had ridden away, leaving her behind in London, and now he feared that she would be in danger.

Brandon had come to the same realisation. "The most important thing of all must be the king's own, sacred life. The Lord saw fit to take your brother Arthur, of blessed memory, in order for you to become king. It was part of His plan. You should rejoice in your good fortune, secure in the belief that He will protect you as His chosen ruler."

But Henry did not look convinced. "Who is to say this is not another part of His plan? He has chosen not to give me the son and heir the kingdom needs. Is this not a great mark of His disfavour? What if He has tested me, tried me, and found me wanting? How little does He value the life of a king to whom He will not grant a son?"

"You must trust in the Lord's plan," Brandon reiterated.

Henry paced again. "I don't know. The books I have read lately. They make me wonder. What if God does not intervene as much as we thought? What if he is more of an observant God, watching while we make our own choices? What if our decisions are not governed by him but are our own free will? Such words I have read, lately, but such minds, which almost addle my own. And who would plant these very doubts in my mind, but God himself?"

There was a stunned silence. Catherine looked aghast.

Thomasin recognised something in the king's words that was close to what William Hatton had spoken of last autumn; a new way of looking at the world. A belief in each individual's ability to choose their own path, rather than to simply follow where they were led. And More's free will.

"Heretical books again?" asked Brandon, half joking. "I thought you had banned them."

"I have been hearing much about this new book by Tyndale, which he is writing in Antwerp. There is something in his ideas about kingship that demands answers. I wonder what advice he would give me, if he were recalled to England."

Brandon was stunned. "But two years ago, you had his translation of the Bible burned in the streets. I remember it well. And have not Wolsey and More and Bishop Tunstall of London all condemned his ideas? They go against the Pope!"

Henry frowned deeply. Thomasin wondered if Brandon had overstepped the mark. "Much has happened in two years," he replied, his voice ominously soft.

Catherine lifted her chin. "My Lord, for years you have been accustomed to coming to me for advice, and I have done my best to advise you, from my faith, my learning and the wisdom instilled in me by my parents. If you would listen to my counsel now, I would recommend other books for your Lordship to read, other minds that might satisfy yours, put you at peace, rather than into this state of turmoil, which befits not a king nor benefits his kingdom."

It was a brave speech, a generous speech, but not one that Henry wished to hear.

"The world has changed, Madam," he pronounced, curtly. "Such books reflect old ways of looking at the world. Rather than counselling me to read your books, you would do better to read mine, then perhaps you might come to understand me better." His words cut through the room.

"My Lord..." Catherine hesitated.

He halted, turned back to her.

"My Lord," she tried again. "Your mind is troubled."

"Indeed it is, Madam, indeed it is."

"These are dangerous ideas, dressed up to impress your mind, but they are subtle masks for heresies."

"Heresy? Heresy? You accuse me of heresy?"

The room was still and sharp as a knife. His words wheeled about them like falcons.

Catherine dropped to one knee. "Of course not, My Lord."

Brandon was on his feet. "Come, Henry, nothing of the kind was said. You are likely overtired by the day's strains. Some rest will restore you."

Henry seemed to accept this, nodding. "I should rest."

But Catherine, as if on a mission, had not finished yet. "My husband, will you come with me, tomorrow morning, to the little chapel, where we can pray together with the cardinal and ask for God's guidance?"

The king turned, his eyes shot through with tension. "You would be better praying for guidance, Madam, but I will be out riding."

Without another word, Henry swept out of the room. The door banged behind him and the flaming brackets on the wall nearby flickered in the draught.

Catherine let out a sigh. One hand upon the back of her chair, she seemed to collapse before their eyes, shrinking and drawing into herself. Her knuckles whitened. Her shoulders shook.

After a moment, she turned to her women. "I will retire. Prepare my bed, prepare my clothes."

Thomasin and Ellen jumped up at once, hurrying to smooth down the sheets and plump up the satin pillows on the large bed. The great white and gold curtains were tied in loops at each of the four corners, in knots that had not been touched in weeks, maybe months.

Brandon moved close to Catherine, speaking in soft tones. "He is troubled. He lashes out at you because he cannot see a solution and he is afraid."

"I know it," Catherine replied. "But he is both my familiar husband and a stranger. You saw how he was when he arrived; the oranges and walnuts, just like his old self."

"He is torn in two directions. I pray that God will guide him."

"As will I. Sometimes I still think there is hope. If only we can use these weeks to reconnect, to remind ourselves of how things used to be, and what God's plan is for us. But the hour advances, I must to bed. I am almost asleep on my feet."

Brandon took his leave. Thomasin and the others helped Catherine to undress and climb into her bed, although none of them believed she would rest easy.

It was late when Thomasin and Ellen finally lay down on the truckle beds on the floor. The embers were dying in the grate and the palace was silent. Even more silent than Windsor, where the sounds of feet and voices had permeated the darkness.

The air in the chamber was thick, from having been closed up so long, and with the presence of sleepers. Catherine's breathing was erratic and Thomasin heard her bed creak as she turned onto her side. Ellen was still, as were Maria Willoughby and Gertrude, who had joined them. Lying on the end bed, under the window, Thomasin caught a little of the light behind the curtains, with that strange luminous silver tone that suggested a full moon. She thought of the oranges and walnuts lying untouched on the table.

In the darkness, her mind drifted back home to Suffolk, among the apple blossom, then to the little chamber where she had slept as a child, with its view over the sheep fields. She wondered if Cecilia was walking in the woods again, finding the first flowers, watching the new lambs. Then she pictured them all at table, in the great hall in the evening, the crackling fire and the slow creep up the winding stairs to the little bedroom. The view over the treetops…

Suddenly, she was wide awake again. Back at Hampton Court, listening keenly to the still night. There was the noise. A sob, light and muffled, followed by another, then a third.

"What is that?"

The sound had woken Ellen too. They listened and it came again.

"The queen," Thomasin realised. "She is crying in her sleep."

TEN

The morning hung heavily upon them. White clouds banked up behind the twisted chimney stacks as Catherine and her ladies made their way back from the little chapel towards the gardens. Catherine looked regal as ever, Thomasin noted, in a gown of grey velvet slashed with carmine and strings of pearls about her throat. No one else would guess she had woken late, after a troubled night of tossing and turning, and had taken no food to break her fast yet.

Thomasin followed her slow progress, grateful to be outdoors. There was no mistaking the change in the season: a real hope of spring in the air, fresh with the scents of greenery and burgeoning life. The world was waking, but it was still waiting, tentative, wondering whether it was safe to bloom again.

As they crossed the courtyard with its dazzling brickwork, there was not a soul to be seen. Thomasin ran her eyes along the first-floor windows of the great hall, searching the doorways and corridors where servants should be scuttling with baskets and brooms. It seemed strange that such a large, impressive palace should be so devoid of people and activity, so still and quiet. Thomasin thought back to the masque she had once attended at Wolsey's magnificent York Place on the river Thames, with its renaissance statues and its cabinet of gold. Such a place as Hampton Court was built for revelry on a grand scale, not for crying at night or whispering behind doors.

The sundial in the middle of the court showed that it was almost midday.

"My Lady?"

Someone was hurrying behind them across the cobbles.

Catherine paused and turned under sufferance.

They had already recognised the voice but the sight of Thomas Cromwell, sweaty and rasping out his breath, was less than welcome.

Catherine held her dignity as the secretary approached, the sun glinting off his gold chains and jewelled rings. He bowed low.

"Why do you seek me out in my quiet hour?" Catherine's voice had a hint of warning.

"My Lady, I am come to take my leave of you."

Catherine waited, offering him nothing.

"The king has granted me his gracious leave to return to my family today, in Chelsea. The area appears clear of pestilence, as am I. I wish to be with them during these difficult times, but I shall remain in correspondence with the cardinal and the king, if this suits you, My Lady. I wish you the very best of health and humbly ask your leave."

Catherine eyed him coolly, knowing that this was a mere formality. This man would not obey any command she might give to stay. His question was for the sake of an empty protocol, with no kindness, no respect, no real regard in it. Purely the courtly game. They knew it; he knew it.

As always, Catherine was more dignified, her thoughts on higher concerns.

"I was not aware that you were a family man."

He kept his head bowed.

"You have children?"

"Yes, My Lady, I thank you. I have a son and two daughters."

"What ages?"

"Anne is twelve, Grace is ten and my boy Gregory is turning eight soon."

"They are well?"

"Very well, I thank you, My Lady."

"And your wife? What is her name?"

"Her name is Elizabeth."

Thomasin tried to picture him with a wife at his side, children at his knee, playing games with them or whispering private jokes, as her father had done. No image came to her.

"And you have concluded your business here, Master Secretary?"

Cromwell paused, as his thoughts ticked over. "The king's business never concludes, but I will continue to serve him from my home. Accounts, advice, letters, whatever needs to be done."

Catherine's eyes darkened. "Do you have letters to dispatch now? Letters the king wrote last night?"

The man's ruddy face did not so much as flicker. "I am delivering the king's correspondence and his orders. There is much to be done to secure the realm amidst this pestilence."

"To secure the realm," Catherine echoed. "Indeed. Do you have the letters? I wish to check them." She held out a gloved hand.

Cromwell's mind was swift. "Regrettably, they are not on my person, My Lady."

Catherine waited, judging how far she might push the man.

"They are among my bags, where my horse waits saddled on the road."

Catherine nodded, as if this was the answer she had expected. It would not be seemly to pursue the matter. "Consider that you have my leave. God speed you from this place."

It was a warmer parting than he deserved.

Thomasin watched him until he passed through the gates, striding in his awkward way, his body somehow both rolling and also tight.

They had left the palace behind and sought the freshness of the gardens where the birds were making melody. The ends of their skirts swished upon the gravel path and their shadows were cast long, in shades of grey and green. As they rounded the corner, three men were visible, shooting at the butts. Down at the far end of the walk, beyond the rose bushes, the coloured rounds were bright in the sun, with their concentric rings. Black, blue, red, yellow. Catherine led her ladies forwards out of curiosity.

Sir Hugh Truegood was standing with his bow drawn, ready to loosen his arrow. There was something in his aspect that was majestic, sculptural even, as he was caught in the act of stretching back. Cotton and Hatton stood by, mere mortals in comparison with Hugh's beauty, leaning on their bows in readiness. Thomasin felt distaste rise in her throat as she saw the latter again, but had no choice other than to follow Catherine as she made her way across the grass to them.

Truegood slackened his grip and bowed as soon as he caught their movement. The other men followed suit, vying to outdo each other by swooping their hats lower.

"Resume your sport," Catherine insisted. "We will take pleasure in watching you compete. Who leads?"

"Truegood leads, My Lady," spoke up Hatton at once, with his usual confidence. "He has hit three bulls' eyes out of five already, compared with my two and Cotton's one."

The flame-headed man made a gesture of humility before stretching back his bow again. His arm arched with power, a

101

muscular curve that held his strength and balance, before the arrow shot straight and true into the heart of the target.

A polite shimmer of applause ran through the ladies.

"Impressive indeed, Sir Truegood; as your name suggests, I think no man here shoots better than you, save for the king himself."

"My Lady, you are too kind."

"I speak as I see. Where did you learn to shoot like that?"

When he turned, Thomasin could see his eyes were the same blazing auburn, his skin pinkish and freckled. The nose was straight and symmetrical, lips wide over white teeth, chin shaven and taut. His expression was honest and open.

"In Flanders, My Lady. In service of the emperor."

"Of course," added Catherine, "you are newly come from there."

"From Antwerp."

"From Antwerp?" she echoed. "From my nephew's kingdom."

"And a fine and beautiful land it is."

"I wonder what made you wish to return home?"

"Business, My Lady, it was only ever business. I am an Englishman through and through, and I longed to see my home in the springtime, when the country comes to life."

Catherine smiled. "That was prettily said. Whereabouts in England is your home, which drew you back here? And why are you not there now?"

A smile played about his lips, tracing a faint line on each side. Thomasin tried to guess at his age, but his fairness was deceptive; he could have been in his mid-twenties or early thirties.

"Glebe Hall, on the Kent and Sussex border. I was to have ridden on there after the Windsor hunt, but the king wished to retain me, as is best, until I prove free of the disease."

"Your wife will be pleased to see you return, no doubt."

"My mother will, My Lady."

"No wife?" Catherine said wryly. "With your handsome face and physique? Even Mister Cromwell has a wife, it seems. Come, Sir Charles Cotton, do you have a wife? I shall not ask William Hatton."

Thomasin shot Catherine a look. Her face was a regal mask, but those who knew her best might have spotted a gleam in her eyes.

"No, My Lady," replied the softly-spoken Cotton. "I have not had the good fortune."

"Well, then," said Catherine with a flourish. "At least show us how well you can shoot."

Catherine went to sit upon the bench while Cotton assumed his position and weighed up his bow. Hatton was a little to her right. Thomasin felt a slight wave of satisfaction that he appeared disgruntled at Catherine's dismissive comment.

"Good positioning," Catherine commented as Cotton placed his feet apart and squared on to the butts. He took up his bow, and although he was a slight man, he managed to convey a sense of strength and ease. The first arrow flowed easily into the red.

"Bravo, oh, bravo," said Catherine, clapping her hands. Thomasin and the other women followed suit. "But can you do it a second time, or was it just beginner's luck?"

"You set me a challenge I will strive to achieve, My Lady."

"And where are you from, Charles?" Catherine asked, as he selected his arrow and checked its flights.

"My family come from the Welsh borders, east of Hereford."

"Is that so? It is a beautiful part of the world. I lived there once, many years ago, and now my daughter resides there."

"At Ludlow, I believe?"

"Yes, at Ludlow. You know it, then?"

"I have occasion to visit it often. Two months back, I saw the princess attending church. I can confirm she was in good health and spirits."

A flush spread over Catherine's cheeks and, for a moment, she appeared incapable of responding. Cotton drew his bow and loosed the arrow. They all watched as it sailed in an arc through the air before striking the black, outermost circle.

"Do not worry, I will permit you another attempt," smiled Catherine.

Cotton drew again, and this time, his arrow flew home to the mark.

"There!" Catherine clapped her hands. "A perfect shot. Two perfect archers."

"Might I take my turn?" asked Hatton, bounding forward with the sun in his hair.

"No thank you, William Hatton," Catherine replied in a chilly voice. "We all know you do not play by the rules."

Thomasin saw the smile transform Ellen's lips and turned away to conceal her own. A flush of pride and loyalty to her mistress bloomed in her chest.

"Come, ladies," Catherine called, rising to her feet. "The hour will soon be upon us."

As she turned to follow, Thomasin caught the glinting amber eyes of Hugh Truegood resting upon her. They left a warm feeling upon her skin that the weak sunshine could not explain.

Henry appeared to have forgotten the unpleasantness of the previous evening. It had melted like snow on his boots before the fireside. He strode into the great hall in his hunting coat just as Catherine was speaking with Maria. Thomasin, Ellen and Gertrude had been relegated to a corner, where they waited to be seated at their low trestle table.

Henry had a glow on him from the ride back. He leapt up onto the dais. "By God's wounds, a splendid morning, a most invigorating hunt and three stags delivered to the kitchens."

The women bowed low at once.

"You should have seen how I killed the last stag," he continued. "It outran us for near on five miles before tiring. Then it stopped, in the middle of a glade, and turned its head back to look at us, as if to surrender. If it could talk, it would have said that the game was up, and we should take it there and then."

"It was a noble creature indeed," added Brandon, throwing off his green cloak. "Worthy of the sport."

"Elevating it almost to an art!" added Henry. "And when I dispatched it with my dagger, it looked into my eyes with an expression that I cannot describe. It quite moved me, the noble beast."

Their words turned Thomasin's stomach: the relish in killing, the creature's death lauded as noble. In truth, it was nothing more than slaughter for the fun of it, or for the sake of eating, and she loathed the way they dressed it up, although such a thought would never pass her lips. And, no doubt, she would partake of the venison pies in a day or two, with a hearty appetite. Yet she had no stomach for the kill, certainly not as the king described it.

Catherine rose quietly. "You have had a fulfilling hunt, My Lord?"

"Less fulfilling than jubilant, God be praised. Utterly glorious. The sun filled the valley as we rode back with such golden light, it almost seemed heavenly."

Thomasin saw Catherine's eyebrows twitch a little. The king's good mood filled them all with relief.

"My Lord." Wolsey was approaching, with the quiet serenity of owning the place.

"Thomas!" cried Henry. "The hunting here is magnificent. We have supplied your kitchens for the coming week."

"I am pleased that it was to your liking."

"More than to my liking; I shall hunt again tomorrow, and the next day, if your woods can bear it."

"I am certain you will find more to your taste."

"Speaking of taste, we are to eat. I have a burning hunger on me now that must be sated. Come, all, be seated, swift as you can. Bring out the food, give the order."

But as Wolsey was about to instruct the servant, Henry caught the man's eye and delivered a firm nod, sending him off to the kitchens. Outranked in his own home, the cardinal blushed the same colour as his robes.

Catherine and Henry took their places side by side, with Wolsey invited to sit a little apart on the same table, as their host. The queen's ladies had their own trestle, which Thomasin was pleased to occupy, between Gertrude and Ellen. Brandon, Mountjoy and Compton, along with Truegood and Cotton, Carey and Hatton, occupied the third. Steaming plates of pork with stewed apples appeared, along with chicken with prunes, egg and herb tarts, dainty quails in sauce, a side of beef and sallets of spring flowers. Servants filled glasses from goblets of sweetened wine.

"He has eyes for you," said Ellen softly, at Thomasin's side.

Thomasin's eyes had been surveying the fare on the table. "What?"

"That Hugh Truegood. He cannot keep his eyes from you."

"Oh, hush, you speak nonsense."

"Nonsense, is it? Just watch him, then you will see for yourself."

"I will do no such thing. If I watch him, then he will be quite justified in saying that I am watching him and will whisper to his busybody friend that I cannot keep my eyes from him."

Ellen said nothing, but raised her eyebrows and reached for the white bread.

Thomasin loaded up her plate, acutely conscious now of the men's table. It seemed to occupy her mind's eye like a heavy weight, but she shook it off as silliness on Ellen's part.

"He is handsome, though — that hair." Ellen had no coyness when it came to looking across the room.

"Stop it! Mind your business."

"I am certain he is speaking of you to Suffolk. The way they smile and look over each time one of them adds a new remark."

"They are most likely commenting upon the tapestries behind me. Eat your food."

Ellen took a sip of wine. "You are not saying you would refuse him, surely? I certainly would not, if he came courting me. Think of all those fine silks and damasks he might have in his warehouses, brought from Antwerp, ready to adorn his future wife."

"I have not said that," Thomasin was forced to admit, "but you are too bold and your imagination runs wild. He would not think of me that way."

107

"Would he not? Just look and see."

Thomasin could not stop her eyes from being drawn briefly across the hall, where they met with the intense amber gaze of Hugh Truegood. He inclined his head slightly to acknowledge her. A small, intimate gesture of recognition, before she tore her eyes away.

But it all felt too much like Rafe Danvers all over again; the stolen glances, the distant admiration, the fixed eyes. Her heart was still fragile. She reached for another hearty slice of beef.

They scarcely noticed the servant enter. A man in Wolsey's livery scurried down the side and knelt in front of the dais before Wolsey bade him speak.

"Please, My Lord, there are people from the village at the gates, bringing gifts for the king."

Wolsey frowned. Henry put down his goblet. The hall fell silent, waiting to see how the king would respond to this potential danger.

It was the cardinal who stepped in first. "You have stayed them at the gates? Not let them approach?"

"Yes, My Lord, a gardener spoke with them at a distance. They bring eggs, cheese and fresh milk, fruit and other items. I did not want to send them away, considering our need." The man looked nervously at the king. "Did I do right?"

Wolsey turned to the king. "What do you wish to do?"

Henry sat very still, deep in thought. "There was no contact of any kind?"

"None, My Lord."

"And a great distance maintained between them?"

"The length of six horses, My Lord. My man had to shout to be heard."

Henry nodded. "Very well. We could use these items at our table. They had the appearance of health, these villagers?"

"The best of health. A mother and child, pink of complexion, tall and sturdy in limbs. They are known to me, and have supplied the kitchens before."

"And they are waiting there still? With the food?"

"Yes, My Lord."

The hall waited to hear what Henry would decide. Thomasin's gaze flickered across the floor. Brandon quietly sipped his wine, Hatton and Cotton exchanged a look, while Mountjoy was alert and awaiting the king's word. At last, her eyes came round to Truegood, but his had just drawn away, as if he had been observing her a second before.

"Tell them to leave the food at the gate and withdraw. Make sure they are out of sight before it is collected. Leave a purse for when they return. And watch them. At a distance."

"Very good, My Lord, I thank you."

The feasting continued, but Henry's mood had changed. He ate with solemnity and purpose, and all his earlier mirth was gone.

Later, the tables were cleared and the minstrels played a quiet song. Thomasin and Ellen were seated close to Wolsey, when Henry drew near. He bent low to the cardinal and spoke in a strangled voice.

"Did I do right? With the food? Did I do right?"

"My Lord," replied Wolsey in surprise, "you are the king. You always do right."

"Yes, yes, I am, I do." Henry drew himself up. "I am the king. My word is right. But then why does God torment me with such doubts?"

"In order to bring you to glory," said the cardinal, rising to his feet, "to aid your path to his side."

Henry was still jittery. "I don't know."

"What do you mean, you don't know? This is all part of his purpose for you."

"Is it?" he replied sharply. "I don't know now. I don't know." And he weaved his way back through the hall and out through the distant door.

ELEVEN

"At least the gardens here are pretty," said Ellen, walking beside Thomasin. "Much nicer than at Windsor, although Windsor had the better grounds. Hampton has more flowers."

"But spring had not yet come to Windsor before we left it," added Thomasin. "We only saw the first flowers."

"I wonder if spring ever fully comes to Windsor. Honestly, am glad to be away from it."

Catherine was ahead of them, with Maria and Gertrude, heading in the direction of the river. On either side the long lawns were broken by pathways and the occasional fountain, or carved statues of heraldic beasts, picked out in gold and white, yellow and red. It was a dazzlingly sunny day. The trees were beginning to blossom and shed their petals prettily, scattering sprays of white and pink across the lawns. They had slipped through the month of April, barely noticing the passage of time. Now May was beckoning, with all its green promise.

The days had passed easily; quiet mornings spent in the queen's chamber, praying, reading or sewing, while the king rode out in the park, hunted or loosed arrows at the colourful straw butts that were lined up at the end of the walk, with Truegood, Hatton and the others. The surface was pitted with holes left by the heads of arrows, from the last time the restless king had taken his sport. They dined simply, with food from the palace larders, supplemented by that which the women left at the gate, before retreating to a safe distance.

Afternoons were passed walking in the grounds, or riding gently along the river. This stretch of the bank was private, so they barely saw a soul on foot. Occasionally, though, a barge might pass, or women might be drying their clothes by spreading them in the fields opposite. Too far to speak, too far for infection. Sometimes they waved in greeting.

After dinner and prayers, the evening hours were passed beside the fire, in letter-writing, singing and playing cards. Thomasin had never understood the skill required for such games, but she was slowly learning the relative value of an ace, a king, a queen, a knave. Once or twice, she had won a hand, laughing in surprise, putting it down to good luck. Sometimes, Henry joined them at the table, although he liked to play for money, so at that point Thomasin would retire, pleading a headache or incomplete sewing, because she had no money to play with. One night Brandon lost five pounds to the king when the cards went against him. *Five pounds*, Thomasin thought in awe, considering all the worldly riches that such a sum might buy.

By the evening, a quiet sort of harmony had descended on the palace, cushioned as it was from the outside world. The queen's chambers, where they had moved on their second day, were rich and comfortable. Thick tapestries on the walls and the crackling fires made them completely silent, impenetrable from outside. Only birdsong reached them in the mornings and the barking of a fox at dusk. Sometimes it was almost easy to forget what lay beyond the gates, although the reports of cases in the city were rising, with many proving deadly. But a fragile harmony had also settled between Catherine and Henry, confined to the hours of dinner and cards, as he sat, flushed and at ease. Only occasionally did Thomasin observe the ghost of strained emotions chasing across his face.

Now, when Catherine turned and looked back towards the palace, she was smiling. The sun shone on her green headdress picked out with pearls.

"The queen looks content," said Ellen, far enough away so as not to be heard.

Thomasin was more sceptical. Circumstances had thrown Henry and Catherine back into each other's company, but the current pestilence would not last forever. Already reports from outside suggested the worst was over. It would soon be time to move, and their quiet idyll would be broken up.

"Such a glorious…" Turning to face the palace, Catherine stopped mid-sentence. She raised her arm and pointed along the pathway they had come from.

Thomasin and Ellen followed her gaze.

The side gate to the gardens stood open. A man dressed in huntsman's clothing was striding through them. In pace with his step ran the king's dogs, perhaps twenty of them, white and brown with their keen, boxy muzzles pointing forward with dedication. At the rear came William Hatton, distinguishable by his bright hair, herding along the final beasts.

The occasional yap or bark of excitement reached the women, but otherwise the pack moved as a group, well-trained, aware of their master's expectations. As the women watched, they travelled along the path down the side of the palace, then disappeared around the far end, through the gap in the hedge.

"Well, the king will be content now," said Ellen.

"As content as he can be here," Thomasin replied, turning her face back to the sun and straightening her bonnet.

Ellen's eyes showed her understanding.

"They will have come from court," Thomasin added, slowly coming to a realisation. "From London."

"Do you think they have brought the infection with them?"

"It is unlikely. They would have chosen the huntsman carefully, for his good health. But he may have brought letters."

The thought seized them. Letters from home, perhaps.

"My Lady," said Thomasin, making so bold as to approach Catherine.

"The kings hounds have arrived," said Catherine as she finally drew near.

"We were wondering whether the huntsman might have brought news, too," Thomasin added.

Catherine considered this. "I suppose we might, if we are careful, head back to find out."

"If you are certain it is safe to do so."

"We shall see," replied Catherine, the light in her blue eyes lifting. "We shall see."

One portion of the stables had been prepared especially for the arrival of the dogs; swept, cleaned and lined with fresh straw and rags. Hatton was standing at the gate as Catherine approached, watching the animals exploring their new home. He bowed low as he saw Catherine coming nearer. She stopped a little distance away, Thomasin looking over her shoulder.

"Mister Hatton." Catherine held her chin high, looking down at the man although he was much taller than her. Her tone was icy. "Is the king here?"

"No, My Lady, he is still hunting."

"Where is the huntsman who brought the dogs?"

Hatton ducked into the stables and returned with a middle-aged bearded man who was wiping his hands clean. He dropped to one knee as soon as he saw Catherine.

"Your name?"

"John Drywood, My Lady."

"To your feet, John Drywood. You have come this day from Westminster?"

"I have, My Lady."

"In whose employ?"

"I serve the cardinal. I am usually employed in the stables at York Place."

"Pray, tell us, are you in good health, no faintness or nausea?"

"I am hale and hearty, as confirmed by Dr Elyot as I left court."

"And what was the condition of things at Westminster? Are there cases at the palace?"

"Nothing for the last three weeks. The place has been emptied and thoroughly cleaned."

"And in the city?"

He hesitated. "I am afraid the cases continue there, My Lady, although they do not increase."

Catherine nodded. "That is something to be thankful for."

"If I may," he added, "I have brought a number of letters. They have been fumigated over a mixture of burning herbs." Reaching inside his doublet, he pulled out a bundle of folded papers.

Catherine's hand shot out to receive them.

"If you please," Drywood hesitated. "There are two that I was given instructions to put into the hands of the king."

"I am his wife," Catherine shot back at once. "Man and woman is one flesh; therefore, you may give them to me. I am also your queen."

Silenced, Drywood handed over the parcel and bowed.

Enfolding the letters in her sleeves, Catherine did not look at them, but held them close to her chest. Her face was a pale mask. Without another word, she turned and headed back to the gardens, but this time she made for the walled space, where an arbour had been created in a sheltered spot. The first roses were beginning to bud through the white and green railings, and the trees were florid and sweet. Intuitively, Thomasin shut the door behind her, then joined Catherine.

Catherine was sifting through the papers. "There are many to me," she observed, "from friends, ambassadors, enemies. One for Maria, one for Ellen, two for Gertrude and two for Thomasin."

She distributed them in turn. Excitedly, Thomasin received the folded pages, yellowed from their journey, recognising the Marwood seal with its crescent moon and single star. These letters had come all the way from Suffolk. She was itching to tear them open and read their news, but as she had learned, she could not do so without direct permission.

But Catherine was staring at her hands.

"What is it?" asked Maria, at her shoulder. For a long time, Catherine did not move.

"Letters for my husband," she replied at length, holding them between finger and thumb.

Thomasin strained to see the seal and the handwriting, wondering who might have sent them. Were they official business or personal? She flushed at the thought and the awareness that followed. Letters from Anne. They must be.

Ellen had also realised who might have written them. She caught Thomasin's eye with a warning look.

With a deft gesture, Catherine tucked the letters inside her bodice. "And here," she smiled, lifting another folded sheet to the light, "is the one I have been awaiting. From Ludlow." She looked up, seemingly refreshed. "You may read your letters now."

It was well-timed. Forgetting Catherine's dilemma, Thomasin hurried away towards the sheltered corner of the walled garden. Here, the plants were coming back to life, with new green shoots opening their leaves, buds bursting on branches and the bushes were red-tipped in the sun. Yet Thomasin saw none of this. The outside world entirely faded away. Her eyes were only for the letter, as she cracked open the seal and carefully unfolded the sheet. It was written in a close, neat hand that she recognised as belonging to her elder sister, Cecilia.

The last time Thomasin had seen her sister was when she'd waved her goodbye in November. Two years older than Thomasin and beautiful with her ice-blonde looks, Cecilia's intended marriage to Henry Kytson had fallen through after her dalliance with William Hatton, which had been encouraged by Anne Boleyn. She had passed the winter quietly at Eastwell, amid the Suffolk fogs and snow, mending her broken heart, and Thomasin wondered how it had changed her.

Cecilia wrote that she was well and so were their parents. She had spent much time with the younger children, reading with twelve-year-old Lettice and teaching Alice her letters, who had just turned six. Digby now had a tutor, an older man, a Mister Glasford from Cambridge, who had moved into the village. He was teaching Digby to become "a real little gentleman scholar" wrote Cecilia, describing how they would translate passages of Greek in the morning and ride through the fields in the afternoons, sketching the plants and creatures they observed there. Baby Susanna was weaned and had spoken her first words.

The park was awakening, Cecilia added, and the walkways were pink with blossom. Thomasin felt a pang as she read this, for spring had always been her favourite season. This time last year, she had been walking in those very avenues as the petals fell into her hair, dreaming of court, never imagining she would find herself at Hampton or Windsor.

Thomasin turned the page. Cecilia had written of her sewing, her walks to the village, of fresh milk from the dairy, a trip to the market at Bury St Edmunds and a new dress from a bolt of sky-blue cloth. She had said little else about her family.

Thomasin turned to the second letter. She recognised her father's wide, generous hand and broke open the seal expectantly. Richard assured her all was well; her mother's health was improving daily and she was able to ride out in the carriage. He was negotiating with a neighbour to purchase a field adjoining their land to the north, to fill with sheep. The king, he added, had sent them the gift of a stag he had killed whilst hunting, which would feed them for many days.

Thomasin frowned. A gift from the king? Yet her father mentioned nothing about being at Westminster recently. Was there a chance that Thomas More had been mistaken? Or did her father not want her to know what business he was about?

She looked up. Catherine was still reading. Maria Willoughby was sitting beside her, listening patiently as Catherine read out sections from her daughter Mary's letter.

Thomasin searched for Ellen. Her cousin had walked away to the far end, beyond the stone sundial, and stood on the distant path with her back to the others. Something in her bearing suggested deep emotion. Refolding her own letters, Thomasin walked swiftly through the lines of green, yellow and white, to the shady spot.

"Ellen?"

When her cousin turned, Thomasin saw that she was struggling to fight off tears.

"What is it?"

Ellen sighed and drew in her breath, unable to speak at first.

"Bad news?"

"From Barnaby," she managed.

Ellen had left her husband Barnaby last autumn, when it had been revealed that he had made her sister pregnant. Thomasin had never liked her self-important, pompous male cousin, whose talents fell far short of his conceit. He had not appreciated the vivacious Ellen, who had improved so much since being at court, shaking off her country ways.

"He is still in the north?"

Ellen nodded. "Far away. But his words can still wound."

Instead of explaining, Ellen simply held out the letter for Thomasin to read. It was covered in a lean, slanting hand that started neatly, then deteriorated as the message progressed. Barnaby Russell had started out by ordering his wife to return home to him in Buxton, then proceeded to beg and implore her to do so. After that, he spoke of her duty and marriage vows; how the anniversary of their wedding was approaching and that this should be the day by which she returned. Then he turned to threats, vowing that if she did not reply, or arrive on their estates by that time, he would seek an annulment on account of their childlessness, after which he would wed her sister Dorothy and legitimise her child. It was the vile letter of an odious, small-minded little man. Thomasin was at a loss to comprehend how her uncle, Sir Matthew, a fine, upstanding gentleman had produced such an heir.

"I'm sorry," she said, returning the letter. "I do hope you will give his words no credence."

"Not at all. I will never return to him. Now I have employment with the queen, I can be of service and I am provided for. I no longer need to rely upon him."

"You are always welcome at Eastwell too, if you ever lack a home," Thomasin added. "I know my parents would welcome you as a daughter."

Ellen's eyes welled up and she attempted to fan away the tears with a flapping hand. "I cannot thank you enough for your kindness."

"You are family, and worth more than that man who, by some unfortunate case, is my own flesh and blood. Will you burn the letter?"

"No, I shall keep it, as a constant reminder of the manner of man he is. When a day comes that I waver, or regret my change in circumstance, I shall read it again and find my strength."

"That is an excellent resolve. And your sister? Will you see Dorothy again?"

"She is with our parents. She has already had more than enough kindness from me and she exploited that. Let Barnaby wed her; they deserve each other."

Thomasin smiled. "You have moved on to better things; you are in the household of Queen Catherine of Aragon now, do not forget it. And I am sure, in time, you will find happiness again."

"Thank you. I do not believe I ever truly had it before. I saw in Barnaby what I wanted him to be, not what he was, but my eyes have been opened now."

Thomasin looked over to the queen. Catherine had stopped reading and was staring across the garden. "What do you make of those other letters the queen slipped into her bodice?"

"From the Boleyn woman to the king?" asked Ellen.

"That's what I thought, too. I wonder if Henry is expecting them."

"Well," said Ellen, "I hope he never receives them. If I were the queen, I should drop them in the fire."

"I hope she does exactly that."

Catherine was looking up at Maria now, who was speaking to her in jolly tones. Catherine replied and both women laughed together.

The sun came out from behind a cloud and lit them up.

Thomasin and Ellen walked around the edge of the gardens, where the rose bushes were bright with new green growth and young thorns.

"Where is Anne, do you think?" Ellen asked.

"Still in London, I imagine."

"At court? Is there still a court at Westminster when the king is not there?"

"For business, I think, little more. I should think she is at the family's London home."

"Waiting for the king?"

Thomasin shrugged.

"What was she like, last autumn, when you danced in her masque and attended her party?"

The memory was like a sour taste in Thomasin's mouth, tinged as it was with betrayal and the time she'd spent with Rafe. "You remember what she did. She played a game with us, encouraged my sister and Hatton, then stood back and blamed all upon her. At least my sister did not chase after a man who already has a wife."

"I do remember," admitted Ellen, "very well indeed. And I remember that the king was none too pleased with her meddling, either. Do you think there is a chance that he will forget her, now they are in this forced separation? Particularly if he does not hear from her, and takes it as a slight?"

"He may quarrel with her," Thomasin admitted, "but he will not forget that he does not have a son."

Ellen looked over the gardens. "There are many women at court who might give him a son. Has he not one already?"

Thomasin had heard word of the young boy, conceived in the heat of passion with one of Catherine's ladies, some eight or nine years back. "I believe so."

"But it is nothing without marriage, is it?"

"No. He cannot inherit. The only way the king will have a legitimate son is if he has a new wife."

At that moment, Catherine rose and stretched with difficulty. From that distance, she appeared small, heavy and old. She was regal, though, there was never any doubt about that, and she was determined, but she seemed suddenly vulnerable.

"Poor Catherine," said Ellen.

"Hush, do not let her even suspect you of pity; she is not of a character to bear it! Come on."

TWELVE

William Compton threw his head back and roared with laughter. The fire in the hearth behind him burned bright and pushed the night away, beyond the windows. "And that was when Francis Bryan rode through the streets of Paris at dawn, singing lewd songs and throwing eggs!"

Henry drummed his fingers on the table at the memory. "The damned fool almost caused a major incident. He is lucky that Francis let him go."

"He has always been more daring than dutiful," added Compton, with a hint of criticism in his tone. "He has been lucky thus far."

"Less than lucky in the joust where he lost his eye!"

"That's true," Compton conceded. "He should have taken that as a warning while he still has one left."

They were dining in the main hall after another bright day in the park, and there was a sense of merriment in the air. Servants were clearing the empty plates and refilling glasses of wine. Thomasin sat back and watched as the company began to relax.

"I wonder how the French fare amid this pestilence," mused Brandon. "They always were more assailed by such illnesses, having many travellers pass through their lands freely."

"But we have the ports, don't forget," piped up Hatton, trying to impress, "with ships arriving daily from all around the world, further than Europe, bringing all kinds of sickness. Perhaps we are in even greater danger."

"But they have more ships from the new world," replied Brandon, frowning, "and merchants from the east."

"It is strange," mused Henry, taking the topic into his own hands. "I wonder about the constitution of foreigners, and I believe the French have one advantage over the English. We are greater in strength due to our good beef and mutton, our fresh air and our breeding; across the Channel, they sicken and weaken with yet another infection or wound, but still they cling to life somehow. I have heard that Francis himself ails with some new condition, always something new, but never anything fatal."

From the side, Compton laughed. "Do you remember how he preened and strutted in Guînes eight summers back? How impressed he was by our golden tents and palace, and then the wind blew the roof off his banqueting house?"

Henry roared with laughter. "I do! His face was a picture. His pride had been wounded, but he tried so hard to wear the face of a lion."

"Not a lion," Compton continued, "a slimy salamander, don't you recall?"

The salamander was the French king's symbol; a strange choice to Thomasin's mind.

"A salamander!" Henry repeated. "Do you remember, Catherine; do you remember his disappointment?"

Catherine smiled gently. "You were most gracious with him, my esteemed Lord, most noble. It was a time when you distinguished yourself with your valour and generosity."

Henry sat back in his chair, basking in her words. His small eyes appeared content, his lips slackening into a smile. "I did, didn't I?"

Thomasin thought how well Catherine knew him; how exactly she knew how to flatter him and lull him to his ease.

Henry turned to his side. "Do you remember, Wolsey? You are a friend of the French even now, are you not? You remember how I outshone him?"

The cardinal inclined his head.

Ellen leaned in, whispering, "I heard that Francis threw him in a wrestling match."

"Shh!" Thomasin looked around. "Really?"

Ellen nodded. "But he will not mention that. Threw him to the floor in front of the crowds. And they say Francis has longer legs, but a longer nose, too. And other things besides!"

Thomasin laughed but paid her foolishness no heed.

Catherine had slowly, with effort, risen to her feet. The hall fell quiet as she raised her glass. "While we speak of such things, I should also like to drink in remembrance of my sister queen, Claude of France, whose soul now resides with God."

It was a clever move. Catherine's own status was delivered amid the act of remembering the dead, so out of respect, no one would dare challenge her self-identification as a queen. "To Claude of France," she added, lifting her glass high.

"To Claude of France," they all echoed, then drank deep.

"Music!" called Henry. "We are not so old, nor so melancholy or weary that we cannot celebrate the evening with a little dancing."

Dreaming away the hours in their gallery, the musicians abruptly came to life and hastily began to assemble.

Wolsey rose to his feet, slowly, in the throes of aching bones. "My Lord, I have letters to write. I will bid you goodnight."

But Henry was too excited to hear him. He had already risen, seized by the impetus to dance. The cardinal slunk away like a wounded animal, leaving the king to occupy the floor. Thomasin saw him pause in the doorway and look back at the young people enjoying his home, as if he was a ghost from a past time, before he disappeared. The last thing she saw was the glint of his jewels, like stars in the shadows.

"We are still healthy and strong," continued Henry. "We have ladies and gentlemen, of good fortunes and spirit; we have, thanks be to God, as yet escaped this terrible scourge. Come, let us enjoy some modest dancing to lift our spirits."

Stepping down from the dais, he extended his hand to Gertrude, who happened to be nearest. At his side, Brandon offered his hand to Maria and they took their positions.

"Another two pairings," Henry insisted. "Come, join us."

William Compton offered his hand to Ellen, who accepted. Thomasin could not stop her eyes from flickering over to Hugh Truegood, but he was on the further side of the hall, trapped behind the table. To her horror, it was William Hatton who reached her first.

"Mistress Marwood? Will you forgive my past mistakes and partner me in the dance?"

Thomasin felt the rage mount inside her. She turned her face away.

"My Lady?" The slight, dark William Carey had seen her discomfort and understood the circumstances. Now, she gratefully put her hand into his and followed him to the floor. Hatton was left standing, with no choice but to wait until the next dance.

The musicians struck the opening chord again and the dance began. Thomasin and Ellen made their low curtseys, then took two steps forward to join arms with their partners and walk in a circle.

"I am very grateful to you for rescuing me," she thanked Carey, when she had a moment. "It was odious for me to receive that man's request."

"It was nothing. I have not forgotten the wrong he did your sister, even though I am sure that most at court have."

For some reason, Thomasin felt tears prick her eyes. She had never really looked at Will Carey before, as he had always been in the background, another young man of the court — fashionable enough, smart, ambitious, but above all, she knew him as Mary Boleyn's husband. His comment was kind.

"She is well, your sister?"

"Well and happy in the country, I thank you."

"She will recover from this, no matter what people say. She has good looks enough to make a good match still. As do all her family."

Thomasin blushed at the implied compliment.

As they linked arms to form the circle, she remembered with a rush that she was dancing with Anne Boleyn's brother-in-law. "This is not so exciting as the masques you must be used to at court, I think, my Lord?"

"I care little for those. They delight my wife more than myself."

"How is Mary? I hope she is well."

"I believe so. She remains in her parents' London house with Anne."

"And your children?"

"They are in the country, at Pleshey, with their nurse. I have heard it is all quite safe there and they are taking every precaution."

"That is best, yes, for children. I am glad to hear they are well."

They turned, parted and briefly paired with another, according to the steps. Thomasin found herself dancing with Compton, while Ellen was with Carey. The king, Brandon and their partners were making a mirror image of the same move.

"Good evening, mistress," Compton smiled. "You are merry tonight?" His breath smelled of wine.

"Merry enough, I thank you."

He squeezed her arm. "And looking most beauteous with it."

Thomasin blushed in surprise, but the dance had already moved on, and she returned to Carey.

"The king is in good spirits," he said. "And the queen, too. It is a rare thing to see, this jollity, that has been brought about by these strange times."

Thomasin wondered at his allegiances. "It is not difficult for you to see? Is it not counter to your cause?"

He looked at her for a moment, with wide eyes. "Oh, Anne's cause. My sister-in-law's cause, you mean. And you associate it with mine."

"My apologies, am I incorrect? Is it not also your wife's cause?"

"It is indeed. But there is no offence taken. My wife has many causes of her own, some which are known to me, others which are not."

They turned, joined arms and circled again. Thomasin recalled rumours she had heard that the Careys' children, a red-headed girl and boy, had been fathered by the king before his infatuation with Anne.

"I serve the king in all things," Carey continued, "and seek to help him bring about his wishes. It is not for me to question what he chooses, or what is inevitable."

"That is very pragmatic of you."

He looped his arm through hers and they began the circular walk again. "I am sure, Mistress Marwood, you have had enough experience at court now to know that it is a fast, unforgiving place. Who am I to urge my wishes, my preferences, if they do not coincide with those of the king who feeds and shelters me, who holds my very life in his hands?"

"The king is fond of you. I have seen so myself."

"Perhaps. He is fond of anyone who agrees with him."

As they turned, Thomasin saw Henry pass round and then come to face her, at a distance. Meeting her eyes, he inclined his head in greeting. She wondered what other emotions were contained; they were difficult to read.

"Most people do not realise," added Carey, making the final steps, "that it is all a game, just as men might play at chess. It requires careful moves made with a cool head. And a prayer that this is enough."

The dance came to a close. Thomasin met Carey's bow with a curtsey, but he still kept hold of her hand.

"Be wary, my Lady," he whispered. "Take advice from one who has lived through this; keep your wits about you. I will be your friend, should you ever need one."

One look at his wide eyes convinced her he was sincere. There was only time for her to whisper "thank you" before the next dance was commencing.

To everyone's surprise, least of all her own, Henry turned to Catherine and offered her his hand. Catherine's face lit up, making her seem years younger, and she gladly, almost girlishly accepted.

"Might I have this dance?"

Thomasin turned to find that Hugh Truegood had appeared on the other side. With a little flush from the wine and pleasure, she smiled and put her hand into his.

His palm was wide, his fingers long as they curled warmly and firmly about hers. There was something calming, some confidence in his energy as he led her into position. Standing opposite him, she dared to look up into his face, noticing the broad cheekbones and square jaw, the rose-pink skin freckled by the sun and the heat in those amber eyes that now caught hers.

She went towards him with a subdued smile. She had noticed it before, but when faced with him at such close quarters, she was struck by how he was built on a larger scale than most men she had known; his height, the length of his limbs, the long hands, the broad chest. Beside him, Thomasin felt small, dainty.

"Good evening." He bowed his head down to hers and smiled.

"Good evening, my Lord."

They took their positions side by side for this dance, as part of a wider circle. On her right, Thomasin was conscious that William Hatton stood beside her, partnering Maria, but she recoiled from him, keeping herself focused on her partner. The chords struck and she followed Truegood's lead.

"Have you been long in the queen's household?"

"Since last November, but the winter and this pestilence makes it feel longer."

"I am sure it does."

They took the steps forward, careful and close, as this dance required. Thomasin noticed that Truegood did not follow easily. Perhaps it was his strength and size, or lack of familiarity with the dance, but here, unlike in sport, he did not move with a natural grace, as she recalled that Rafe or even Nico had. There was a power to him, an intensity of physicality, that made him too self-conscious when it came to dancing. As they turned, and he drew her back to him, she wished he could soften his body a little, so taut and wooden he felt.

"Have you been much at court yourself?" she asked, trying to help him relax.

"Barely. Does this count?"

"You have been more concerned with business, I understand?"

"Yes," he replied, then paused to allow another pairing to pass. When they came back together, he caught her eyes and beamed down into them. "This is another world."

"That's what I found when I first arrived. I had no idea how things would be."

He nodded and moved alongside her. She waited for his reply, but none came.

Eventually, as they turned together, she asked, "How do you find it?"

"Oh," he replied, "I suppose this is not typical of court life, shut away here?"

"It is not, no. If you ever go to Westminster, you will find things quite different."

They continued to dance. Their feet moved through the motions, but the words fell stilted between them.

"So, do you think you will ever go to Westminster?" Thomasin tried again.

"I shall do what the king requires of me."

It was a closed response. She stepped to the side as Hatton and Maria passed them by. As Truegood came back, face to face, he beamed his broad smile again, before moving slowly and deliberately through the steps.

"What is it like in Antwerp?" she asked, after a time.

"My time there was very productive."

"And you were welcomed there?"

"Very much."

She waited for him to tell her more: the people, the places, the colours, the smells in the street, the strange customs, even his work with rippling silks, dyed cloth, intricate lace. She would have settled for knowing what it was like to take a ship across the waters from one country to another, or to ride under foreign skies, to taste foreign food. But he did not expand.

Thomasin concluded the dance with mixed feelings. It was flattering to think Truegood was interested in her, and with his auburn hair and warm eyes, his powerful build and strength, he cut an imposing figure. He had lived an exciting life of travel, and had prospects, and must have had experiences to share. Yet his words were clipped and tight as buds before spring. She wondered at the reason why. Perhaps he was simply unused to company, unused to opening up and sharing. Perhaps it was his character to give little away.

He bowed low, showing her his full, gleaming head of beautiful red hair. "Thank you, my Lady. May I?" He offered his hand and led her back to the table, where Ellen was waiting, brimming with expectation. She waited until Truegood had moved out of earshot.

"He is so handsome!" Ellen whispered, as Truegood sat down beside Brandon.

Thomasin could not disagree. "But he can't hold a conversation."

"Nor dance," added Ellen. "I did notice that, which is a surprise. He did not hit the target, then?"

"Not this time, no."

Ellen sighed. "It's a shame. Perhaps he will improve upon acquaintance."

"Perhaps."

"The king and queen danced, you saw?"

"I did." Thomasin looked over to where Catherine and Henry were now speaking by the window, listening to each other with expressions of kindness and warmth. "It feels as if the outside world no longer exists."

"Oh, but it does," said Mountjoy, appearing behind them. "I fear this is just the calm before the storm. Brace yourselves, ladies, brace yourselves."

Thomasin was passing along one of the darker corridors, returning to the queen's chambers with fresh water. The castle was eerily quiet. Wood beams creaked, taking their ease. As she turned a corner, her way was suddenly blocked by a figure standing in the gloom, forcing her to draw up short, spilling a little of her water.

"My deepest apologies, my Lady."

The voice was familiar. It took her a few seconds to recognise William Compton, his eyes glinting devilishly.

"No, my apologies, my Lord, I did not see you in the darkness."

"Water for the queen?"

"What is left of it, yes."

He smiled, briefly, coldly, as if that was nothing to do with him. Then, she could not help noticing, his eyes ran over her body.

"You are quite charming, if I may say. Do your parents have a match arranged for you?"

Thomasin felt her face grow hot with the intrusion. "No, they do not, my Lord."

He nodded. "How old are you?"

"I am almost eighteen summers."

"Quite old enough, then."

She stood, clutching the water jug between them, hoping he would let her pass.

"Is there any young man who has caught your eye? Anyone whom you might have encouraged?"

Thomasin lifted her chin, determined not to answer his impertinent questions. He saw her response and softened.

"I only ask because in such a position as yours, the king might be of assistance, to arrange terms favourable to a match. He likes to be aware of the amours of the queen's women, for the sake of discretion. There is no young man you are meeting, while you fetch the water?"

"Absolutely not! The queen awaits me."

"You are sure?"

"Quite sure."

"You will not return, to dally a little?"

Thomasin shuddered with distaste. "The queen awaits me."

"Of course."

He stepped aside to let her pass. She hurried by him, relieved to arrive in the better-lit quarters, where the torches on the wall brought her back to Catherine's chambers.

As she opened the door, Thomasin almost collided with a dark figure immediately on the other side. She was ready to call out, before realising it was the queen.

"Mistress Marwood? Please accompany me."

Catherine had pulled a robe over her nightdress and stuck her feet into slippers. Her hair was loose and long down her back. Thomasin was alarmed, but it was not her place to question the queen, so she followed obediently.

After a short way, it was clear Catherine was heading for Henry's chambers. The guards at the door stood to surprised attention and parted to let her access the door. She knocked softly, before the king called from within.

Catherine slipped inside, leaving the door ajar in her uncertainty. Blushing for her, with some idea of her intentions,

Thomasin pulled it to, and stood blocking the view inside. The guards stared at the floor.

Snatches of their words reached those outside.

"At this hour?" Henry was saying.

"Were you sleeping?"

A muffled sound suggested the king had got up from his bed.

Catherine's voice was higher. "Let me come to you this once, for all the times we have been happy together as man and wife."

"You know my scruples about this."

"How can it hurt, after all these years?"

"But what is the point? You can no longer conceive a child; you no longer bleed."

"It is not unheard of. Think of St Elizabeth, who bore John the Baptist long after her childbearing years were thought to be over."

There was more muffled movement. Thomasin felt acutely for Catherine.

"You must leave. You know why."

"You are mistaken in that. There is no fault, no impediment between us. Please, husband."

Thomasin heard the name Arthur spoken, and her mistress let out a little cry. "It is not so. Shame on you." Swiftly, she appeared in the doorway, pulling the robe about her short frame, and hurried back to her chambers. The king's door closed softly.

Thomasin turned to the guards. "Say nothing of this, or I will see that you are dismissed." Then she sped after the retreating queen.

THIRTEEN

Catherine rose early with the light. In the still of the chamber, Thomasin and Ellen fumbled with her clothing, tying her laces, lifting her rippling skirts down over her head. The material came down in blue waves before settling about her feet. In silence, with rumbling stomachs, they followed her, shivering, to the chapel. Wolsey was waiting at the door to lead them in. It was a small, tight space. Dark and chilly for a spring morning. The cardinal had already spoken to Henry of his plans to improve it: to extend the far end; to put in bigger windows and an entrance chamber.

Thomasin and Ellen squeezed into a pew with Gertrude and Maria, while Catherine knelt before the altar. Before her, Wolsey in his rich red robes spread his hands wide and began to murmur the opening prayers. Catherine bent low, heavy with worldly burdens, as the words washed over her. Before long, Thomasin felt her cousin's head droop upon her shoulder and her breathing grow deep and regular. The words continued to flow from the cardinal's mouth, in a stream of holy images and blessings, and the candles flickered, until Thomasin also closed her eyes.

She came to as the chapel rose to its feet. Wolsey held out a hand, to help Catherine to stand. On either side, Ellen, Maria and Gertrude stretched slowly up from the pew. Thomasin rubbed her bleary eyes and waited for Catherine to pass, before following her out into the daylight. Catherine was serene but subdued. She gave no indication of what had transpired the night before, and Thomasin knew how to keep a secret.

"I have drawn up designs for a new ceiling, and a gallery," Wolsey was saying, "with a large altar window to be devoted to a saint of the king's choice."

Catherine's face was impassive. "In the same location?"

"Not necessarily. I favour a grander scale, with a wider entrance and space for an antechamber, perhaps even a gallery."

Catherine looked at him suspiciously. "And why exactly does God need a gallery?"

The cardinal judged her tone and melted away.

Catherine passed through the arch and into the colonnade. Behind her, Thomasin and Ellen blinked in the sudden light. It looked as if it was to be a fine morning: there was a fair blue sky marred only by a few pale clouds. The roses alongside the stone walk were beginning to show their buds and birds sang in chorus. The smell of warm bread drew them towards the hall, where Thomasin was looking forward to breaking her fast.

"My Lady, a beautiful day," said William Carey, joining them on the path.

He shot a smile at Thomasin, his tanned face suddenly uplifting. She realised she had never noticed his warm eyes before.

"Good morning, Master Carey," replied Catherine, continuing her progress.

Carey fell into step with Thomasin. "I was wondering whether the queen has plans for today?"

"None that I know of yet."

"Then do you think we can persuade her to take a boat on the river, downstream a little way, to the meadow at Lea's corner? It would be pleasant, don't you think?"

"Oh, I am not sure. It does sound nice, but to leave the grounds, given the pestilence? Would she wish to?"

"We can but ask. Or if not, perhaps you might obtain leave to go with me, just the two of us?" He read her expression of surprise and continued, "You see, I have a plan for a little pastime. You know how much the king and queen have loved to dress up to hunt?"

Thomasin shook her head. "Remember, I am new to court."

"Of course, forgive me. It was always their delight to ride out in costumes, to hear music and feast outdoors, a custom they have forgotten of late, which it would be pleasant to revive, whilst we are here."

"That does sound pleasant. I am sure the queen would be happy at the prospect."

"Then shall we try and visit the meadow? Would you like to?"

Thomasin blushed at the prospect of the pair of them together, but it was not an unpleasant idea to her mind.

"Only if you think it proper. Your cousin could chaperone you."

Chaperone? Her mind was stirred in confusion. Did she need a chaperone? After all, Carey was a married man.

"Apologies, I think I have spoken out of turn. It was kindly meant, as a friend."

Thomasin was about to reply that it had been kindly taken, as one friend to another, but at that moment, the peace was broken by a roar.

"Madam!"

They heard Henry before they saw him. Catherine had almost reached the hall, while the king approached from a side passage, walking swiftly, holding himself taut. Catherine paused and curtseyed, awaiting his approach.

The king was angry. All could see, but it was a cold, controlled fire that showed in his clipped movements, the thin lines of his lips and eyes. Thomasin felt a jolt of fear through her stomach.

As he drew near, he focused only upon Catherine, until he was close enough to speak. His voice was low but powerful, like a blow. The laughing, happy Henry of late was unrecognisable.

"Have you been honest with me, Madam?" he asked tersely.

Catherine was visibly shaking as she met him, face to face. "I am, My Lord. What sort of a question is this?"

"A valid one," he spat back. "So there is nothing you have concealed from me? Nothing I should know about?"

"I cannot imagine to what you refer, but it is not fitting to speak to me thus. I am coming from chapel."

"Not fitting?" Henry's small eyes had become dark slits in his face. "Not fitting, Madam? So where are my letters? You know the ones I mean. Where are they? I know they arrived at the palace in the hands of the houndsman."

Catherine lifted her chin with dignity.

"The letters, Madam," Henry persisted. "From Bishop Foxe and Mistress Boleyn. What have you done with them?"

"You speak her name to me?"

"I do, Madam. Do you deny that you kept her letters from me?"

Catherine spoke slowly as she struggled for control. "Your letters are no concern of mine."

"No, Madam, they are not, and yet you interfere with them? I suppose they are gone for good? Burned in your hearth? She writes to me, asking why I have not replied to her. How can I reply to letters I have never seen? Do tell me. Perhaps I should write back that my wife has stolen them!"

His voice rose to such a level that it was impossible for those around not to hear him. The queen's ladies, and Henry's gentlemen, were stilled by the angry accusation.

Catherine gathered up her skirts and swept past her husband with dignity, in the direction of the hall.

"Nothing to say, Madam?" Henry called after her. "Nothing? Where are my letters?"

"Come now, My Lord," Carey attempted. "Surely this is a misunderstanding."

"No misunderstanding," Henry spat back. "Deliberate interference in my personal affairs. Was there nothing from Bishop Foxe, concerning the Pope? You do not want those letters seen, do you? What did the Pope say? Is the marriage null and void? Do not forget, Madam, that we are not husband and wife. That was a mistake. We never have been." He paused to let his words sink in. The onlookers stood silent, aghast. "You are not my wife, in the eyes of the Church and the law," he bellowed so that Catherine would hear him, "and I am not your husband. You are the dowager princess, wife to my brother, and I am your king. It is treason to steal the king's letters. Treason! Treason!"

Catherine did not make it to the hall, where her meal awaited her. She staggered, one foot before the other. Tottered round the corner, leaned against the wall. Her ladies gathered around her, but she batted them away like flies. An antechamber stood empty, usually a waiting room used by servants, with a table and benches. There, she collapsed onto her knees in the rushes, shaking with sobs. Swiftly, Maria pulled the door closed behind them.

"Please, My Lady."

Thomasin knelt with the others round her, offering their words of comfort. Catherine spluttered, voicing half words, suffused with pain. She convulsed again, sobbing uncontrollably and quite unable to answer them. They fetched wine and cordials to revive her, herbs to calm her, and finally managed to seat her on a chair, although her hands were still quivering.

"Fetch bread," urged Maria after a while. "She has not broken her fast."

Thomasin hurried out, almost straight into William Carey, who was positioned near the door.

"The queen is within?"

"She is indeed, but do not speak of it to anyone."

"I will not tell a soul. I take it she is not well?"

"Not well at all. I have come out only to fetch her bread, for she has not yet eaten, coming lately from chapel."

"Then I will not detain you. Poor Lady. I hope she fares better soon." He hesitated, lowering his voice. "That was savagery."

Thomasin nodded and turned, but Carey gently touched her arm. "Wait. I hope you and I shall have the chance to speak again before long."

For a moment, he held her with his eyes. Mid-brown eyes, warm and safe. Not the intense dark pools with which Rafe had held her captive, nor the dancing golden stare of Nico, almost like a caress; the eyes of William Carey were welcoming and gentle. They invited trust.

"Yes," she heard herself breathe. "Yes."

It was quiet outside by the time Catherine was strong enough to venture back to her rooms. Ellen and Thomasin were sent out first, to check that the corridor was empty, looking up and down through the gloomy stone passage. Only shadows met their gaze. Catherine had fortified herself with wine and bread from the kitchens and dried her tears, and her ladies had straightened her bodice and headdress. In the doorway, she took a deep breath, straightened her back and lifted her chin.

With Maria on one side and Thomasin on the other, Catherine walked shakily but swiftly, leaning on Maria's arm. They were fortunate to see no one on the way to the hall stairs, and then Ellen went ahead, to clear the way through the courtyard. Servants melted away, glimpsed only in shadow or in the ripple of a gown. A broom was left abandoned, leaning against the wall. The palace was unusually quiet, but they were grateful for the small window of peace in which to make their journey. Under the stone arch, Catherine paused and caught her breath before attempting the steps. She held her hands to her side and winced.

Maria was beside her. "What is it, My Lady?"

"A pain. It will pass."

They waited for a long time, while Catherine kept her palms pressed upon her waist. Then, she unfolded a little and nodded that they were to proceed. Maria offered her arm, but Catherine declined. Finally, the safety of her apartments came into sight and the door was closed behind them. The cool comfort of lavender and ash enveloped them.

Catherine eased herself into her chair, nestling down between the cushions. Thomasin hurried to stoke up the fire while Ellen removed her shoes. Maria and Gertrude gently unpinned her headdress, lifting away the heavy folds of fabric that hung down her back.

"I wish to lie down."

Catherine's hands clutched the chair's arms. Slowly, she rose and swayed a little. Thomasin looked at Maria in alarm, but her face was calm and composed, setting the tone. The queen's bed was in the adjoining chamber, and between the women, they managed to make her comfortable.

"Pull the curtains. I want darkness."

The bright, glorious day, which had previously held so much promise, was instantly blotted out. Thomasin heard a bird singing in the garden as she pulled the last drape over the light. Darkness encircled Catherine.

Once Catherine was settled, Thomasin crept into the main chamber. The windows stood open, with the scent of the spring day. Wine, pasties and bread had been brought to the table, and Ellen beckoned her cousin over.

"Come, eat, you have had nothing yet."

Thomasin ate and drank gratefully.

"The queen sleeps?"

"Perhaps. She does not want to be disturbed."

"What do we do if the king comes to be admitted?"

"There's nothing we can do. We have to obey. But let's not worry about that unless it happens."

Presently, they took up embroidery, tracing intricate black patterns with their needles across white collars and cuffs. The hours passed slowly, in a mood of unease. As Thomasin pulled her thread in and out in rhythm, William Carey's words mingled with those of the king, and his final accusation rang through her head again: treason, treason!

"Did the king speak merely in anger," she wondered aloud, "or did the queen commit treason in keeping his letters?"

Ellen looked up from her work. "What letters?"

"The letters that…" Thomasin began, but then she realised what her cousin meant. "Of course. I do not know to which letters the king might refer."

143

"We were so occupied with letters of our own that we scarcely had time to notice any that the queen might be handling, which were not our business."

"Not our business indeed," Thomasin agreed.

"And I thought he would never be so harsh as to say what he did in public like that."

"To reject her? To say she was not his wife?" Thomasin felt deeply for Catherine and the pain those words had plunged her into. "No, that was cruel."

"He has clearly been holding that thought in for some time, and the letters brought it out."

"Poor Catherine. She will never accept it."

"She may not have a choice."

The room was quiet. Maria was dozing in a chair, and Gertrude was reading.

"Where is Mountjoy?" Thomasin asked, realising she had not seen Catherine's chamberlain for some time.

"A servant from the king came and summoned him, while you were with the queen," said Gertrude, "but he has been gone these two hours. I wonder what it can be about."

A slight sense of unease crept over Thomasin at the length of the man's absence, but there was nothing to be done. She picked up her needle again and tried to forget it.

"What was Will Carey speaking of before?" Ellen asked. "Before the king arrived."

"He was hoping to arrange an entertainment."

"Oh, that would be nice. I do hope it is not spoiled now, by all this."

"It depends how long the king is angry."

Ellen lowered her voice so the others could not hear. "But he seemed to show particular favour to you. Carey, I mean, not the king."

"Did he?" Thomasin did not look up from her needle.

"I think so. He paid you most marked attentions, did he not?"

"Perhaps he did. I scarcely saw."

When Ellen kept her silence, Thomasin looked up. "What? It was just a conversation. He wanted my opinion." But Ellen just smiled in an infuriating way. "That is all, there is nothing to smile about."

"Of course not," Ellen replied, "nothing at all. That is why you are blushing."

"I am not blushing!"

"If you say so."

"I am not. Definitely not blushing."

"They say he and his wife lead separate lives. She takes other lovers, now the king is done with her."

"Enough, stop it. This is not my concern. The Careys may do as they wish."

"I am sure he will," Ellen giggled.

Thomasin decided not to answer, but she could not help but wonder whether Carey's attentions to her had been so marked as to reveal interest on his part. She was not sure how that made her feel.

It was mid-afternoon, and the day had clouded over. Catherine had not yet emerged, nor called for assistance, from her dark chamber. The women were still engaged in their sewing when a knock came upon the door. It swung open at once, and Wolsey came gliding in with a proprietorial air, pausing in the middle of the room and looking about him impatiently.

"Where is the queen?"

Thomasin and the others had risen, dropping curtseys as protocol dictated.

"She is resting in her chamber, not to be disturbed," spoke up Maria, who stood between the cardinal and the closed door.

"I have a message for her."

"My Lord, she is sleeping."

"At this hour?"

Thomasin was shocked at his disrespect.

Maria looked the cardinal straight in the eye. "The queen is indisposed."

There was an uncomfortable moment, when each wondered what the other would do. Then, a noise from the inner room broke the silence and the queen's door opened a little.

"What is this noise?"

"My Lady?" Wolsey urged, before anyone else had the chance to speak. "I must speak with you."

"*Must* you, my Lord Cardinal?"

They all noticed her emphasis.

"I have important news."

Catherine emerged a little from the doorway, wrapped in a gown, her head bare. "Important indeed, to wake a queen. Tell me, is London burning? Has the flagship sunk? Have the Turks landed?" Thomasin was pleased to see she had recovered her spirit.

For a moment, the cardinal hesitated.

"Well, come on, man, you have not woken me for nothing. What is it?"

"It is the king, My Lady. He has left Hampton Court and rides for Greenwich."

The chamber fell silent. Thomasin was shocked.

"Left?" echoed Catherine, eventually. "He has left?"

"An hour since, My Lady, and all his household."

"Without leaving me word?"

"This is his word. I am the bearer of it. And you are most welcome to remain here, as my guest, for as long as you wish, and enjoy my gardens and hospitality."

Catherine needed no more time to think. She turned to her women. "Begin to pack. We depart for Greenwich in the morning."

"But, My Lady..." began the cardinal.

"We leave at first light."

FOURTEEN

Thomasin had not forgotten the last time she'd travelled on the Thames. Last autumn, she, her father and Cecilia had made the short trip in Wolsey's barge to an entertainment held at York House. It had been a cold night, bright with stars overhead, a night that promised excitement, but the rolling motion of the boat on the choppy water had unsettled her stomach and made her feel queasy.

This stretch of the river, though, was gentle and meandering. Now it was late spring, not autumn, mid-morning, not evening and the wide, flat-bottomed craft moved at a gentle pace so that their leisurely progress through the green fields was almost a pleasure. The queen's ladies sat on cushions, with blankets across their knees for warmth, Thomasin and Ellen on the right-hand side, with Maria and Gertrude opposite. Catherine herself sat on a low chair set in the bow, covered over with furs. Her face was composed. The rhythm was set by the rise and fall of the oars, smoothly handled by the team of eight rowers in the cardinal's livery. In the boat behind rode Mountjoy and Wolsey himself, who had declared it his duty to accompany Catherine on her journey.

It was another sudden departure. Thomasin felt the strangeness of it, this glittering life of upheaval. Last time, they had been fleeing from the danger of the sweating sickness, but now they were in pursuit of the king, all concerns about infection set aside. Catherine had needed little reassurance. The men insisted that all at Greenwich were healthy and that no new infections had been reported in the area in the past three weeks. She had allowed herself to be guided into the boat and heaped with furs with a sense of quiet desperation. Surely Henry had fled to Anne. The letters were merely the catalyst for his desire. And where Henry went, Catherine would follow, as befitted her station, as she had done for almost twenty years.

Thomasin was surprised to find the journey so enjoyable. Along the banks, they saw the occasional houses, or people walking, washing and leading horses, church towers and the spokes and wheels of wind and water mills, but the countryside had come to life, in a riot of greenery and wildflowers. Sheep and cows stared back at them from meadows, grazing contentedly and once, a flock of swans glided serenely downstream.

Catherine was in tune with her thoughts. "There is no more beautiful time in England than the month of May." She indicated the bank with a sweep of her hand. Willows overhung the water, trailing their leaves. "I did not notice it until I had been in England two years. The first May, I was widowed, and lay in my chamber in the darkness, but the next year, I travelled to Greenwich for the first time. There is an incomparable beauty about it. I never saw the like in Spain."

"Nothing like," echoed Maria Willoughby, her accent still heavy with her own Spanish youth.

Thomasin sat up. It was rare that Catherine spoke about those early days in England. "It must have been a very difficult time for you."

Maria shot her a discouraging look, but the question had already been asked.

Catherine paused. "Perhaps the hardest time of my life. So far."

Thomasin waited. All the women waited.

"It was hardest because I could not see God's plan for me. I had always known what I was born to be, but there were times when it seemed as if this would never come to fruition. It had been given to me, then suddenly taken back."

"You were widowed very young," Thomasin encouraged.

"I was just sixteen. A child, still."

"What was he like? Your first husband?"

Maria tried to intervene, but Catherine lifted her hand to stop her. "He should not be forgotten. Especially not in times like these, when we are grateful to have survived the pestilence once more, thanks be to God." She sighed deeply. "He was even more of a child than I. Only fifteen, but so gentle and serious. He tried so hard, did his best to be the little king in the making. A good, noble soul. Truth be told, we spent very little time together. After all these years, I barely feel I knew him at all."

"He was a great prince and would have been a great king," interjected Maria.

"But God took him, God chose him," replied Catherine. "I do remember that Easter, at Ludlow. We went to the local church, and washed the feet of the poor. The next day, we both fell ill."

"I remember," Maria nodded. "But you could not have known. I saw no danger in it either."

"Sometimes I wonder," Catherine continued, "what would have happened if we had stayed in the castle that day. There were reports of illness, but not in the town centre, and being young, we had no thought of our own mortality. We were newly married; we would be king and queen; we did not think we could die. Not yet."

"And yet you did become queen," said Thomasin.

"Seven years later. And in all that time, it was never certain. I thought I should be set back to Spain."

"They were hard years. And yet you came through them. You are England's queen. That was God's plan for you all along."

"And what about now? More tests? More hardship? I am no longer young. I wonder what we will find at Greenwich. I fear my husband's last words."

"He spoke in haste," Maria reassured her.

"But I am old; my beauty has deserted me in the service of my husband. Child after child, until I can no more. And now this: treason."

The women in the barge were silent. There was little comfort to offer when the king had been so cruel.

The palace lay around a bend in the river. After the sweeping fields, it was an imposing sight, with its long red-brick frontage stretching along the bank. The squarish gatehouse had turrets rising to the sky and a line of windows caught the sun. Beyond, the roofs of more buildings were visible, with their twisted chimneys, giving way to tall trees and the rising slope of the park behind. The place looked busy. Small craft were arriving and departing, offloading items at the side steps, where barrels were being rolled round to the cellar.

The queen's barges drew gently alongside the steps. Thomasin was relieved to have arrived after the long journey, setting her feet again on solid ground. She had heard much of the magnificence of this palace, rebuilt by the king's late father, and the sight of it did not disappoint. Yet, like her mistress, she was apprehensive about their reception.

Catherine shot a look upwards at the apartments running alongside the river. The largest, finest windows were on the further side, and Thomasin guessed that was where Catherine expected Henry to be. She wondered if he had seen their approach.

Catherine did not wait for Mountjoy and Wolsey to disembark. She had spent much time in the palace, and she headed through the gate with the air of one who had returned home. Beyond lay a courtyard, where beds were planted between railed paths. Gardeners pruning the weeds dropped to their knees as she passed. Water from a small fountain in the centre played softly against stone. Catherine headed for her apartments in the wing facing them.

"My Lady." Brandon appeared in the doorway, bowing low. "This is a surprise, My Lady." Despite his usual composure, he appeared flustered.

"I trust my rooms are ready this time."

"Of course. But, Catherine, wait…"

His use of her forename stilled them all. All the ladies halted. Catherine held herself erect, her head turned slightly towards her brother-in-law.

"She is here. The lady."

Thomasin was close enough to hear Catherine's slight intake of breath.

"Lodged with her father, for the time being."

Catherine gave a curt nod of appreciation. Then, in full sail, she swept through the doors and up the stairs.

Hurrying up behind her, Thomasin felt the news as a twist in her stomach, both for the queen's sake and for her own. Now there would be an awkward triangle again, curtailed by protocol and politeness, but with pain and rivalry simmering below the surface. She winced to think of the tense moments that were bound to arise, in eating, dancing, passing through the shared spaces, in the chapel and gardens. The space would again be shadowed.

On a personal note, Thomasin did not relish seeing Anne Boleyn again, either. Once she had enjoyed being at her side, thrilled to dance in her masque or attend parties in her private rooms, but Anne's callous role in her sister's downfall had revealed another side to the king's paramour. Now she did not care to see the lady again, nor witness the progress of her relationship with the king and the distress it would cause her mistress.

"These rooms were designed by the late queen of blessed memory, Queen Elizabeth, and the gardens too," pronounced Catherine, walking into her chambers.

The air was heavy and the grates were cold. Servants rushed in behind her, straight to the hearth and inner rooms, ready to sweep and dust.

Mountjoy had caught up with them. "My Lady, would you care to retire and let the servants do their work?"

"I will sit in my little closet and take some wine. They may be about their business at once."

Thomasin followed Catherine into the little chamber. Lined with wood, with windows open to the gardens, it had been turned into a personal chapel with the altar draped in cloth of gold and bright candlesticks. A painted tablet of the Virgin stood centrally. Catherine knelt before it to give thanks for her safe arrival.

The women knelt behind her, accustomed to her devotion.

"I was married in this very room," Catherine said eventually. "Those days afterwards, that summer, were so sweet. Such innocent happiness."

Thomasin looked about her in surprise. It was hard to imagine that his little chamber had witnessed such an important event.

Ellen was equally surprised. "Why here, My Lady?" she asked. "And not in the chapel, or the cathedral?"

"The late king married at Westminster, and my first marriage was at St Paul's, where hundreds flocked to see us. This time it was a private matter, a love match." Her face clouded over as she remembered the occasion.

"It was a beautiful occasion," Maria reassured her.

"And then we had our joint coronation, two weeks later," Catherine continued. "That was held in public. The crowds could barely be contained."

Mountjoy appeared in the doorway. "My Lady. I bring news from Bishop Mendoza. He is making his way to Greenwich now and hopes to arrive within the week."

"Within the week? It must be his gout flaring up again; he is accustomed to using a litter when it is at its worst."

"It will be a comfort to have him, though," added Maria. "Poor Inigo."

"A comfort indeed," Catherine agreed. "My countrymen are few and far between."

Gertrude led Thomasin through the door and down the stairs. "The queen's kitchens are below her lodgings, barely any distance. And no one should be using this entry, save for those supplying her table."

Thomasin held onto the smooth stone wall at the side. The circular steps were dizzying, coiled into a tight shell. She could not imagine having to carry plates of food up and down them.

The final step left them in a corridor, leading into a red-brick chamber, where two serving hatches at the far end revealed the activity within. The warm air rushed up to hit them, bringing the scent of meat.

"The design is not ideal," Gertrude said, "but it means the food arrives faster and hotter than somewhere like Hampton."

They waited at the hatch until the chief usher came to speak with them. Thomasin peeked past him to see the long table where onions were being chopped, the blazing bread oven with its tiny door, and the great hearth where a pig was being turned on a spit.

Gertrude was used to instructing servants. "The queen is now occupying her lodgings. She will require the regular supply of bread, wine and spices, breakfast at seven, to be taken in her rooms, and a light supper at nine, unless she is in the hall. She will usually dine at ten and four in the hall, as is the king's custom."

The usher nodded. "Very good, my Lady. I will assign servants to her special care. Does she have her own cook?"

"He remains at Windsor, due to the sickness."

"Very well. We will accommodate her in all her wishes. If I recall, she is especially fond of game meats but dislikes sharp sauces. Creamy dishes too, she likes. I believe we still have jars of preserved Seville oranges from her last visit."

Gertrude was impressed. "Your attention to detail will be most appreciated by My Lady."

"I will ensure that the provision of coal, water and linen is sufficient. How many ladies accompany her?"

"Just four."

He nodded again. "And is there anything she requires right now?"

"Wine and spices, to revive her from the journey. But we are but two hours from dinner, so perhaps a little bread and meat?"

"I will have it sent straight up."

"Thank you. Where might we find the laundry mistress, to speak with?"

He pointed down a corridor to their right. "I believe Mistress Arnold will be in her chambers, below the raying room, at this hour."

"I will convey your excellent service to the queen, Mister…?"

"My name is John Tandy, my Lady."

"Mister Tandy. Thanks and good day to you."

Thomasin followed Gertrude, impressed by her business-like manner. "You are good at this."

Her friend shrugged off the compliment. "So will you be when you've been in service long enough."

The laundress's room was empty, but a door led into a courtyard outside, from where the scent of soap reached them. They stepped into a small, brick court, hidden away from view of courtiers, with a central pump and trough. Here, a pair of girls were scrubbing what looked like horse blankets amid a cloud of soap suds. They jumped up and curtseyed upon seeing Gertrude and Thomasin.

"We seek Mistress Arnold."

"She is in the drying room," stuttered one, pointing across the way to another door.

"Thank you. Be about your work again."

Mistress Arnold was inspecting the dry laundry, folded in neat piles on the wooden table, smelling sweetly of lavender. She was a middle-aged woman with grey hair beneath her cap and a sharp look about her. She turned her black eyes upon Gertrude and Thomasin. "The queen has arrived?"

"This hour. We are come to inform you there are currently four in her household, in addition to our Lady, increasing to eight, probably the day after next."

"Very well. We will provision the rooms accordingly. Does the queen have any laundry that she requires washing today?"

"If you could send up a woman to collect her intimate linen. The remainder of her wardrobe has been sent for, from Windsor. When it arrives, she will require her current attire to be attended."

Mistress Arnold nodded. "And her favoured scents are?"

"Lemon and cedar wood."

"Very good, Madam."

"And are there any garments or jewels of the queens stored in the wardrobe here?"

"I will summon the clerk of the wardrobe to investigate at once, and have them sent up to her chamber."

"With as much haste as can be mustered. The queen wishes to appear properly dressed at dinner."

Mistress Arnold inclined her head in understanding. "I will make it my priority. May I add it is a pleasure to see the queen back at Greenwich again."

Again, Thomasin was left in awe at the smooth running she observed in the other side of palace life, that which was barely seen, but necessary to maintain the fresh, pristine look of the court. Under the surface, the wheels kept turning, manned with such efficiency.

"Let us go around to the gardens and gather some flowers and herbs," suggested Gertrude. "We have time, and the queen will be gladdened by them."

A small arched doorway led them into another courtyard, where barrels and firewood were being unloaded from a cart. A great muddy brown carthorse of huge dimensions looked down its forelock at them. It was very similar to the horses Thomasin remembered from Suffolk, and she wondered where this one had come from.

Beyond lay the kitchen garden. Rows of vegetables and leaves were pushing their way up to the sun, unfolding wide leaves. To one side they found lavender, rosemary and mint, gathering a few handfuls of each, scenting their palms with sweetness. Another arch led through to a formal rose garden, where marigolds and tall pink and purple hollyhocks grew around the sides. Against the wall, a honeysuckle had started to flower. Gertrude went straight to it. Deftly, she plucked a few strands where the tiny white and golden trumpets had opened.

"And look, beyond," she said, gesturing to Thomasin to follow. A gate in the wall looked out across the park beyond, a wide sweep of green dotted with trees. Beyond, the land rose up to a hill. "A goodly sight, do you not think?"

Thomasin was impressed. "Truly beautiful."

"I hope we shall have the pleasure of spending some of these early summer days there. The view from the top is spectacular. The king has a hunting lodge there, do you see it?"

Following her direction, Thomasin saw the distant frontage of a small castle-like place against the sky. "Perhaps we shall get to enjoy a banquet after all, since we were unable to finish the one at Windsor."

Gertrude seemed less enthused. "But it cannot be so happy as that one might have been, because the Lady is here."

"Anne Boleyn?"

"And she will take her part in any entertainments the king plans."

"Even before the queen?"

"Right under her nose, as if there are two queens here. I do not know how our Lady will bear it."

As they looked out across the park, a small party of riders crested the hill and began their descent. There were four of them, noble in bearing, but not royal, on well-dressed horses, taking the air. They were distant at first, but drew nearer as they headed for the stables.

"There. Thomas Boleyn and his son," Gertrude identified. "Do you mark them?"

But Thomasin's attention was fixed upon another rider in the group, squinting to make out the dark figure with broad shoulders and black hair under his feathered cap. Her heart began to beat faster as she felt a chill of recognition. Once again, she remembered those intense eyes that held her spellbound, the intoxicating scent of him, the pressure of his lips: the way he made her feel. There was no doubt. The way he sat high in the saddle, the shape of him, his movements. Rafe Danvers was here with the Boleyns. The man who had captivated her and broken her heart last autumn.

She took a deep breath. She need not worry: Greenwich was a large place and there would scarcely be a moment when she was not required by Catherine. She must act as if the man did not exist, and surely he would understand this and keep his distance. He had ignited in her such a dangerous passion that she had felt her self-control slipping through her fingers, and had almost surrendered herself, body and soul. But she had drawn back in time, sought spiritual guidance, remembered her place. Yet she had not forgotten how close she had come to sharing her sister Cecilia's disgrace.

"Come," said Gertrude, "I'll show you the tiltyard. It is bigger than the one at Westminster."

And though her hands were shaking, Thomasin made an effort to turn her back on the distant figure of Rafe and walk the other way.

FIFTEEN

The noise from the hall reached them as they came down the staircase. Catherine had summoned Mountjoy to walk at her side, with her ladies ranged around them. They moved together, aware of the battlefield lying ahead.

Catherine had been delighted by the items sent up by the wardrobe department. There was a gown of deep red velvet, another of tawny sarcenet with green sleeves and a black and silver headdress mounted with pearls. She even found a pair of her embroidered yellow dancing slippers, worn at the toes with use. But best of all was a dress of gold tissue, shot through with silver, an item Catherine had worn to welcome the Imperial ambassadors some five years back. It was an evening that called for such a gown. Among the jewels that were sent to her in a little casket, was a string of diamonds set in gold; the perfect complement to such a regal dress, and golden buckles, which her ladies attached to her shoes. It was hard not to be dazzled by the queen, as she shone from head to toe in gold.

Catherine looked with satisfaction into the mirror before departing her chambers. "Let us show there is but one queen at Greenwich and one queen in England."

It was heartening to see her spirit, thought Thomasin, slightly ashamed of her own ash-grey gown, pinching her cheeks to redden them as they approached the great hall. Her stomach was knotted with fear of what, or who, they might encounter.

A trumpet announced their arrival.

"Her Royal Majesty, Queen Catherine of England. Make way for the queen!"

At least the heralds were still using her official title.

The hall was thronging with people and light. Henry was seated at the dais at the top, under a cloth of state.

For a moment, Catherine paused, nervous to see if the king would accept her announcement as queen. After his cruel dismissal of her at Windsor, this would be a turning point. Either he would let it go, and there was still hope, or he would denounce her title here, before all assembled. That would mean all was over.

Henry did not flinch. If he held doubts, he judged this was not the time or place. Thomasin heard Catherine exhale in relief, then begin her walk towards him. All eyes were upon them.

The hall was busy. Visitors had come from outside to see the king again. Those who had already taken their seats along the trestles at the side rose and bowed as the queen and her ladies passed by. Thomasin recognised several from court the previous autumn, but none whose names she cared to recall. Her heart beat a little faster, as she could not stop herself scanning the hall for one particular face, with its dark, glowering looks. As they progressed, Catherine's appearance drew admiration, and conversations halted mid-flow, as her subjects could hardly draw their eyes from her, friends and foe alike. Sparkling in her regal gold, she reflected all the warmth in the place, truly and spectacularly a queen.

One look was sufficient to tell Thomasin that Anne Boleyn was not present. Not yet. The mood, and the response of the crowd, would have been quite different otherwise. As they progressed through the hall, though, she noted the broad back of Thomas Boleyn and his tall son George, who half turned towards Catherine and doffed their hats in a feigned show of deference. The hypocrisy of it turned Thomasin's stomach. Catherine, however, did not even look in their direction.

Ahead, Thomasin spotted the poet Thomas Wyatt in conversation with another man she had seen before, although she had never been formally introduced to him: Thomas Grey, Marquess of Dorset, fifty and greying, cousin to the king on the York side. His head was bent towards that of Francis Bryan, a feisty and roguish companion of the king, who wore an eye-patch following a near-fatal accident in the joust. Again, as Catherine passed by, the three men fell silent in a demonstration of respect for the queen.

Thomasin remembered Wyatt's ready wit and the laughter that had flowed around him in Anne's chambers. She would have enjoyed spending more time in his presence, but given his allegiance to the Boleyns, it was a necessary sacrifice.

Seated behind the top table, Henry had his eyes fixed on them. Catherine's approach was slow, as she had planned it to be, capitalising on the drama of her entrance. Thomasin could not read the expression on the king's face, but the importance of this critical moment made her legs tremble. He had stormed away from his wife only the day before, with the worst accusations. What kind of welcome would he offer his wife now? Had his temper cooled? Would he denounce her in public?

Nor could she forget that terrible feeling, walking with her family towards the chapel for Cecilia's wedding, then watching the mood turn. The laughing eyes, the derision, the burning shame at the empty altar. Thomas Boleyn had had the last, cruel laugh, and it had contributed to her mother's collapse on the way out. The current moment had the potential to be as explosive, if Henry chose.

On the next table to the king, Thomasin noted the presence of Cardinal Wolsey, with whom Henry had been in conversation. Wolsey's acknowledgement of Catherine was to incline his head and clasp his hands, as if in blessing. It felt distant.

Further off sat an old friend of Catherine, the dour-faced but erudite Bishop John Fisher. Thomasin was pleased to see him, recalling the rare instance of his wit, in the company of Thomas More and Catherine, and the way a smile unexpectedly lifted his serious countenance. The bishop rose to his feet and bowed low to Catherine, despite the infirmity he suffered in his back. In response, Catherine sent him a kindly look.

The opposite table was occupied by Thomasin's recent companions from Hampton: Charles Brandon, William Compton and, she particularly noted, William Carey, who caught her eye with a grin. At least one person was pleased to see her, Thomasin thought. Behind them were the flame-headed Hugh Truegood, and the little, drab Charles Collins. Perhaps there were friends to be found here, after all.

Reaching the steps, there was no way to avoid the king directly. Nor could Henry escape the moment. Catherine made a deep curtsey before her husband, and her ladies followed suit. Henry was dressed in green and gold, a reminder of happier May days. His hair was pushed back under a cap with gold aiglets and a deep red ruby; his cheeks were flushed but those small, pale blue eyes were troubled.

One thing the king hated, Thomasin had learned, was being forced into a position, put in a situation that made him uncomfortable, his choices taken away. She hoped he would not lash out now because Catherine had engineered such a public meeting.

Henry spoke as courtesy demanded, but it was only brief and made no acknowledgement of her appearance or position. "You are welcome to court."

Then he rose, offering his hand to the queen. Catherine took it, visibly relieved, and placed herself in the seat beside him, over which the gold canopy hung. They sat stiffly, side by side, without exchanging a word. Eventually Catherine tried to speak to her husband, who gave her his attention, but only a short reply.

"I fear this is no true welcome," whispered Ellen.

Thomasin nodded, following her to the empty table. From there, she permitted herself a look around the room, her stomach still turning. Thomas Boleyn was standing, watching the top table with interest, perhaps awaiting the arrival of his daughter. Thomasin turned to the table opposite, to Brandon and Carey, where she hoped to find greater understanding, even friendship. She was not disappointed that Truegood was present, as a potential ally, a port in a storm. Casting her eyes around again, she noted with relief that the face she had been dreading to see was not there. There was no sign of Rafe Danvers, whom she had glimpsed in the park earlier.

The hall was on edge. At first, Thomasin wondered if it was due to the lateness of the food, or the tardiness of the diners in seating themselves. Servants circulated with wine and spices. But no-one seemed to be in a rush to eat. They appeared to be waiting. Boleyn kept occupying the central space again, sometimes with his son George, who wore a look of impatience, and more than once they exchanged a few inaudible words before the whole court.

A few more courtiers appeared, slipping into empty seats, and a jester threatened to start tumbling and talking to a monkey sitting on his shoulder, which drew a few laughs. But still the food was not served.

"What is wrong?" whispered Ellen. "Is the dinner hour later at Greenwich?"

"The king has not given the order to serve."

"Why not? Is he unwell?"

"Or does he seek to humiliate the queen in this way?"

Presently, Mountjoy approached their table. "Apologies, ladies, but it appears you must move. This table is reserved."

"Then where must we sit?" asked Maria indignantly, looking around them. No one else was seated on their trestle, so close as it was to the dais.

"I am afraid you must move to the next one down, and squeeze upon the end."

Thomasin looked at the indicated table, which was already busy, where Wyatt, Grey and Bryan had placed themselves among other diners.

"My Lord, it is hardly seemly..." Maria began.

"Nevertheless, those are the orders."

"From whom?" Maria looked to the dais. "What if the queen needs us?"

"She will indicate her need to you."

"But there is no one else requiring this table," Thomasin pressed. "It is empty."

"But not for long. I am very sorry for the inconvenience, but I must urge you to move."

When the doors opened again at the far end, Thomasin realised why they had been displaced. At once, she felt like a fool.

Anne was dressed in grey and silver, with scarlet sleeves. Even from a distance, the colours were striking, and the light caught the places on her headdress which sparkled with diamonds. In the doorway, she paused, ensuring that she held everyone's attention before she entered, but there was hardly any need as all eyes were already upon her and the shadowy figures behind her.

Thomasin felt a sting of pain for her mistress as Anne started her walk through the hall. Comparisons were unavoidable. It reminded her of the time she had first seen Anne, when she'd arrived at court with her family and watched the woman in red dance seductively with the king, as if no one else was present. It was also the night she had first met Rafe, when he'd rescued her from a fire in the gardens.

The tension between Henry, Catherine and Anne was palpable. Dazzling as she was in her gold, Catherine could not compete with the brightest jewel her rival wore: that of her youth.

Anne approached with a stately bearing. She had always been commanding, even captivating in the way she moved, but there was something more to her now, as her manner seemed to contain a sense of entitlement.

"She has been practising her walk," whispered Gertrude.

Behind her, Thomasin recognised Jane, George's wife, pretty and delicate but completely overshadowed by Anne, and an older woman with dark hair, still in possession of striking good looks, and such similar features to Anne that Thomasin realised it must be her mother, Lady Boleyn. Behind them came two gentlemen; the smiling Henry Norris, with whom Thomasin had danced in a masque and the dark figure she had been dreading. Rafe Danvers followed Anne down the hall, his handsome head held high, his dark eyes, which had always been intense, now filled with insouciance. In his wake came the odious William Hatton, prancing merrily as if his soul was light as a feather.

Thomas and George Boleyn bowed to Anne as soon as she drew level. Then, with the air of ownership, they proceeded to occupy the table from which Thomasin and the others had just been evicted. She saw Rafe approach, but being tucked behind Gertrude, she managed to avoid him seeing her. However, Rafe took a seat on the opposite side to her, between Wyatt and George Boleyn, so it was probably only a matter of time before he did.

Anne dropped a low curtsey before the king and queen. Protocol dictated that she still showed reverence to Catherine, queen or not, regardless of their circumstances. She looked long and hard at Henry, before sweeping her eyes away and resting them on Catherine.

"You are here, Mistress Boleyn," said Catherine in measured tones.

"I am," she replied and paused, before adding disingenuously, "My Lady."

"Then I look forward to your good service. You may report to my household in the morning. I have lacked for company, especially those who can sing and play cards."

Anne's cheeks flamed red and Henry shifted uncomfortably in his chair, but neither dared to challenge Catherine directly. Catherine had seized the moment and defined Anne's role at Greenwich. It was a clever and daring stroke, well suited to the woman she had become of late.

Catherine turned to Henry. "Summon the servers."

As the first servants appeared with their plates, there was little Anne could do other than retreat to her table, where she sat fuming. Soon, Thomas Wyatt walked over and distracted her with whispers.

Thomasin caught Ellen's eye and the pair exchanged a smile.

"Don't let her see you," whispered Gertrude in warning, "or she will turn her anger upon you."

It was strange to see Anne again, thought Thomasin. Last autumn, she had seemed to have the upper hand, but Catherine's time at Windsor, despite its stormy ending, had breathed new hope into the queen. Perhaps the king's outburst on the last day had been merely that: a surge of temper. Thomasin kept her eyes on the table, and dared not linger on the Boleyns, in case she drew Rafe's attention.

At last the plates were placed before them, releasing their rich, inviting scents: beef, mutton and spices, herb custards and hot pies. Thomasin divided the portions with Ellen, with a growing hunger. On one occasion, looking up, she spotted William Carey speaking with Thomas Grey, and he offered her a smile of greeting.

Catherine and Henry ate in regal silence, while the hall around them was alive with sound.

It was not until the first set of plates were being cleared that what Thomasin had been fearing happened. Both fearing and yet, somehow, on an instinctive level, anticipating with a churning stomach. Rafe's eyes found her. She felt rather than saw them, because it was the heaviness of his gaze that she became aware of, almost suffocating, just as she remembered it. There were a number of people between them, and he had been occupied with the Boleyn circle, partly turned away from her until now. Thomasin sat back to allow the dishes to be removed, but from the corner of her eye, she could see the pale ellipse of his face markedly facing her. Although she tried her best to ignore it, he did not look away, challenging her to respond. She stared over to the other side of the room and fixed her eyes on the middle distance, as Hugh Truegood was holding up his glass for more wine.

The second course brought mixed dishes of fruit and cream, custards and savoury tarts, which were placed within her reach.

"I know you have seen him," Ellen whispered. "You are doing admirably well."

Thomasin stiffened, unaware that Ellen had known of her association with Rafe. "It is not too hard. I simply do not allow myself to look."

"Your strength of will is admirable. Has he tried to make contact with Cecilia since?"

Thomasin realised her cousin was speaking of William Hatton, seated among the Boleyns. Her secret was still safe. "Not that I know of, and I hope he will not."

"I am not looking at him either. We will support each other in this."

As she turned back to her plate, Thomasin was aware of Rafe again. She stared into her glass but a figure was crossing the hall, and Will Carey settled into an empty seat before her at the table. If she did not already have the attention of the Boleyn faction, watching one of their own, she did now.

"Ladies, I thought I would come and welcome you to Greenwich. I am glad your journey here was a safe one."

"We came by river," Ellen offered.

"Most dignified; a wonderful route. I am pleased you decided to follow the king. I had wondered when we would meet again."

Thomasin felt uncomfortable. "You are not sitting with your family tonight?"

"My family? Oh, you mean the Boleyns?" He turned to acknowledge them on the next table, with all their eyes needling him.

Thomasin was unable to stop herself from mirroring his gesture, almost as if his eyes dragged hers with them. Sure as she had predicted, Rafe's black, burning gaze met her for a second and flushed through her chest and cheeks. His look was one of driving questions, almost unbearable.

"I am part of the king's company, as I have told you, a gentleman of the Privy Chamber; my allegiance lies there."

Thomasin handed him a plate of wafers. "Then eat with us, for they all stare."

He smiled and bit into one of the honeycomb shapes. "I suppose they do. They will have their use of me at the appropriate time."

"Your wife is not here?" asked Ellen.

"No, she remains at Pleshey, our Essex house, as young Henry has been ill."

"Nothing serious, I hope," said Thomasin.

"Just a childish illness. It will pass. I will visit in a few weeks, when my term here is up."

"Master Carey." The strong tones of Thomas Boleyn called to them across the table. "There is a place for you here."

Carey turned slowly. "I thank you, but I am intent upon eating all these young ladies' wafers."

Thomasin and Ellen giggled.

Boleyn did not desire his son-in-law's presence sufficiently to push the matter.

"I hope we do not get you into trouble," Thomasin said, smiling at Carey in spite of Rafe's eyes, yet buoyant at her own strength in refusing to meet them. The months apart had certainly helped. She felt his presence like a distant temptation, but within her was the strength to resist him.

"Not at all," he replied, taking another wafer. "I am capable of doing that all by myself."

It was no surprise to those present that Anne Boleyn was not content to sit and eat quietly while Henry and Catherine ate upon the dais. Not even the wit of Wyatt nor the wisdom of her father could hold her attention. As soon as the plates of sweets were brought out, she picked up a dish of gilded gingerbread and made her way up to the top table in a long, sinuous walk designed to draw attention. Stopping before the king, she made a long pause, holding his eyes with her own, before proffering the treat.

"My Lord, I know you have a fondness for gingerbread."

Before Henry replied, Catherine gave a terse smile. "Thank you, Mistress Boleyn, but we already have a whole dish to ourselves."

Anne did not flinch. "I am sure you do, My Lady, but these would taste all the sweeter for having come from my hand."

A smile twitched over Henry's lips.

"Perhaps they may do," Catherine responded, swift and sharp as a pin, "and so as our guest, we cannot deny you the pleasure. Please do return to your table and allow your family to enjoy them. That would give us both the greatest of pleasures, as your hosts."

It was a deft move. Anne had not expected to be outwitted. She turned to Henry with a look of expectation. "My Lord?"

But the king did not wish to escalate the gingerbread into a scene. "Please," he replied, with a wave of the hand. "Enjoy them."

Anne struggled to conceal her pique. "I will do as you wish, My Lord. They will fortify me for when we exercise our dogs together later. I am sure both Your Majesties would wish me to be hale and hearty for that occasion."

She did not return to her table, as Henry had intended, but crossed the floor to where Brandon and Compton sat, and Truegood and Collins looked on, sharing the gingerbread with them and throwing back her head in laughter. Thomasin thought it a transparent attempt to rouse Henry's jealousy.

The king, though, was not to be drawn in today. He beckoned to Bishop Fisher to come and sit on a low seat beside him, and soon the pair were deep in what appeared to be an earnest conversation. Presently Wolsey joined them, nodding in agreement, with a most serious countenance. Anne's laughter did not even penetrate.

Thomasin watched the king and queen for a while, comforted by Catherine's small victory. Then, her line of sight was broken by a figure on the next table rising to their feet. Rafe was standing in the way, in response to the musicians beginning to sound their instruments, and she was unable to escape him. He looked very much the same, his hair swept back under a cap, his dark clothing familiar across his broad shoulders. She had forgotten how tall he was.

That gaze was impenetrable, expressionless, save for the control it exerted. Thomasin felt the power he had once held over her; the intensity of her feeling, the physical response that almost bordered on obsession. But then his final cruel words from last autumn returned to her, twisting her guts. "You little fool … to whose household do I belong? Who pays for my bed and board? To whom do I owe my allegiance?"

She pulled her eyes away. But, to her dismay, he was coming closer.

Thomasin squirmed in her seat.

"Will you dance?"

Her heart leapt into her throat. How dared he approach her, ask her? Did he think she would even speak with him, or pick up the threads of their former intimacy?

Anger flooded through her, almost making her burst, and she shook her head in fury.

Rafe turned away. She did not see his reaction, but instead, he offered his hand to Jane Boleyn and led her through the trestles to the empty part of the floor.

"The dance!" announced Henry, with an air of forced jollity. "Let those who will, take their partners. It is a long time since we have danced like this." Yet he made no move to rise from his seat and participate. Seeing this, Anne held out her hand to her brother. George cast her his infectious smile, and they assumed a central place on the floor.

The men were on the move now, taking their partners. Charles Brandon stood up with Maria Willoughby, Gertrude was claimed by Hugh Truegood and Ellen blushed as Henry Norris approached her.

"Shall we?" asked Will Carey, nodding to Thomasin.

She accepted happily and they joined the formation at the far end, closest to the king and queen. Close enough to be just within earshot, if she turned her head on the side.

"Do you not wish to retire now?" she heard Henry ask Catherine. "You must be fatigued after your journey."

"Thank you for your kindness," Catherine replied, "but I am quite well. I am looking forward to watching the dance and I am hoping for a few rounds of cards before I sleep."

Thomasin noticed Henry's swift glance towards Anne and understood his motives.

The musicians struck up the first notes, a lilting melody that rose and fell before the refrain, redolent of love and summer. Thomasin vaguely knew the dance but was a little unsure how to start, so she waited with the line of women until they made their first steps, parading about in a circle on the spot whilst the men looked on admiringly. Next they closed in towards their partners, linking arms, and began their pattern of steps, back and forth. Carey was a good dancer, as Thomasin had observed before. She was able to follow him with ease and, as fortune dictated, Rafe was on the further side of the group.

"You did not wish to dance with Mister Danvers?"

Thomasin coloured. "I did not mean to appear rude."

"No, not rude. Just certain. You may dance with whoever you please, or not."

This was a refreshing response. "Thank you."

Carey shook off the topic. "So what do you make of Greenwich?"

"I have seen little yet, but it all seems to be beautiful, far more so than Windsor. Maybe even Hampton."

"Well, the cardinal will not like that," he smiled, nodding to where Wolsey sat. "He has not smiled once since he arrived here."

"He smiles?" laughed Thomasin. "I did not think him capable."

"He will smile well enough when he has his minion Cromwell back at his side to do his bidding. Or when the king has rewarded him with some new estate."

"He is coming here? Cromwell?" The thought of the odious man filled Thomasin with distaste.

"Not so far as I know. He has returned to London for the time being. Wolsey is trying his best to repair his relationship with the king. But I must not speak of that here."

As they turned at the far end of the dance, Carey nodded to indicate the proximity of Henry.

"Greenwich is beautiful." Thomasin took the hint and changed the subject. "I hope to see much more of it before long."

"The king is planning a tilt, so there will be plenty to see then."

"Oh, shall I look forward to it. Will you ride?"

"I hope so."

They turned and paused. The dance required them to join the next pair to form a square. To Thomasin's relief, it turned out to be Ellen and Norris. Out of the corner of her eye, she saw the flash of Anne's red sleeves rising in the air. Beyond her was the darkness of Rafe's habitual black as the second square was made.

"Mistress Marwood," said Norris as rose from their bows, "it is good to see you again. I trust you are in good health?"

"I am, sir, thank you. I trust you are the same."

"I am indeed. And you are in the service of the queen now?"

She noted that he referred to Catherine by her title. "I am, and find it most pleasant employment. She is a most regal and worthy lady."

"That she is," he echoed promptly.

She turned away, reconnecting with Carey, as Norris did with Ellen. When they came back together again for the second time, Norris took her arm a little closer. He was a distinguished-looking man in his late forties, but still light on his feet.

"I was sorry about what transpired with your sister."

His words took her by surprise. "Thank you, sir."

"It was a most unfortunate event."

"It was indeed."

He released her arm and bowed low. "I thought her a nice girl who did not deserve such treatment. I do hope you will not associate me with it in your mind."

"You were not a party to it, as I recall, so I do not."

He flashed her his handsome smile and returned her to Carey for the final steps. The group walked about in their circle, first one way, then the other. Briefly, Thomasin felt Rafe's eyes again as they broke apart to bow in their pairs, but she reserved her smiles for Carey.

"Would you like to dance again?" Carey asked. "With me, I mean?"

Thomasin was surprised to find his placid, kind manners were having the most positive effect upon her. She could almost forget that Rafe Danvers was in the room, and the tension between the king and queen, when she was sheltered by his kind attentions. He was easy to be with.

"I should like to, yes."

"Then wait here; I am just going to take a drink. Can I bring you anything?"

She smiled and shook her head, enjoying the moment before the music resumed.

But as he turned away, Thomasin felt the space around her change. A figure sidled up to her, and a gentle voice purred close by. Anne was standing beside her, speaking, but her eyes were fixed on the king.

"That drab grey doesn't quite suit you, does it, Mistress Marwood? Your complexion deserves a warmer colour, like brown or tawny, don't you think?"

Thomasin decided not to rise to the bait. "Good day, Mistress Anne."

"It is a surprise to see you here, an even greater surprise to see your mistress. I had thought you all confined to Windsor, or at least to Hampton. Yet you show your faces here."

Thomasin flushed with anger. "The queen is free to go to whichever of her palaces she chooses."

"Yes," she murmured. "A queen would be. How do you like being in service?"

"Very well."

"I expect it is very quiet and dull."

"Dignified and peaceful, to be exact."

"It is not so long since I was hoping you might enter mine."

"My sister too, if I recall." Thomasin could not stop the retort escaping her lips, although she knew it was ill-advised to start a quarrel.

Anne laughed unpleasantly. "Your sister too, once, as she appeared keen to play the game of love, but she turned out less adept at it than I had hoped."

The rage boiled over in Thomasin. She knew her own passions well, and it was best to walk away from Anne right now, before she risked slighting someone of higher standing than herself.

She turned and bumped straight into Carey, returning after slaking his thirst.

"Have you changed your mind about dancing?"

"I must get some air. I am suddenly unwell."

Over her shoulder, he saw the reason at once, and communicated his sympathy with his eyes.

Turning their backs on the hall, they passed through the far doors and out into the courtyard. By the central fountain, Thomasin paused to get her breath.

Carey looked at her in concern. "What did she say? Her sharp tongue has become intolerable of late."

Thomasin nodded. "I had to leave before I spoke out of turn."

"What did she say?"

"Something touching my sister."

He nodded. "Of course. She is trying to reassert herself, afraid she has lost her influence while the king and queen have been together."

"Has she?"

He sighed. "Who can say? The king hardly looks moved by her tonight. It is long since I kept up with the changing emotions of that family. Shall we head this way? The gate takes us to the rose garden."

Thomasin accepted his arm.

They walked through the fresh evening, with the last rays of light bleeding behind the trees. Inside the garden, the gravel walks were threatened by encroaching greenery, newly sprung before the gardeners came to tame it. The air smelt clean and full of life. An occasional rose had opened its petals but most were still in bud.

"You were not too upset by her, I hope?"

"I will recover."

"You will have seen," he offered, "that I am not highly valued by that lady or her family. It is my own fault, in part."

"I'm sure that cannot be the case."

"For years I stood by, did not question or challenge, accepted my lot with gratitude, although I did not know then how high the family would rise. I feel less of a man for it."

Thomasin was silent, unsure how to respond to his confession. "Oh, no, that last part is not true."

"Wait before you decide that. My marriage was an arrangement that suited us both at the time. Eight years ago. I was close to the king, so I complied. I come from a disgraced Lancastrian line, not so far back."

They turned to follow the curve of the path.

"I professed myself satisfied with a beautiful, lively wife, whose star was on the ascendant, but I turned a blind eye each night she was conducted to the king's bed."

Thomasin was not shocked, but the words were brutal to hear.

"I thought it temporary, that she would return to me in time. I told myself I was doing it for the king, or because I loved her. But I have never had the love of my wife. After the king tired of her, there were other men. We live most of the year apart. My children are such on paper alone."

"I am sorry."

He shook his head. "It has been my misfortune. My cross to bear."

"I am still sorry for it."

"Thank you. But now the Boleyns seem set to rise further, I find myself caught. Rise with them or keep my distance."

"Surely the king will value you for your own sake, as a gentleman of his chamber?"

"I hope so. To be honest, I have spent the last two decades serving Queen Catherine. It is hard to see her treated thus, although it would do me no good to voice my thoughts."

"It is a time when people must practise diplomacy."

"Which is why you walked out of the hall."

Thomasin nodded, smiling slightly. "I will be missed soon."

"You have a few more minutes, I think. Catherine will not leave the hall while Anne remains. She will leave them no chance to spend time together in her absence."

"Will it work?"

Carey shook his head. "Most likely it will only prolong the pain. Unless she is hoping Anne will give up, in which case she does not understand Anne's character." He turned to the sky. "See, a sliver of moon."

"Like the mark of a fingernail on the sky," she added poetically.

He gave a short laugh, looking at her intently. "And what of you, Mistress Marwood? What are your hopes? A husband with a title? A country estate and children?"

"You missed the most important thing off the list."

"What is that? Money? Fine dresses? No, that is not you. Happiness; I'll bet you want a happy marriage above all."

"You are not far wrong," she admitted. "I hope one day to be able to love the man I call husband."

"Then you will be the envy of many, but no more so than he would be. It would be a fortunate man indeed who could win your love, Thomasin."

His use of her forename surprised her. The air was turning chilly, but his eyes showed his desire to keep her outside for longer.

"I must return to the queen; my time is not my own."

"Of course, let me accompany you. I apologise for having kept you, for pouring out my private matters."

"Not at all." She took the arm he offered. "There is no apology needed. You may speak freely with me."

"Perhaps I will," he said wistfully, "one day."

Outside the hall, Ellen was waiting. She hurried up as she saw Thomasin approach. "There you are! The queen noticed your absence and sent me to find you. She is taken ill and has retired to her chamber."

Thomasin felt uncomfortable, caught out in the neglect of her duty.

"It is entirely my fault," added Carey. "I detained her without thought; I send my apologies to the queen. No harm was meant."

"Hurry now," Ellen urged, and Thomasin picked up her skirts and followed after her.

SIXTEEN

Catherine was lying on her side on her bed, while Maria and Gertrude attempted to remove her outer garments.

"Here we are," announced Ellen as she and Thomasin entered, "both of us."

Catherine groaned as Maria tugged at her reluctant shoe.

"My Lady, can you please roll forward, just a little."

But Catherine remained immobile. The evening had taken its toll on her, despite her best efforts.

"Come here," she barked, "round here where I can see you. Now, round here."

Thomasin and Ellen edged round the bottom of the bed, to the other side, where Catherine's angry, red face was pressed into her pillow. Maria was still trying to remove her shoe.

"Well, explain yourself. You!" She jabbed her finger at Thomasin, who had never seen her in such a rage.

"My Lady," faltered Thomasin.

"You are in my service; your duties are to wait on me. Did you get my permission to leave the hall? To walk in the gardens with a man, a married man? What kind of scandal are you trying to bring into my household?"

"My Lady…"

"Was it that woman who put you up to this? I saw you talking with her. Was it her idea, to send you out walking with her brother-in-law? Have you compromised yourself? What was her intention? What did she say to you? She will use you like your sister, remember that. I took you into my household to give you a fresh start, away from those rumours and questions, but you revert to type as soon as you get the chance."

The unfairness of Catherine's accusations stung Thomasin deeply. She could barely form words in her own defence, so shocking and unjust the comments were.

"Well? What do you have to say for yourself, girl? Speak!"

At that moment, Maria succeeded in removing the shoe she had been pulling, causing Catherine to groan and draw up her feet. The other shoe remained on her foot, and Maria stood back in despair.

At the sight of Catherine sprawled so piteously, in pain, Thomasin realised that her anger was misplaced. Catherine felt hurt, slighted, afraid, and those emotions caused her to lash out.

"I offer my profound apologies for leaving the hall, My Lady; no disrespect to yourself was intended. That woman spoke to me unkindly, and I wished to remove myself from her presence at once."

"You left the hall without my permission."

"I apologise. I had not realised I needed to seek it at that moment. I was only gone a few moments."

"Long enough." Catherine paused, shifting her hip and shoulder. "What did she say to you?"

"Please, My Lady, it was a slur upon my sister."

Catherine grunted. "Maria, finish your work and remove my shoe. Prepare me for bed. Why can I no longer dance? I long to dance again."

Thomasin waited, her head clouded with emotion and anger, but her interview with Catherine was clearly over. As Maria and Gertrude attempted to dress her for bed, she slipped into the antechamber with Ellen.

"Do not let her words upset you," said Ellen. "She was slighted by Anne after you left, and Henry did nothing. I am sure her anger towards you was part of that."

"I am sure it is," said Thomasin, sitting down in the window seat and pulling the pins from her headdress. "But I have never heard the queen speak that way before."

"It was harsh, I agree. Here, do you want some wine to help you sleep?"

Ellen poured the dark liquid into a cup and Thomasin drank it gratefully.

"I am sure her words will hang on me into the small hours."

"Ellen! Thomasin! The queen's nightgown?" called Gertrude from within.

Ellen put a hand on her cousin's shoulder. "I will go. It will all be better in the morning."

"Thank you."

Thomasin turned to the open window for some relief. Night had fully fallen and the air was sweet and clean-smelling. On this side, the queen's apartments overlooked the neighbouring friary and friars' garden, which were joined by a gate to the orchard. The only lights were those gleaming from within the church windows, muted as the friars performed their late-night rituals. Thomasin breathed deeply, filling her lungs. She stood outlined in the window, with the cool air rushing over her.

Catherine was still being undressed, with complaints and groans, but Thomasin picked up her wine glass and blotted out the sound.

The evening had left a sour taste in her mouth. For the first time, she felt unhappy in the queen's service, and she understood the reasons why. Tonight, she had been caught up in the tension between the three of them, the triangle of Henry, Catherine and Anne, even though she had always tried to act for the best. Being in the queen's household at Windsor or Hampton was one thing, but here, with the Boleyns in attendance, the dynamic was completely different. She did not doubt there would be more uncomfortable scenes in the coming days.

If only the situation could be resolved, but Thomasin could not see any outcome other than that of suffering for her mistress.

Thomasin did not have to wait long before the tension surfaced again. The following morning, Catherine was cool and detached as her ladies dressed her in her best red velvet gown, carefully arranging her skirts and pinning her pearl headdress into place. Thomasin's fingers worked swiftly, but she avoided meeting her mistress's eyes and Catherine said very little, and nothing about their conversation the previous night. It was a fresh, cooler morning, and Catherine elected to break her fast in her chamber, in the company of Bishop Fisher, who had called to pay his regards.

Around mid-morning, Catherine and her ladies were returning from chapel when Thomas Boleyn turned down the corridor ahead. He gave a little pause of recognition, as if it had crossed his mind to turn away, but his pride, or etiquette, made him continue. Catherine glided towards him serenely, as if he was part of the stonework.

As Catherine approached, Boleyn stood aside and bowed, expecting her to pass by.

Instead, Catherine paused then spoke boldly. "Sir Thomas, send your daughter to attend upon me, as soon as possible."

Boleyn's face showed he was taken by surprise. "But, My Lady…"

"What?" Catherine turned to face him. "She is not too busy, or too important, to obey a summons from her queen?"

Boleyn knew when he was beaten. To defy Catherine openly would be to compromise his position. "I will pass on your message."

"And your wife and daughter-in-law must come too. As ladies at court, they should have followed the custom of waiting on the queen." She did not wait for his answer, but surged past, leaving him standing.

"My Lady, are you sure you want to have that family in your chamber?" asked Maria, as they approached the stairs.

Catherine held up a hand to silence her. "If she is with me, she cannot also be with him."

It was three in the afternoon when stillness was broken by a knock upon the queen's door.

Catherine was playing cards with Ellen, while Thomasin sat with Gertrude and Maria, sewing in the window seat. The afternoon had ticked past slowly. Thomasin, certainly, had felt tense with anticipation, and one look at Ellen, who kept making mistakes in the game, confirmed that she was feeling the same.

"Come," called Catherine, not looking up from the cards splayed in her hand.

Everyone's eyes except Catherine's were on the door. It was opened by one of the guards from outside.

"Lady Mary, Countess of Essex and Lady Catherine Willoughby."

As the pair entered, Maria gave a little cry of surprise and jumped up to embrace her daughter. The pair had been stuck at Windsor since the outbreak of the sweating sickness, only now able to travel to Greenwich to rejoin Catherine.

"Oh, what a pleasure to see you both," said Catherine, rising to her feet in genuine delight. "I hope you are in good health and your journey was not too arduous."

Mary curtseyed. "We are both well; neither of us succumbed, thanks be to God, and the sickness is now completely gone from Windsor."

"That is wonderful news indeed," said Catherine, smiling as Maria held her child close.

"Thank you, thank you," said Maria, "for keeping her safe and bringing her to me."

"She was good as gold," smiled Mary, "no trouble at all."

"That was a blessed action," said Catherine.

Mary turned to Catherine. "We brought some of your books and a few more items from your wardrobe. Bishop Mendoza was also of our party, but he is now resting after the journey. His gout is causing him to suffer."

"Of course. I shall visit the good bishop in due time but come, be seated, take some refreshment."

No sooner had Mary done so, than a second knock was heard.

"Come!" replied Catherine, with less trepidation than before.

However, this time, the door opened to reveal a trio of Boleyn women, decked out in their brightest and best. Anne was resplendent in white and green, her face glowing proud under an arc of pearls.

Catherine's demeanour changed at once. Regaining her composure, she regarded Anne's mother, a woman with finely chiselled features and wide, dark eyes, as beautiful as ever in her late forties, dressed in a russet gown. As a young woman, she had served Catherine in her first years as queen, alongside Elizabeth Marwood. Once, they had even been friends. Thomasin looked with interest at Anne's mother.

Catherine chose to address her former lady. "Lady Boleyn, you have arrived at a happy hour. We have new arrivals from Windsor, returned to us safe and sound."

Lady Boleyn inclined her head. It was difficult to read the gesture, be it submission or sarcasm.

"Come," said Catherine, "sit and take some wine." Then she added, pointedly, "All of you."

"My Lady," began Anne, "I have come to pay my respects, but I fear I cannot stay."

Catherine turned slowly and let her eyes fall heavily upon Anne, who tried not to be daunted.

"I had promised to play bowls this afternoon and watch the king at tennis…"

"Hush!" It was her mother who interrupted Anne. "Your bowls and tennis can wait."

Catherine did not let a muscle of her face flicker. "The king, my husband, has been playing bowls and tennis since you were a babe in arms. He can manage perfectly well without you."

It was on the tip of Anne's tongue to answer, but the eyes of the whole room were upon her, and she was not yet emboldened enough to challenge Catherine directly. Thomasin wondered if her relationship with the king was at a low point, and she lacked the confidence to fight her cause. It was one thing to do so in the hall, but quite another in the queen's own chambers.

"Sit," ordered Catherine. Anne and Jane went to occupy the other window seat, while Lady Boleyn took the chair at the card table vacated by Ellen.

The air was thick between them, like smoke. Thomasin could feel the presence of the Boleyn women as she tried to concentrate on her sewing. From the corner of her eye, she was aware of the hems of Anne and Jane's dresses, green and white, and blue, rippling as they twitched their feet impatiently. How Catherine managed to bear their presence, was testament to her inner strength.

Catherine drew out a pack of cards and began to deal. "Let us play, Lady Boleyn, like the old days. What game shall we choose? Do you know this new game called Primero, or should we choose one of our old favourites?"

"Whatever My Lady wishes."

"A goodly answer. Then let us play Imperial, as we used to years ago. I recall it was a favourite of yours."

The room watched as Catherine finished doling out the cards. Then she cast her eyes meaningfully around the room. "I am sure I do not need to remind anyone here of the rules, only that I insist upon them being followed meticulously."

Thomasin saw Anne turn her head towards the window, as if this could deflect the hidden meaning that was meant for her.

Taking the lead, Catherine laid the first card, and Lady Boleyn followed suit.

"I do remember," she continued, "once when your children were small. That first summer here, we had a passion for playing dice, endless games of dice, and we took the board outside, while your children were visiting from the country. We played while they fought battles in the orchard." She placed her next card very deliberately. "They must have been just nine or ten. Your Mary lost her poppet. Who would have thought it?"

It was a statement, not a question. Catherine took the trick and swept the cards away.

"And you, Mistress Marwood, you were yet within your mother's belly and your sister a babe in arms."

Thomasin looked up in surprise, suddenly connected to the past, and the court, in a way she had not expected.

But Catherine had turned back to the table. "Shall we play again? And let us have some music. Send for the lutist."

A brief calm settled. Catherine and Lady Boleyn played several hands while the soft tones of the lute took the edge off their suffering. All save for Anne, who twitched and shifted as if she was being prickled by hedgehogs, her eyes drawn to the window, despite its view offering her only the friary and nothing of the court.

Presently, Catherine looked about and spotted the jug of wine on the cupboard. "I am thirsty," she pronounced to the room.

Ellen rose to her feet at once.

"No, no." Catherine waved her back down. "Anne can fetch my wine."

The room fell still. All eyes were turned upon the window seat. For a moment, Thomasin thought that Anne would refuse.

"I will fetch it," offered Jane softly, barely within earshot.

But Anne shook out her dark hair under her bonnet and rose to her feet. Without a word, she walked across the floor, lithely, with grace, plucked up the wine and brought it back to the card table. Without so much as a glance at Catherine, she filled her glass, then that of her mother. Then she returned the jug and resumed her seat, still full of grace, as if she had been rehearsing the steps of a dance.

Catherine did not touch the wine, nor thank Anne, but played on.

Thomasin and Ellen sewed steadily and the lutist continued to pluck.

Presently, Catherine looked up. "Let us widen the game into two pairs. Anne and Jane, will you join us? I hear the Lady Anne is a most dedicated player."

"Oh, My Lady," blustered Jane, "I have no skill for it, and no one should be made to partner me, for I always lose. Pray forgive me."

"She speaks the truth," added Anne, in a cynical tone. "I won five pounds from her the other night."

"Of course she speaks the truth," said Catherine at once, swift as a blade, "because she is speaking to her queen."

"I will join, and make up the four," said Thomasin, rising and putting her sewing down, hoping to defuse the tension. It was a game she had learned during the long winter months at Windsor. She took a seat opposite Anne, partnering her as Catherine and Lady Boleyn made the other pair.

The first hand she was dealt was weak. One knave of clubs, but the rest were small numbers. It was not going to win her any tricks, and she hoped Anne had better cards in her possession. She looked up at her partner, whose dark eyes were cast down upon the table, with the air of a contained animal.

Catherine took the first trick but Anne claimed the following two, then Lady Boleyn won another. Thomasin was poised to play her knave, in the hope that she may win the round, but it sat uneasily with her. It was only a card game, she told herself, but it meant that she was siding with Anne against Catherine. Still, she had few hands left, and it meant nothing really. She lay down her knave upon Catherine's ten of clubs. Lady Boleyn threw away a three in the same suit. Anne was the last to play.

It was a surprise to all when she placed the queen of clubs over Thomasin's knave. The trick was already theirs.

Thomasin looked up at her sharply.

"I had no choice," replied Anne with nonchalance. "It is the lowest of my remaining cards."

"I see the Lady Anne will not stop at a knave," said Catherine, "but she will have a king if she can."

Her implication was unavoidable. Yet if it shocked her, Anne merely twitched her lips and returned to her hand.

Piqued, Catherine turned to Anne's mother. "Lady Boleyn, you are to be commended for having raised such, what is the word, such loyal daughters. So loyal they would do anything to advance their family. First the one, then the other."

It had been before her time, but even Thomasin understood that she was referring to Mary Boleyn preceding Anne as royal mistress.

"And such a blessing," continued Catherine, "that the younger does not mind treading where the elder has already been."

The sting in her words was sharp. Lady Boleyn blushed a deep shade of red. Anne, though, put down her cards and rose from the table.

"What means this?" Catherine asked at once. "You have not been given leave to rise."

Anne's face was pale but set within it, her eyes were large and dark. "I am indisposed."

"Enough that you are unable to finish the game you started?"

"The game is making me indisposed."

"Then you would be well advised to withdraw and consider the wisdom of engaging yourself with more experienced players."

Anne shot a look to her mother, but Lady Boleyn's eyes would not offer her consolation. Rather, they seemed to suggest this was a situation of her own making. She dropped a curtsey, but as she rose, added plainly, "I will take my leave. I am sure experience is a great advantage, but there are some offices that only youth can perform."

The others could only gasp after her as the green and white dress sashayed out of the room.

"My Lady, my deepest apologies," began Lady Boleyn. "This is a strange situation, indeed, and not of my choosing."

Catherine waved her away, and Lady Boleyn hurried after her daughter, with Jane bringing up the rear.

SEVENTEEN

Will Carey hurried through the crowd as people took their places for dinner. The hall was filling fast, and tapers burned on the walls although it was still broad daylight outside. The season of midsummer would soon be upon them at Greenwich.

"I had hoped to find a place by you," he said, squeezing in at Thomasin's side while Ellen sat on the other. He flashed the smile that transformed his plain face. "You have been closeted with the queen all day?"

"Indeed, as she wished. There was an altercation between her and Anne. I am not quite sure who came off better."

"Really?"

They both looked up to the top table, where Catherine sat alone awaiting Henry's arrival. Her face was a perfect mask and her headdress studded with pearls, despite having grumbled and pouted all afternoon following Anne's departure.

Wolsey hovered nearby, also waiting for Henry, no doubt with some opinion or advice to impart.

"I believe them to be playing bowls," whispered Carey, "him and Anne, although I did see her chiding him earlier."

"Chiding the king?" Thomasin was surprised.

"In the antechamber of the chapel. I passed when they thought themselves unheard."

"And did you hear her words?"

"I could not avoid them. She was upset and did not show restraint. She chides him for keeping her and Catherine under one roof at Greenwich, where she is forced to show deference to the queen."

"And the queen is forced to take impertinence from her."

Carey held up his hands. "I am in complete agreement with you there. Anne and her party should be elsewhere. No one likes this unease. We go from one painful situation to another."

The doors opened at the end and Henry strode in, followed by Charles Brandon. His face looked heavy as thunder as he approached the dais, bowed his head to Catherine and took his seat beside her. At his signal, the trumpet sounded and the servants began to bring in the plates of food. There was no sign of Anne.

"Oh dear," said Carey. "He does not look happy."

As Thomasin watched, Catherine inclined her head towards her husband and spoke a few gentle words.

Henry did not turn, but listened acutely, as if absorbing them. They seemed to calm him, although he did not face Catherine, but reached for his plate.

"Oh, lovely!" Carey looked down at the table with pleasure. "I have such an appetite tonight, as if nothing will sate it."

The servants had placed beef with prunes and pork with orange between them, along with a dish of pastries and another of larks.

"Seville orange slices," Carey noted. "The kitchens have not forgotten who is queen."

Thomasin looked about. None of the Boleyn faction was present. Presently, though, George arrived, leading Jane by the hand, followed by Rafe.

Again, her heart gave that little catch. The imprint of him had not entirely left her. She could recall that ardent pressure of his lips and the way he filled her dreams at night. But it was not to be. No matter how strong her feelings had been, he was a dangerous man, unscrupulous, disloyal. She turned away.

"Oh," said Carey, "here we go."

Thomasin realised with a beating heart that George Boleyn was leading Jane towards their table. With Will Carey as their only family member in the room, they sat down opposite him, with Rafe following. He had little choice but to take the empty space on the other side, almost opposite Thomasin. She squirmed inside at the proximity.

"Master Carey," nodded George Boleyn, "ladies. Good day."

"Good day," Thomasin muttered back.

"Well, damn, I am hungry. All this business gives a man an appetite." George Boleyn reached for the plates of food before Thomasin or Will had had the chance to take their portion and started to gather a spoonful, as if no one else was there. "Here, Jane, bring your plate closer. I know how fond you are of this beef. It will lift your spirits and put colour in your cheeks."

He loaded a generous portion onto her plate. Carey's face paled as the food began to vanish.

"They will not always be like this," George Boleyn said to Jane. "It will ease. At some point soon it will be resolved."

Thomasin realised they were speaking of Anne and her situation.

"It's too fatiguing," breathed Jane, seeming exhausted. "All this arguing, constantly."

"It is essential that you rest and eat well. Perhaps we should go to New Hall for a while. We cannot risk your health."

"Here," spoke up Carey, reaching for a plate, "pork for you, Thomasin, Ellen?"

He served each of the women, then himself, but George Boleyn had already claimed the dish of larks. Once again he was piling Jane's plate high with delicate concern.

Thomasin watched Jane as she ate. On the few brief occasions they had met before, she had never really taken a close look at George Boleyn's wife, Anne's sister-in-law. She had a light complexion and pale eyes, her features perfectly symmetrical and small, pretty enough, but with nothing to make them distinctive. There was something gentle, mild-mannered about her mouth, nothing of malice in it, but an innate intelligence. And something else too, difficult to identify, but perhaps an edge of vulnerability. It was a face she found hard to dislike.

As if she felt Thomasin's eyes upon her, Jane looked up.

Thomasin smiled. Jane hesitated, as if unsure what etiquette demanded, then let her lips twitch in response.

"Eat up," said George Boleyn, "eat up."

Seated beyond Jane, Rafe Danvers was eating in silence. Thomasin tried to draw back as far as possible, to shrink into the space towards Will Carey, to distance herself from his overwhelming presence.

"Mutton?"

Thomasin started. Rafe was holding a plate towards her, from the end of the table, noticing that the Boleyns were intent upon taking more than their share.

It was a reconciliatory gesture. She wanted to accept, it was polite to do so, but that might imply forgiveness, even friendship renewed. She stared dumbly into the meat, then took the dish with a nod of thanks.

After she had loaded up her plate, Thomasin handed it politely back. Rafe was apparently waiting for the moment and spoke softly.

"You are still in the queen's household?"

"Yes." She kept her eyes on the table.

"Does it suit you?"

"Well enough."

He cleared his throat, drawing her eyes to him. "I suppose it is not possible to get close to you now."

"No." She turned her head away.

"You are looking well."

Thomasin did not reply.

There was a murmur in the hall as the king rose to his feet. Henry was looking more satisfied than earlier, and he smoothed down his beard with a hand glinting with jewels.

"Tomorrow, the Venetian ambassadors arrive at Greenwich. We will host a tilt in the yard. All challengers must submit their arms by noon."

He resumed his seat and the bubble of conversation erupted.

Thomasin looked past Will Carey to Ellen, then caught the eyes of Maria and Gertrude on the far side. The Venetians were daring to show their faces again at court, after trying to entrap Queen Catherine to supply information about the emperor, and her ladies to spy upon her and report her movements.

"I can hardly believe it," Ellen hissed.

Thomasin looked to Catherine. Once again, Catherine was composed, but Thomasin knew that the significance of this was not lost upon her. Nor had she forgotten that the ambassadors had left Windsor expressly against her orders. Briefly, the queen turned and caught Thomasin's eye. A silent understanding passed between them.

"They are not good news, these Venetians?" asked Carey.

"We entertained them at Windsor, before the spring," explained Thomasin, "and, let us say, we were initially impressed by their manners, but swiftly came to realise their intentions."

"Oh dear, that does not sound good."

"No, they are either slippery as eels or clumsy as oxen."

"I am stunned that they dare show their faces again," added Ellen. "I wonder what they can want. They cannot possibly come without good purpose, when they should be retreating with their tails between their legs."

"The Venetians?" chimed in George Boleyn, overhearing their talk. "It may be to do with the Pope. Any day Henry expects the return of Edward Foxe, his ambassador to Rome. While Clement and the emperor are at such odds, I expect they are waiting to hear his judgement. What the Pope and emperor do has a direct impact upon Venice."

"Really?" asked Carey.

"You will recall that Rome was sacked last year?"

Carey nodded.

"And the Pope was imprisoned by the emperor?"

"Yes."

"Well, Venice feared a similar fate from unruly Imperial troops. They lost a major trading partner back then, and were forced into an Imperial alliance, for self-protection. But now the Pope is free, they are torn between two masters, not knowing which way to turn. Perhaps the Doge has instructed his ambassadors to woo both sides."

Thomasin let this insight sink in. If the Venetians were unsure who to follow, their task in England was a difficult one indeed. On one hand, Henry was appealing to the Pope to annul his marriage, whilst on the other, his unwanted wife, Catherine of Aragon, was aunt to the emperor. This polarised the Venetians along the lines of the royal dispute. And they, like everyone else, were unsure who would win.

Suddenly it all made sense. The expensive gifts, the flattery, the attempts to gain informal information. They were trying to play both sides until a decisive victory was reached. Thomasin could understand them better now, and itched to impart this information to Catherine.

"A tilt tomorrow, eh?" said Carey, breaking into her thoughts. "What do you think of that? George, will you ride?"

"I shall indeed. Rafe?"

He nodded, and Thomasin briefly caught a glint of his dark eyes before she looked away. He was still the same, with his dark slanting brows, the brooding looks, the blue-black hair. There was no doubt he was the most handsome man at court, outdoing the likes of Hugh Truegood and George Boleyn, who was reckoned to be beautiful by the ladies, and even, dared she think it, the king himself.

"I will ride," he confirmed, "if the ladies promise to come and watch."

"Will you?" asked Carey, turning to Thomasin, then to Ellen. "Will you ladies come and watch over our vain efforts?"

"Will you be strong enough?" George Boleyn picked up on the question and asked Jane, solicitously, before anyone else had the chance to answer. "We must bring cushions and a blanket for you, but you will sit with Mother, and she will bring you back to our rooms if you require it."

Thomasin looked again at Jane. She did not appear unwell, or frail. Then it suddenly struck her. Perhaps Jane was with child? It was not seemly to ask, but she resolved to watch her closely for signs, especially if she needed attending to. It was an interesting development but one, Thomasin was aware, that was not her business. She must keep Jane's secret, if such a secret there was.

The plates were being cleared away now. There would be no dancing tonight. The king was heading to his rooms to prepare for the tilting in the morning, and Catherine was rising to her feet, ready to retire.

"Look," urged Thomasin to Ellen, "up, up we go." To Will Carey and the others, she bade a general goodnight, casting her net wide enough that Rafe was also included in it.

As she hurried after Catherine, another thought occurred to her. The return of the Venetians meant another reunion for her. No doubt the golden-eyed Nico Amato would be amongst them.

Catherine did not head straight back to her apartments. She took a detour through the corridor and across the court, over which hung an orange sky, to the strip of apartments where visitors were housed. The architecture here was on a smaller scale, with plainer carvings, unpainted and ungilded. There was noise here too, of voices, and a clatter which sounded like the movement of barrels or irons.

Thomasin and the others followed without question. She paused outside the third door, knocked and waited until a voice inside bade her enter.

Following Catherine, Thomasin found herself in a dark, smoky room, with a small fire in the grate and a single bracket burning upon the wall. Before the hearth, a bent-over figure was struggling to rise, although Catherine bade him keep his seat. It took Thomasin a moment to recognise Bishop Mendoza, the Spanish ambassador, Catherine's fellow Castilian, newly arrived from Windsor. He was looking tired and unwell.

"Keep your seat, I pray," Catherine said, guiding him back down, then taking his hands, glinting with gold. "Dear old friend, I am so pleased to see you here, safe from the sickness."

"As pleased as I am to see you, My Lady," he replied, "although not free from all sickness; my gout made the journey a trial."

"I will order anything you need. Food, medicines, comforts. We shall not expect you to appear until you are quite rested enough."

"Thank you for your kindness."

"How have you been? Did they look after you at Windsor after I left?"

He nodded slowly. "Well enough. The sickness took a few, but I kept to my chamber, admitting only the one servant, in whom I trusted well enough. I have left bills unpaid…"

"Do not worry," she replied. "They will be seen to."

"The place was in chaos, I heard," he continued. "Those ambassadors left in haste, leaving their goods behind them, for goodness knows where, then the castle was closed up. No one was permitted to leave and none to enter, save for the delivery of food. How did you manage at Hampton? I wrote there, but I dared say nothing of import, as I know the man Cromwell had oversight of all the letters."

"Not quite all," Catherine replied, "but I received none from you, none from his hands."

"Is that true? Then he is the very devil. I wrote twice a week, offering sustenance, prayers, verses to fortify you."

Catherine shook her head, her lips tightening. "No, I received no such letters. But your news alleviates my conscience somewhat regarding others. And those ambassadors are expected here tomorrow, where they shall come face to face with me again, and will need to make their apologies."

"Here, tomorrow? Those dancing clowns?"

Thomasin tried to stifle her laugh.

"Those dancing clowns will be here," Catherine smiled, "and we shall see how they dance for the king now, once their duplicity is exposed for all."

"But be careful," said Mendoza. "It is a delicate situation. We do not want to make an enemy of the Doge."

"Not at all," Catherine replied, "or else we should have no more supplies of golden lace," and they laughed again.

"Is Mountjoy here?" asked the bishop, after a moment.

"I shall send him to you, shortly."

Mendoza leaned forward in his chair, the firelight highlighting the lines etched in his face. "My Lady, for all our laughter, I do urge caution. I have received letters from friends in Rome. The Pope is a free man again, no longer under the control of your brother, but still in fear of him. Henry has been sending non-stop letters and ambassadors to plead his cause, but he prevaricates, pleads and weeps."

"Weeps?" asked Catherine. "My husband has made the Pope weep?"

"So my sources claim."

"I am almost undone by this knowledge," she replied, profoundly moved. "I cannot but think of the danger to his soul, his immortal soul. We must pray for him, and for the removal of the terrible Boleyn woman who has brought him to this."

"I have prayed for his delivery and yours day and night, My Lady."

"Thank you. We shall do so tonight, and again in the chapel come morning. It is a wicked thing indeed to see a once great king so ensnared by temptation that he imperils his very soul."

With a pause in the conversation, Thomasin felt emboldened to speak. "My Lady, if I may, we overheard George Boleyn at table, saying that the ambassador was expected back any day. He called him Foxe?"

Catherine nodded. "Edward Foxe, Bishop of Hereford, Wolsey's man, of course, and I believe Stephen Gardiner was also sent with him. So they are due back soon? They are already in England?"

"It may be so. Boleyn seemed to think their arrival imminent, Foxe at least."

"They must have achieved something, to be returning so soon. I wonder what the Pope has to say on the matter. Well, we shall see." Catherine rose and pressed the bishop's hands again. "I will have more firewood and wine sent to you, and will visit you again in the morning. There is an apothecary here, too, so do not hesitate to order anything you require; it will be added to my account."

"I thank you, gracious lady."

Catherine drew her skirts around her. "Come, ladies, let us take a little air in the park before we retire."

It was a beautiful summer's evening. The air was mild and sweet as the birds swooped low, seeking their roosts and mates, filling the trees with their chatter. Thomasin breathed in the scent of grass and flowers, undercut by the freshness of water, a constant reminder of the proximity of the river. A line of trees in full leaf shaded their path. The land rose up to the hunting lodge behind, a curious red-brick building that Thomasin was interested to explore.

"The view from up there must be wonderful," she nodded to Ellen. "You must be able to see all along the river."

"It's a fair climb, but worth it, I am sure."

"I am looking forward to the tilt tomorrow."

"And the arrival of the Venetians," Ellen added with a wicked glint in her eye. "I wonder how they will be treated."

"And we," mused Thomasin, thinking of Nico and the kiss he had given her in the garden at Windsor, "should we acknowledge them?"

"I suppose we must wait and take our cue from the queen."

"My Lady?"

They turned at the voice. Will Carey was hurrying along the path behind them. Thomasin realised she was pleased to see him, as he was to see her, rushing straight to her side, but dropping his bow to Catherine.

"I saw you from the window, so I thought to come and walk with you, should you wish it."

Catherine looked with interest at Thomasin. "You are welcome, Mister Carey. In all our long acquaintance, I have found you to be sensible and discreet."

It was a sincere greeting, allowing Carey to take his place between Thomasin and Ellen as they walked along, speaking with enthusiasm of the tilt tomorrow. Carey had recently been in the king's chambers and heard of his plans.

"The seamstresses, painters and tent makers will be working through the night," he began enthusiastically, continuing with a more detailed outline of the arrangements as they headed along the path.

From time to time, Thomasin noticed that Catherine turned and looked back at them, as if keeping her in her special notice. It made her more conscious of her actions, and perhaps her replies to Will Carey were a little more quiet than they would otherwise have been. Ellen chatted away merrily, though, about fabrics and spangles and chariots.

They took the path towards the gate in the wall. Above it, the moon loomed large in the deepening sky, more than half full but not complete.

Passing through, they caught the scent of the bush on the other side; a honeysuckle twining up around the arch, with its white and golden trumpets. Carey paused, captivated by the scent, and reached up to pluck a strand.

"Here, smell it." He held it up to Thomasin's nose. The sweetness was indeed intoxicating.

She took it from his fingertips and tucked it into her bodice, to carry the scent with her as they walked on.

"So tell us, Mister Carey, how the king fares tonight," said Catherine, drawing alongside him.

"Very well, I believe. He is in good spirits and full of plans for tomorrow."

"And how has his day been? How did he pass the afternoon?"

"In playing bowls, I believe."

"Bowls? I'll wager his partner was Suffolk, who always manages to beat him."

"Not today."

"Oh," replied Catherine in mock surprise. "Did he actually beat Suffolk today?"

"No, but he was beaten by Mistress Anne, which I do not think was to his liking."

Catherine fell silent, and Thomasin shot Carey a look. He took it as encouragement. "I believe it led to an argument between them, outside the chapel."

Catherine raised her eyebrows. "Is that so, Mister Carey, is that so?" She did not wait to hear the details, but walked on.

"Should I have told her?" asked Carey, but Thomasin could only shrug, uncertain whether or not he was right to have done so.

The waves of honeysuckle wafted over her again. Laughter from an upper window somewhere reached them.

Catherine was by the doorway. "I am to retire. Maria, Gertrude, come with me. Thomasin and Ellen, through the far gate is the knot garden, if you recall. Gather some fresh scented bunches and come straight up. Mister Carey will vouch for your safety, I am sure."

Thomasin dropped a curtsey, surprised at the sudden freedom, and watched as Catherine departed from view.

"Well, that was unexpected," said Ellen. "We had better find some suitable flowers."

"More honeysuckle?" suggested Carey, motioning back along the path.

"Oh yes," Thomasin agreed. "You go first, Ellen. We will follow on."

Carey went next. Thomasin let her eyes rest on his broad shoulders, on the slashes in his sleeves, white in the evening air, on the thick mane of hair on the back of his head.

As they were enveloped in the scent, he turned and caught her looking. "Thomasin? You look serious."

She smiled. "Do I?"

He laughed. "A little. Why has the queen been watching you so closely tonight, but has now left you with me? Do you think she will chide you later?"

"Oh, you think this is some sort of test?"

"Do you? Will she warn you, later tonight, to stay away from a married man? To guard your tongue before a member of that family?"

"I don't think of you as being part of that family. You seem separate. You said so yourself."

"But she may still see the ties, and may distrust me. How do you see me, then?"

"As a friend," Thomasin blurted out quickly. "As someone I feel comfortable with."

He nodded. "Someone you can trust? A confidant?"

"Yes, I suppose so." She reached up and plucked some honeysuckle.

Carey stepped back and sighed. "Always everyone's friend, dependable, plain Will."

She looked at him curiously. "Is that not a compliment? What more would you wish for?"

"To be seen, valued, for my own self."

It was an easy reply to find. "Well, of course I do. You are valued for yourself, for your kindness, your company. I am pleased you are here."

"Really?"

"Of course, I would not say otherwise."

"Do you not fear being out here alone with a married man?"

Thomasin could not help but smile. "Fear? You? No, not at all. Why should I fear you?"

He stepped closer, his eyes darkening. "You do not fear talk? That your reputation might be compromised? An innocent girl and an experienced man?"

She stepped back, brushing against the bush. "That's not what anyone would think."

"No? Not me? Not you?"

She looked at him anew, this gentle friend with the damaged heart and the warm eyes. She enjoyed his company, but he had never moved her in the way that Rafe had, or even Nico; she had never felt captivated by passion when she was with him.

Could he really be suggesting there might be something between them?

"Do you not see me in any other way than as a friend?"

Thomasin shivered, seeking an answer that would not clarify.

"Come on!" Ellen had emerged from the garden with a handful of flowers.

"I had better go," Thomasin said, with a sense of relief. "The queen will be waiting."

"You have no thoughts about my words?"

"I don't know. I had never… It is complicated."

He held up his hands.

"I must go. I'm sorry, I don't know."

She carried the honeysuckle away with her, the bunch in her hand, and the little twig she had tucked into her bodice. William Carey? Mary Boleyn's husband? Did he care for her? Did he desire her? It seemed as strange as being told that day was night, and night was day.

EIGHTEEN

The waiting was different this time. Tinged, coloured. Conflicting emotions were balanced on a knife's edge. The mood was waiting to settle.

Somewhere in the palace, the ambassadors were getting closer. Gold glinting, eyes smiling, lips curled. They dusted down their breeches, picked stray hairs from their sleeves. Looked at the carved initials, the linked H and C in stone, breathed the air with the roses and honeysuckle and smoke. Along corridors of stone, they followed the set route, trying to bring the glitter and spice of Venice into an English afternoon.

Thomasin sat, with Ellen and Mary, Duchess of Essex, Maria and her little daughter Catherine, poised on a bench down one side of the hall. Opposite them, was the odd assortment of Lord Mountjoy, the Duke of Suffolk, Bishop Mendoza and Thomas Grey, ranged before William Compton, William Carey and Bishop Fisher. They had been assembled for half an hour, after the Venetians had been spotted on the road. Henry, seated in gold on the dais, did not insist upon silence, but chatted to Wolsey, who stood awkwardly at his side. Catherine, as ever, the picture of a painted statue, gazed into the middle distance as the moments slipped past. Tension played about her mouth.

It was still early. The morning was cool, as the sun had not yet climbed, but it promised to be warm later. Out in the tilt yard, preparations were continuing: fresh sawdust scattered, the ground raked over, cushions and carpets draped on chairs and benches.

Will Carey had greeted Thomasin as usual, with polite formality, but did not linger on this occasion to exchange words. He looked tired this morning; she imagined his sleepless night, turning over their comments in the garden, his fears and doubts. But she chased that image away; she could no more imagine what he was thinking than she could read the mind of Catherine.

Into the silence came footsteps, heels upon stone flags. But they were erratic, singular, not the oiled fleet of Venetians in step.

Anne burst through the doors, followed by her brother and father.

"Are they here?" She took a few steps into the hall, flaming in orange and gold, then stopped at the silent wall of faces ahead. Her dark eyes scanned back and forth for allies.

Thomasin saw the king tense.

"They are not here yet. Step aside."

Anne made a show of turning and looking about her. "Aside? I should step aside? Which side?" Her father put a warning hand upon her arm, but she shrugged it off. "Where is my place, please? Where was it planned that I would stand?"

Henry rose. "Had you been here in good time, you would have been included. Now, we expect them at any moment. There are seats in the window, there."

Anne pretended to look in disbelief. "In the window? At the side?" She looked back at the sea of faces, from cardinal to bishop, to queen and ladies-in-waiting. Her eyes lighted upon Wolsey. "Will you not speak for me, Cardinal? You who have never loved me and never seek to make a friend of me? Here I stand without a place. Where should I go?"

"Enough now." Henry rose. Thomasin was conscious of Catherine at his side, who remained erect throughout. She never let her eyes rest on Anne, as if the woman simply did not exist.

But Wolsey, unexpectedly, stirred and turned to the king. "Perhaps the Lady could be accommodated beside me? As a gesture of my good will."

Despite the silence, the surprise could be felt. It was an extraordinary move on Wolsey's part, a signal that he intended to take Anne seriously, and a blow to Catherine.

But footsteps were approaching. The proposed shift had come too late, as the ambassadors were already at the door. They were held in place behind the guards, but their jewels and faces sparkled in the gloom of the antechamber.

It was good timing. To diffuse the tension, Henry merely waved the Venetians forward. Wolsey went unanswered and Anne had no choice but to follow her father into the window space. Yet Thomasin wondered at Wolsey, and what this shift might mean.

There was little time to dwell on that, though. They rippled forward like a shimmering wave, a flock of dazzling geese, with Marco Vernier at the front, splendid in black, white and gold, decked with gold chains and a velvet hat topped with white feathers and pearls. In one orchestrated movement, as a glittering cloud, they bowed low, but Thomasin knew that among them must be Matteo Vitruvio and Nico Amato.

Henry left them bowing for a long time. Before he signalled for them to rise, he exchanged a brief glance with Catherine. Thomasin wondered what had passed between them.

The herald announced them, and Henry gave the necessary wave of his hand.

"The Ambassador to the Doge and Signoria of Venice, Signore Marco Antonio Vernier and his company."

"Signore Vernier," said Henry slowly, "we meet again. I see that your company has been fortunate in surviving the recent sickness."

Vernier doffed his hat with a flourish and sparkled as if he had no shame. "We were fortunate indeed. I thank the good Lord that you were also spared, My Lord, My Lady."

He was at the back. Nico Amato with the yellow eyes. Thomasin spotted him as soon as they rose. He looked less well, less bright, than before. His star had been dimmed. She recalled his final comments about hoping to remain in England and leave the employ of the ambassador.

"It was God's will. I suppose given all your travels, you have little left to offer us."

Vernier was thrown slightly. "My Lord, we have already given you our best silks and laces, but we did trade a little on our travels, and offer you spiced cakes, oranges, rose water…"

"And where did your travels take you?" pressed Henry, before turning to Catherine in a show of unity. "I believe they left Windsor in some haste, did they not?"

"Against my express wishes," Catherine added, buoyed by Henry's support, "and without taking their leave."

"Without taking their leave?" Henry turned back to Vernier with a calculated intensity. "Surely that was not the case? They would not have been so disrespectful?"

Vernier squirmed before them, half turning for support from his companions, the wind knocked out of his golden sails. "My Lord, My Lady, no disrespect was intended. The sweat arrived at Windsor and the whole castle was being closed up. We were given to understand that you had departed for Hampton."

Catherine looked as if she would speak again, but Henry got in first.

"No doubt, now you are at Greenwich, you will be anxious to prove that there was no disrespect, merely misunderstanding."

"Of course, My Lord, of course, no disrespect." Vernier threw in another bow for good measure.

At that point, Anne made a movement. It was slight, perhaps the rise and fall of a hand, or a shift in weight from one side to the other, but it caused her orange skirts to ripple in the light. Thomasin caught it out of the corner of her eye. If it had been designed to get Henry's attention, it was successful. Once she had his eyes upon her, she pursed her lips and turned away. There was a pause.

"My Lord," Catherine said softly. Only those closest could hear. "Shall we proceed to the joust?"

Henry turned back to the hall. "By eleven of the clock, the challengers must hang their shields upon the tree. You must all be in your seats by then, and we shall commence. Be about your business. The ambassadors will attend upon the queen."

Henry left the dais and walked past the Venetians.

Passing Anne, with a mixture of impatience and interest, but barely fixing her with his eyes, he said, "Come, Madam."

For a second, Anne hesitated. But Henry had merely taken two steps further when she slipped into pace behind him, like his shadow as he withdrew from sight.

It was an unsatisfactory ending. Henry had backed Catherine's position in public, insisted that the ambassadors give her the respect she was due, but then he had asserted his private preference, before all those watching.

Even from a distance, Thomasin could see Catherine's bottom lip trembling as she struggled to maintain her calm front. But Thomasin was not alone in seeing her distress; the queen's devoted Maria was at her side, speaking softly, offering her arm as Catherine rose.

Vernier was still on his knees before her. She looked down upon the top of his head. All the emotion seemed to rise in her. "Is there anything else you would say to me, Signore?"

Vernier looked uncomfortable. The remaining members of court fell silent.

"You will not find me so forgiving of the slight you gave me."

"Please, my Lady…"

"Nor the way you intended to use my ladies, to gain information about my movements, my thoughts, through the means of encouraging them to write you letters. And offering them gifts to do so, in secret? Whatever did you mean by it?"

"It was merely a way to build a closer relationship…"

"Nonsense. It was little less than espionage. What did you hope to hear? Did you think to get news about my nephew, the emperor? Or were you merely playing myself against my husband, waiting to see whose cause to back? You have been premature, Signore Vernier. Premature indeed, with your gifts and requests. I have long wished to return this to you." She reached into her sleeve and drew out the ballas ruby on its gold chain. "Take it."

Vernier stumbled forwards to receive the jewel. "My Lady, I…"

Rising, Catherine looked down at him. "You will not address me again in all the time you are here, and you will depart as soon as possible."

The Venetian appeared as if he was about to speak, but Catherine walked past him, signalling that the discussion was over. Thomasin and Ellen jumped up and hurried after her, but not before Thomasin had briefly met the golden eyes of Nico

Amato. They somehow seemed to be speaking to her, but their message was impenetrable.

Out in the tilt yard, Catherine shook off her dark cloud and made for the stands. Thomasin was delighted to see Thomas More and his daughter and son-in-law, Margaret and Will Roper taking their seats, along with Bishops Mendoza and Fisher. Margaret saw her approach and waved, but for now, Thomasin had to sit with Catherine in the opposite section, decked out in red and green flags. Catherine occupied the carved chair, made more comfortable with cushions, but at least there were thick carpets draped over the benches where her ladies were to sit. From a service tent painted with gold apples and pomegranates, servants brought them dishes of pastries and glasses of wine.

Henry was seated in the next portion of the stands, already deep in conversation with Wolsey. At one side, Thomasin also noted the familiar figure of Thomas Cromwell, listening intently to his master. His time with his family had clearly come to an end, and he had judged it safe to return to court. Catherine would not be pleased at his return, thought Thomasin. Hopefully it would not resurrect the unpleasantness about the letters at Hampton.

Beyond the king, in the final third of the left stands, Thomasin caught the flash of Anne's orange skirts. Surely her parents were among her party, and Jane Boleyn and their hangers-on. No doubt, though, their young men, Thomas Wyatt, George Boleyn and Rafe Danvers, would be riding in the lists.

The arena lay before them, freshly sanded and marked out by palings painted in green and white. Brightly-coloured rings were suspended from a handful of scaffolds, which the competitors would attempt to spear. Opposite, the right-hand stand was filled by the non-royal parties.

The Venetians had been directed to sit at the furthest end, the worst seats with the worst view, looking a little uncomfortable and uncertain of their welcome. Nico was among them, Thomasin noted, but the distance was too great for any meaningful communication.

Further along were more of the king's gentlemen, beside Mountjoy and More's party, and a swathe of faces she did not recognise: visitors to the palace for the day and other royal staff.

She returned her eyes to Margaret Roper, who was looking well and happy enough, chatting with her father. Servants were circulating with drinks and people were shifting about to find their seats, or swap for a better view. Suddenly, joining them from the steps behind, came two more figures whom Thomasin recognised. Young John Dudley, her friend from last year, and beside him… She blinked. It could not be … the unmistakeable person of her own father.

Thomas More beckoned Sir Richard Marwood into an empty seat beside him. Thomasin could hardly believe her eyes; then she recalled what More had mentioned whilst they were at Windsor — that her father had been at court back before the spring. Was it a coincidence that he had returned at the same time as Cromwell?

It was the first time Thomasin had seen her father in six months, the longest she had been apart from him. He was not looking her way, but as Thomasin watched, barely able to contain herself, Margaret leaned across, spoke a few words and then pointed at the opposite stand.

Richard sought his daughter with his eyes. He was looking well, in a brown and red doublet and feathered cap, but his beard was greyer, and there was a look of tiredness about him. Finally, he found her, raised his hand to wave and broke into a smile.

Thomasin waved back, enthusiastically.

"Look," she said to Ellen beside her, "my father is here, look."

Ellen was waving too, but there was an edge of doubt to her voice. "But your uncle is not?"

Thomasin's uncle, Matthew Russell, was the father of Ellen's estranged husband Barnaby. He had welcomed them all to his London house last autumn, and had always been kind to Ellen, especially after the truth had emerged about Barnaby's betrayal of her with her own sister.

Thomasin scoured the crowd. "No, I see no sign of him."

Ellen looked relieved. "I don't think I am ready to face him yet, especially after that unpleasant letter."

"I understand, but he is most ashamed of his son, and you are always welcome at Monk's Place. I wonder why Father is here, though."

"Perhaps More invited him."

"Maybe."

But Thomasin could not escape the sinister connection that Cromwell had also reappeared at the same time, recalling the way the minister had pressurised her father to work for him last autumn.

Trumpets announced the first challengers. The crowds on both sides of the lists grew attentive. At the far end of the field, where flags fluttered from striped tents, the riders appeared, all co-ordinated in red and silver. In a line, they rode slowly around the outside of the field, visors up, while the herald announced their names: Sir George Boleyn, Sir Henry Norris,

Sir Francis Bryan, Sir Thomas Grey, Rafe Danvers and Henry Courtenay, Marquess of Exeter.

"Gertrude's husband," Ellen whispered, as the final gentleman passed them by.

Thomasin watched him pass. Courtenay was a cousin and close friend of the king, raised alongside him. The two men did not look dissimilar.

As he passed by, his eyes were searching the stands, and Thomasin saw the moment he spotted Gertrude and raised his hand in greeting. In response, she lifted out of her seat a little and gave a restrained but genuine wave, one eye upon Catherine.

"No doubt they'll have the chance to reunite later," whispered Ellen, who had also observed their exchange.

The dazzling riders took up their positions on the opposite side, with squires clustering about them to tighten saddles, adjust straps and offer wine. It was not difficult for Thomasin to pick out Rafe Danvers from among them, and now she had the chance to observe him while he was occupied, she indulged herself, watching his back, his wide shoulders and long limbs. Briefly, he removed his headpiece and she saw the blue-black locks, thick and full, returning her straight to the memory of running her fingers through them, of the intimate kiss they'd shared at her uncle's house. It would have been so easy to give in, to grant him what he desired: what she had desired too! But that would surely have led to her ruin. She would not be here, in the queen's household, but back in the Suffolk countryside, waiting for the scandal to pass. She knew she had been right, but passion deep inside her still yearned for him, longed to feel his touch. Those dangerous ideas she had chased last autumn, of an individual setting their own path, could so easily have tipped into self-destruction.

No, she thought, straightening in her seat, she had been right to control her desires. Catherine's example had taught her the value of discipline and restraint. It became a lady far more than the passionate outbursts that seemed to define Anne Boleyn and her interactions with the king. At that moment, Rafe turned and looked right up to the stands, as if he had felt her eyes upon him. And there it was again. That shiver of desire, for all her convictions. Those dark brows, the deep pools of his eyes, the brooding lips. She pretended to pick at a thread on her gown.

Were there two conflicting selves within her? The one which was ruled by prudence, judgement, experience, and the other like a well of desire that threatened to bubble over? Would it ever be possible to reconcile them?

The trumpets came again, followed by the voice of the herald announcing the defendants. Into the field appeared the opposition, in white and green: the Duke of Suffolk, Sir William Compton, Sir William Carey, Sir William Hatton, Charles Collins and Hugh Truegood, riding in slow procession, their horses trapped in silver and white, embroidered with green leaves and hung with little bells.

Ellen broke into Thomasin's thoughts. "He is handsome, isn't he? In spite of everything."

At once, unbidden, Thomasin's mind flew back to Rafe. How could Ellen know the desires she was suppressing?

"Hugh Truegood? Don't you think?"

Thomasin realised her mistake. "Hugh, why yes, there is no denying that."

"I know you found him difficult…"

"Not difficult exactly, more hard going. He's nice enough. We just didn't seem to connect."

"Are you sure?"

Thomasin turned to her cousin and saw the brightness in her eyes. "I am sure. But, it seems, so are you. I believe you are sweet on him."

Ellen blushed. "Is it wrong? I am still married to Barnaby."

"Not wrong, not at all. Barnaby treated you in the most shameful manner, and now has threatened to divorce you. Why shouldn't you start again and be happy? You are still young enough."

"Do you think?"

"Yes, of course."

"And you have no further interest in…"

"None at all. You should make yourself known to him, if he is the one you desire."

Thomasin felt the irony of her words, soaked through with her restrained passion for Rafe. But there were no such issues between Hugh and Ellen, all was simplicity.

"But how? I feel so uncertain around him. All the things I can think of make me feel like a fool."

"What did you think of?"

Ellen smiled. "Perhaps a letter, or after dancing with him, I could invite him to walk in the gardens, should the queen not object, or I might wait where he will pass."

Thomasin could not help but laugh. "You need no ideas from me, cousin. I think he could be wooed, won and betrothed by the week's end."

"Oh, look, William Carey is riding by."

Ellen was nodding at the approaching riders, among whom they saw Carey's eyes searching the crowd. When he saw Thomasin, he nodded and smiled, before riding on to take his position.

"There," pronounced Ellen, "he was looking for you. I am certain he would give you the favour from his lance, if he had been able to."

"He could not do so as a married man."

"No one believes in that sham of a marriage anymore. Where is his wife?" Ellen leaned in closer and lowered her voice. "No longer in the king's bed!"

"Ellen, hush!" Thomasin looked round, afraid that Catherine would have overheard her indiscreet remark, but the queen was talking intently with Maria. The Spanish gentlewoman held her young daughter close to her side, unwilling to let her go after their separation.

The trumpets sounded again and the crowd fell silent, looking to the king and queen for approval. With the colourful competitors lined up, lances pointing forward, the tilting was ready to begin. Henry broke away from Anne, who had moved her chair closer to his side, and stood before the crowd. With one majestic flourish, he lifted his arm as high as it might go, then brought it down in a swoop. The first hooves thundered down the track.

NINETEEN

The dancers moved in formation, crossing and re-crossing the hall in a complex ritual that Thomasin didn't recognise. Anne's bright orange skirts swirled about her as she led the way, head thrown back, body moving elegantly to the rhythm. She offered her hand to her brother, George, resplendent in his cap covered in gold aiglets, then joined with Francis Bryan to perform a different manoeuvre.

"Apparently it's a new dance she has developed based on a French format," commented Margaret Roper at Thomasin's side. "A favourite of Francis himself."

"There seems to be a lot of swapping of partners," Thomasin observed, as Anne was now side stepping with Henry Norris, who then handed her on to William Compton.

"Oh, I am sure that's why he liked it," said Margaret wryly.

Thomasin raised her eyebrows.

"You must have heard of his reputation, the king of France? Anne's own sister was one of his conquests. I wonder if that's what gave her the idea."

Thomasin thought at once of Mary Boleyn, and then almost immediately of Will Carey. Was this yet another painful secret he'd had to turn a blind eye to?

"You know he had Da Vinci staying at his court?" Margaret continued. "He lived in a house in the grounds of Chateau Amboise, while Anne was there."

The name meant nothing to Thomasin. Margaret saw her confusion and laughed.

"Da Vinci has not yet reached Suffolk?"

"I confess I have no idea of who he is. A courtier of some kind?"

Margaret's eyes lit up. "Where shall I begin? I will have to show you sometime; Father has copies of a few sketches he made. He is nothing less than *the* renaissance itself. The universal man, the polymath, artist, inventor, scientist, architect."

"Will he ever come to England?"

"Sadly he is dead these past ten years. Such a man we shall never see again. Father speaks of him often." She turned to Thomas More, as if to speak of it, but he only smiled gently, deep in conversation with Bishops Fisher and Mendoza.

The chords changed. Before their eyes, the dancers whirled about, stopped and froze. There was a moment of unexpected stillness, immobility, in the heart of the dance. Conversations stopped, heads turned. Then the dancers sprang to life again and leapt into the air, much to the delight of the crowd. Laughter and a burst of applause rang out at their athleticism. Anne landed elegantly, and was at once snaking around the circle, brushing past Thomasin with the hem of her dress, so that her golden slippers were visible. George Boleyn followed, his long, toned legs in white stockings.

There was an unfamiliar rhythm to the music too, Thomasin thought, tuning her ear to the rapid change of chords, which had slipped into a minor key. It was not an unpleasant sound, but it felt an odd mixture to her; upbeat and swift, then suddenly overwhelmed by melancholy. No doubt the latest in French fashion, far too complex and shifting for solid English tastes, where songs were more predictable and formulaic. Cecilia had once joked that the court songs liked a good thump before finishing with a burr, like the death of a heart. Thomasin had always found it easier for her feet to follow known patterns, rather than be tripped up by sudden change, but this new style intrigued her.

Henry seemed enraptured by the performance. While Catherine had retired to the dais with Maria for company, the king was standing by the fireplace, watching intently with his narrowed eyes, clapping his hands on occasion, as if he was committing the dance to memory.

It did not appear easy. As Thomasin watched, Gertrude whirled past, led by her husband. Henry Courtenay had called upon her to take part, even though she did not know the steps, but he was keen to be beside her after six months apart. It was a little inconsiderate, Thomasin thought, as she saw Gertrude put one wrong foot after another and blush. Courtenay was more concerned with his own pleasure than her discomfort. Yet all eyes were upon Anne, so scarcely anyone saw Gertrude's awkwardness.

The dance drew to a close, the final chords sounded and the participants formed an outward-looking circle, with glowing faces as they made their curtsey or bow.

Henry stepped forward, clapping his hands sharply to the musicians. "Again, again, I have it, I have the steps, let me show you. Play it again."

"Are you sure, My Lord?" asked Anne. "You do not wish to see it one more time?"

"I can't wait. I have it, or most of it. You will guide me. I must dance!"

Francis Bryan withdrew so that Henry might take his place, and the dancers lined up for a second time. Anticipation settled on the room as the king replicated the first steps with Anne at his side.

Catherine turned away.

"Here you are. Not dancing?"

Thomasin turned to see William Carey, changed from his tilting colours into a soft grey doublet.

"Not dancing to this, I do not know the steps. Neither are you, though."

"Again, it is not a dance I know, and Anne no longer invites me to participate. I am no longer a favourite." His playful smile betrayed that he considered this no great loss.

"You did well at the tilt," Thomasin offered in consolation.

Carey had acquitted himself with grace and success, scoring highly against Thomas Grey, his pairing from the challengers.

"You saw?"

"Of course. Everyone saw. You did very well."

He seemed pleased that she had noticed, but quickly tried to bury his pride. "It's been a while since I rode at the ring, with the sweat and other business. You should have seen me joust in France, at the Field of Gold; that was my finest hour. Still, it pleased the king. He is in a good mood."

"He is indeed," Thomasin smiled, watching Henry make a complex turn and quickly shuffle his feet to keep pace with the others. She shuffled along the bench to make space for her friend. "You must be tired now; won't you sit down?"

"You are very thoughtful, but I am thirsty before I am tired. I was about to offer to bring you some wine?"

Thomasin had grown a little warm in the crowded hall. "I would be grateful, thank you."

Carey nodded, loosening his collar. "It does seem unusually hot in here, and I am not even dancing. Mistress Roper, a glass for you too?"

Margaret turned in appreciation. "Thank you, yes."

He smiled. "I will not be a moment."

The women watched him go.

"He is rather attentive," Margaret commented. "Mary Boleyn's husband, is he not?"

Thomasin was unsure whether or not to feel a criticism in the observation. She felt a rush of protection towards Will Carey. "He is a true gentleman."

"I can see that. I couldn't help but hear him, too. A good man, I think."

Something about her judgement pleased Thomasin, although she could not have explained why.

"But this dancing is awkward," Margaret continued. "I feel for the queen."

The dramatic moment came again. With a sudden pause, the dancers froze, waited and resumed. Henry held the stillness with them, then laughed aloud as they resumed their steps. Even in his slashed velvet and gold chains, Henry was a skilled dancer, quick to pick up a new routine, yet he still looked to Anne to guide him in this. As the women watched, he turned the wrong way and almost collided with Henry Norris, before drawing back to correct himself.

"I will have it," he protested. "I will conquer it!"

The dance seemed to bring out some competitive element in him, rising to a challenge. Perhaps, thought Thomasin, it had been brought on by the tilting earlier, and now he needed to master what Anne offered; a thinly veiled display of his personal desires.

"My Lord, you will keep us dancing until midnight if that's what you need to conquer it!" William Compton laughed. It was a daring comment, verging on criticism. Only Compton, with his close friendship with Henry, might get away with it.

Fortunately, Henry was in high spirits, his mood robust. "Have a care, Compton. I shall keep you dancing until dawn if I require it."

Across the hall, the troop of Venetians arrived in their colourful ensembles, taking up a position together and holding back while their eyes searched the room. Vervier seemed particularly on edge, and eventually wove his way through the crowd towards Catherine.

"Who are they?" Margaret asked.

"Ah," Thomasin smiled. "These are the notorious ambassadors from Venice. I met them before at Windsor, but they displeased the queen there."

"It would seem he is trying to make amends now."

As they watched, Vervier knelt before Catherine, hoping for her attention. Without breaking off her conversation with Maria, though, the queen merely inclined her head very slightly, and turned away. The snub was undeniable. Vervier, the slick, polished Vervier, who had so charmed her before with his honeyed words and gifts, who had danced and strutted his Venetian heart out, rose slowly and adjusted his hat, before creeping away. He did not make it back to his fellows, though, as Thomas Boleyn, with his arch smile, was waiting to intercept him for private words. Thomasin wondered what he might have to say.

Henry's laughter rang through the hall. He had Anne by the hand and was turning about with her, until they were dizzy. The complex dance had been interrupted, usurped for his own purpose, and those around them paused, uncertain of what to do next.

"Play something else, and we will dance," Henry commanded. "One of my favourites; we'll have no more of this French puffing like peacocks. Play on!"

The musicians rapidly struck up a new chord and the formation on the floor changed again.

That was when Thomasin saw her father enter the hall. He was looking well, if a little careworn, and his expression was serious. Richard Marwood had once held a prestigious role at court, close to the king himself, in his much younger days, but he had shied away from intrigue and politics, preferring the life of a country Justice of the Peace. Behind him came Thomas Cromwell, steering Richard slightly with a touch to his elbow. From his body language, Thomasin sensed her father's discomfort, and felt at once that his presence at Greenwich was not through his own choosing.

She half rose in her seat, trying to catch his attention. Richard was looking around, and he caught her eye and made his apologies to Cromwell.

"My daughter!" He came forward to embrace her, his face splitting into a wide smile. Thomasin stepped into his arms. She had always been closer to her father, sharing the same pragmatic temperament, whilst her elder sister Cecilia was more like their mother, Elizabeth.

"How are you? What brings you here?"

"I am well, very well. As you look, too. All is well at home, I assure you."

"With mother? Her health is good?"

Last autumn, Elizabeth Marwood had consulted some of the best doctors in London about the malady in her chest, which had been afflicting her for almost two years.

"She is living very simply, as the doctors advise, and her pain is much reduced."

"Oh, that is good to hear. And Cecilia, and the younger children?"

"All well and happy. It is so good to see you. Still in the queen's employ?"

"I am, as is Ellen over there." Thomasin gestured towards her cousin, who was sitting with Hugh Truegood further down the hall. "We have moved around to escape the sweat, with success so far."

"That is excellent news. We had heard about the illness and were most anxious about you. But we received your letters, which reassured us greatly."

"And I received yours. They were such a great comfort. We are well, thus far, thanks be to God. But Father, what brings you here?"

Richard nodded and took a seat. "I was summoned by Cromwell, as you may have deduced. He wishes to pick my legal brain, but I have not been able, or willing, to assist him."

"About the king and queen's marriage?"

"The very same. Because my particular jurisdiction has included marital cases, he wishes for my assistance. I had to assist in the Church courts, after the sweat wiped out almost a whole monastic community at Bury St Edmunds, so I became more learned in the matter. Truly," he said more quietly, "there is more to it, of which I cannot speak here."

"Of course not," Thomasin acceded, taking his hint. "You see More is here, and Margaret and Will, and John Dudley?"

"It is almost like old times," her father admitted. "And how is the queen?"

Thomasin looked up at Catherine, resplendent in her jewels upon the dais. She had insisted upon heaping on her diamonds and pearls after they had arrived at Greenwich, since she was back in Anne's company. She had stopped speaking with Maria and now watched as Henry and Anne partnered each other amid the dancers.

"She is sad," admitted Thomasin truthfully. "This is a torment to her. She is a good woman, a queen, and she is being treated most cruelly."

"Hush," said Richard at once. "Do not let anyone hear you speak so, as it can be construed as speaking ill of the king."

"I understand. But it is the truth."

"Now, here is your wine, my Lady." William Carey had reappeared, holding one glass. "I have delivered the other to Margaret. Good day, sir, am I right in thinking you are Sir Richard Marwood?"

"Indeed I am, and you are William Carey. A good day to you too, sir."

"Alas, I bring you no wine, only my most heartfelt greeting and gratitude for the company of your daughter."

"Is that so?" Richard raised his eyebrows and looked searchingly at Thomasin.

"Can I go back and bring you a glass?"

"No, thank you, I am well."

Across the room, Thomasin became aware of Nico's eyes upon her. He stood at the side of the Venetian group, watching her interaction, as if judging his moment.

No doubt at some point she would have to speak with him, but not at the present time, not before all these people, especially not her father.

"That was well done," cried Henry, as the dancers slowed to their final positions. "Another, play another, play 'Love's Idleness', let's dance again."

He had Anne by the hand and was looking about the hall, flushed in the face, as if he had forgotten who or where he was. By his side, Anne's face was glowing, her eyes lit bright.

"Shall we?" asked Carey, recognising the tune.

"Oh, I hardly know. My father…"

"Go on, dance," said Richard, taking her wine from her hand and placing himself in a chair beside Thomas More. "It will give me and my old friend a chance to catch up."

Thomasin allowed herself to be led onto the floor, in formation beside Jane and George Boleyn. The musicians struck up their chords and Thomasin joined the women in curtseying to the men before them.

Dancing with Will Carey was always a pleasant, civilised matter. He led and she followed in agreed formation, but it was more out of deference than the combative attitude of some dancers. It was elegant, simple. He would have been slow in comparison with Rafe or even with Nico, but he was easier to partner than either of them. Carey always made her feel comfortable and safe, so that she could be herself. He was always attentive, never distant or troubling. Perhaps, after all, that constant sense of easiness was better than the brief intensity of passion.

He took her hands and smiled as they walked in a circle. Briefly, Thomasin then had to partner George Boleyn, while Will Carey partnered Jane, bowing and striding forward arm in arm.

"Good evening, Mistress Marwood," Anne's brother ventured.

"Evening, my Lord," she said back softly, always uncertain of his moods, but never of his allegiance.

The dance moved on. Carey appeared before her again, moving in step with the men. They joined hands and turned one way, then the other. Then, the circle rotated again and Thomasin was disappointed to see him replaced by William Compton, with his wide, lascivious grin.

"Mistress Marwood, as delectable as ever."

She took his hand reluctantly. He put an unwelcome arm around her waist and pulled her close to him. She smelled the wine on his breath.

"Tell me, you little tease, when can I see you in private?"

She pushed him away. "Never."

He laughed. "I can advance you beyond your wildest dreams, for the sake of your family. You just need to be nice to me."

"No, thank you."

"You'll change your tune."

With great relief, she was returned to Carey, who was looking concerned.

"Was he bothering you? I saw him seize you about the waist."

"I have plainly refused him."

Carey shook his head. "He is well known at court. Most of the women avoid him."

"I intend to do the same."

The final chords played and Carey bowed low, as Thomasin dropped her curtsey.

But Henry had not finished; he was laughing loudly, galloping around with Anne still on his arm. A quick look up to the dais showed Thomasin that Catherine was aware of it too, and was following the pairing with disgruntled eyes. Yet, for once, Henry seemed oblivious, as if he had forgotten his surroundings.

"Shall we?" Carey offered her his arm.

As they turned, Thomasin noticed William Hatton on the far side of the hall. He was in conversation with Thomas Wyatt and a group of ladies, laughing and throwing back his head, without a care in the world. The familiar bitter sensation arose in her stomach, but she turned away and put on a smile.

Carey led her over to rest on seats by the open window. The summer's day was still clinging to light, although night advanced.

"Tell me," he said, "do you like art, Mistress Marwood?"

"Art?" The topic threw her. There had been portraits hanging on the walls at Windsor and Hampton, but she had scarcely paid them much attention. "Paintings? Of kings and queens?"

"Yes. And miniatures? Do you know what those are?"

"I know what the word means, but little more."

"It is one of my passions. You see how I shall lecture you now: I am excited by a new artist, who paints in this style. Have you seen no miniature paintings in the queen's chambers?"

"I suppose not. You mean small ones? Not the ones that hang on the walls?"

"Exactly those. Small enough to fit in the palm of your hand. A few years back I brought a young artist over from Ghent. Lucas, his name is. He has painted the king many times, and the queen earlier, myself also. His work is incredibly skilled."

"I should like to see it."

"Really? You will, you will. Mary thinks it frivolous."

Thomasin noted the implied comparison with his wife. "Of course I would."

He was engaged. "But listen, I have made a fascinating discovery. You don't mind me telling you?"

"Please, continue." Thomasin was enjoying this new side to Will Carey, more passionate and excited than she had ever seen him. "Go on."

"I have found out that there is another talented artist in his family. His own sister, Susannah. Can you believe it? Her work is outstanding, truly; her touch is exquisite. I have one picture;

I assumed it was her brother's, but he tells me by letter that it is hers. It is of the queen, and I plan to present it to her upon the anniversary of her marriage. It falls in just over a week."

"That is thoughtful of you."

"I will show it to you before then, to judge the woman's skill for yourself."

"I don't know if I can be much of a judge in that."

"Oh, you will be. You need no experience, only your eyes." He looked at her intently. "Your very beautiful eyes."

The words were deliberate, full of meaning. Thomasin did not know how to respond.

"I should return to my father. It is so long since we saw each other last."

"Of course, please do not let me keep you."

It wasn't that, she thought, making her way round the outside of the dancers. Will Carey was a strange mixture; gentle and warm, passive and accepting of his wife's family and her choices, independent, and now this sudden rush of passion he wished to share with her. She did not know what to make of him, or rather, of his clear feelings for her, which she could no longer ignore. She felt drawn to him, but for all his circumstances, he was still a married man, and what future could he offer her unless he divorced Mary? She did not want the taint of such a scandal, especially not one so close to the throne.

Thomasin shook her head. Such a path seemed impossible.

"Dancing, my Lady?" Her father appeared at her elbow. "I have been waiting for this chance to dance with my daughter for months."

Thomasin smiled and took his arm. As they moved into the new formation, she once again caught Nico's eyes from the side of the hall. He stood alone, slightly separate from the other Venetians, who spoke among themselves.

"Now, you will have to lead me," Richard pleaded, "as it is so long since I danced in public."

They were barely a few minutes into the dance when a sudden movement caught their attention. A woman in pale green had fallen, careening down to the ground as those around her clustered to break her fall. The dance, and then the music, halted abruptly.

As Thomasin got closer, she saw it was Jane Boleyn, surrounded now by her family.

George Boleyn was kneeling beside her, propping up her head as she looked about with confused eyes.

"Stand back, allow her some air!" commanded Thomas Boleyn, waving the dancers away.

"Is she unwell?" Henry was overlooking the scene. "Overheated? Giddy with the dance?"

A dozen pairs of eyes stared down at Jane's flushed face.

"It is the warmth in here," replied George Boleyn, "and she has danced much tonight and drunk little. We will retire."

Between George and Thomas Boleyn, Jane was brought to her feet.

"She does look warm," added Henry, peering closely at her. "You have no headache? No other pains?"

They all knew what he was fearing.

"No, My Lord." Jane's voice was very faint.

"Take her, take her," Henry urged them.

Jane hobbled out, surrounded by her friends, but the mood had changed. Henry was looking around with uncertainty, rubbing the front of his doublet. The dancers caught each other's eyes, wondering whether to leave the floor or resume their positions.

"I will retire," Henry announced. "Seek your beds, all of you. I bid you a good night."

And he strode from the hall as fast as his legs could carry him.

TWENTY

Henry's departure signalled an end to the evening. Servants moved rapidly into position to begin the process of clearing away the signs of revelry: glasses, cushions, and benches were all swiftly removed. The hall was almost clear of guests, but Catherine lingered in her seat to speak with Bishop Mendoza. Thomasin's father was making earnest plans with Thomas More and William Carey had disappeared, having been recruited by George Boleyn to assist him with Jane.

Night was stealing in through the far doors as Thomasin wandered down to the landing overlooking the staircase. A sweet, mild scent of early summer mixed with woodsmoke and fresh herbs beckoned her to abandon the palace and stray outside.

There was nothing she would have liked better than to roam the gardens at this hour, in the soft, cool green places and among the roses blooming greyly in the moonlight, with the stars spread above. Yet she knew better and paused, having to be content to look down the steps and imagine that world. Others, though, were bolder.

At the bottom of the stairs, embraced by the darkness, two figures stood in conversation, heads bowed close, drawn together, although you could still have passed a hand between them. Thomasin drew back when she spotted Ellen and Hugh Truegood, unwilling to break up their meeting and interrupt whatever was passing between them. Her cousin looked happy but earnest as she spoke, and Thomasin guessed that she was explaining her difficult situation. As she continued, Truegood took both of Ellen's hands in his and said a few words of comfort. Thomasin retreated under the archway, pleased to see their obvious connection.

"My Lady?"

Nico had approached her on silent feet. He slipped into her wake like a shadow, his former brilliance somehow dimmed, the light in his golden eyes reflective of resentment or shame.

"Nico Amato. I wondered whether you would appear here at Greenwich."

He made a low bow. "I go where I am bidden, as do you."

"And is the palace to your liking?"

"It is a most beautiful palace, greatly to my liking, although my service is less so."

Thomasin raised her eyebrows in a question.

"Much has happened since I last saw you, my Lady. But believe me, I have thought of you often."

Thomasin could not deny that she had thought of him too, but she was not about to admit that. She eyed him suspiciously, the butterflies in her stomach stirring. He was as handsome as she remembered, with that lean, sleek look, the groomed head, the elegant limbs combined with sturdiness. The memory of his lips upon hers in the garden at Windsor returned. Yet his eyes were sad.

"You have not thought of me?"

"I have been busy, very busy, about the queen's business."

"Of course you have, moving from one place to another. It must be a change from your life at Windsor."

"Yes, the sweat has done that."

"And it has allowed you to spread your wings a little. No longer the chained bird you once were, I think?"

These words were unexpected, and Thomasin did not know how to reply. She recalled how astute, how perceptive Nico could be.

"You received a harsh welcome from the queen, did you not?" she asked.

"It was not undeserved."

She gave him credit for the admission.

"The old gentleman is your father?" he asked.

"Yes, my father, Sir Richard."

"He is very proud of you, it is plain to see."

Thomasin looked back to the hall.

"And the situation between the king and queen rumbles on. I see there is no end in sight, no relief whilst he is torn between the queen and Lady Anne."

"You are right there; it is an unhappy situation for all."

"And you, Thomasin?" He pronounced her name slowly, dwelling on each syllable. "Are you happy?"

Happiness was not something she had dwelt on lately, as she had been so busy observing it, or the lack of it, in others.

"I'd hoped to see you before we left Windsor," he continued, without waiting for an answer. "I assure you that I had no choice but to follow where Vernier led, as dependent upon his favour as I am. I had no part in that move, but the sweat made it essential for us to leave at once. You understand that, I am sure."

"And the plot? To gain information about the queen to undermine the emperor?"

He held up his hands. "I knew it was too clumsy to go unnoticed. Again, it was not of my doing. Vernier can take the credit for that. The Doge was fearful that the emperor would take Venice in order to control the port, so he wanted any news of the queen's doings, any transgression or opposition to the king that he could use as leverage. He was hoping to turn the emperor's attentions towards England and distract him from Venice. I never thought it would work."

"All down to Vernier? That's convenient."

"Not all, no, I admit."

Some vital truth was within her grasp. "Who else was behind it? Does Vernier have a friend here? Did someone try to influence him? Suggest you visit Windsor?"

Nico sighed. "You cannot guess?"

Thomasin's heart beat faster. "Not the cardinal?"

"Not he, no."

"Really?" She had been so sure.

Nico looked around. "You must not tell. It was the lady's father. Signore Boleyn. He approached us at Westminster, suggested we went to Windsor and offered us a handsome reward. He wanted information. Secrets. Anything we could gain from the queen, especially her dealings with the emperor, when it came to her marriage."

It took a moment for Thomasin to process all this. "Thomas Boleyn?"

Nico nodded. "I am sorry for my part in it."

A rush of anger broke through Thomasin's reserve. "The queen did not appreciate being manipulated in such a way. Any information that was passed on from her, or about her, would have been compromising. If it was used against the king, it may even have been treason."

"Yes, I understand, but she is an intelligent woman who will not be made a fool of."

"It is a shame you were not aware of this before."

"Believe me, I was, and I advised against it at the time. Vernier insisted no harm could come of a simple exchange of letters with willing ladies. He made us believe it was our duty, to use what he called our Venetian charms." Nico took a step closer, tried to look into her eyes. "Have I lost your good will forever? Can you ever look upon me as a friend again?"

"I don't know."

"I am trying to find a different position, a permanent role at the English court, so I can be free of this diplomacy. So I no longer am caught in this web."

"I am afraid there is always a web. You will be exchanging one for another."

"But perhaps another may be preferable. I have approached Wolsey in the hopes that he will employ me as his secretary."

Thomasin frowned. "You know that Thomas Cromwell already holds that role, and he is ruthless. He speaks Italian too."

Nico nodded. "I had hoped there would be work enough for two, given how busy he is, with all these negotiations. I could go as an envoy to the Pope for him. I would not be taking bread from Cromwell's mouth. Or Bishop Fisher, I might try instead."

"I am not qualified to advise you."

"But do you approve? Can you give me hope that if I transferred to the court, you would be my friend?"

"You must do nothing on my account. I can make no such promises."

He looked hurt. "Then there is no hope, no chance to regain your good will, or anything more?"

"I did not say that much, only that you must do these things on your own account, not on mine."

"Can you look upon me as a friend again? Do you not remember that night in the gardens at Windsor? How many times I have thought of it!"

"Yes, I remember, but you must stop now."

Nico looked at her ruefully. Again, his physical beauty struck her, but she knew better than to be swayed by that alone.

Passion had led her into trouble before and she was older now, and wiser.

He tried to take her hand. "Can we not be friends?"

Thomasin moved her hand away.

"Is it that man you danced with? Master Carey? Is that why? I will not give up, I will win you back."

"I am not yours to win back, nor any man's. Now, I must go."

Thomasin turned back to the room just as her father approached, to bid her goodnight. After him came Thomas More, Margaret and William Roper. Nico melted away.

"I will travel back with More," said Richard, coming to take her hands. "He has kindly asked me to stay at Chelsea, before I return to Suffolk."

"Will you not be back at court again?" Thomasin asked.

"It is unlikely. I am meeting with Cromwell at his home, and have no official need to come back out to Greenwich. I trust that you will remain in good health and spirits. It has been wonderful to see you, even for a brief visit."

"Please give my love to Mother, Cecilia and the others. Safe journey back."

He bent to embrace her, unleashing that scent of woodsmoke and wine that clung about his beard and furs. "Write to us. Remember to hold up your head and follow your path truly."

"I will, Father."

"There is one thing more. I hesitated earlier, but you should know. Ellen's husband."

"Barnaby Russell?"

"My disgraced nephew. Ellen's sister has borne his child; it is a boy. I will leave it to you to decide whether or not Ellen needs to know."

"Thank you. I will hold fire, for now, as I think she may be on the verge of new happiness."

At that moment, over Richard's shoulder, she saw him approach. The fluid, easy gait, the shock of fair hair. She could not quite believe her eyes, but they told her that William Hatton was actually approaching her father, his face signalling his intent.

"I cannot…" she muttered, in warning, "look out."

"My Lord?"

Something in Hatton's voice alerted Richard. He turned slowly. Hatton's beaming face drooped to read the sheer disgust there.

"Can you possibly be addressing me?"

"My Lord, I have wished for some time to make my peace with you, to offer my sincerest good wishes and ask for your blessing."

The silence around them was thick as midnight. Thomasin could scarcely believe her ears and sensed the bolt of anger coursing through her father. All the pain and shame of the previous autumn came rushing back.

Richard turned, his thick eyebrows set heavy, his jawline steely. "Peace? Good wishes? Blessing?" He almost choked on the words. "How can you presume?"

"My Lord, I had hoped… The time has passed, and all is well. I had hoped the wounds may heal."

"You had hoped? Hoped for all those things, without offering any word of contrition or apology, daring to approach me in this brazen way?"

"My Lord, I…"

"There is nothing you can say that I wish to hear. You have no concept of the impact your actions had upon my family, upon my wife and daughter, as your life continues unaltered.

Your arrogance is breath-taking. Any person of any sensibility will always note it."

Hatton made a short bow. "My apologies for disturbing you." He withdrew into the hall.

"Father!" said Thomasin in awe. "You were magnificent."

Richard nodded, containing his rage. "I can scarcely... Will you walk with us to the carriage? Is that permitted?"

Thomasin threw a look into the hall. Catherine was still deep in conversation. Five minutes would not hurt.

They took the main door down the wide stone stairs and out into the courtyard. The Venetians had left and Ellen had returned to her duties, leaving Hugh Truegood sitting in reflection upon the bottom step. A bright moon was hanging overhead as the horse hooves clattered over cobbles. More's carriage drew up before them and the footmen jumped out to open the door.

"It was wonderful to see you again," said Margaret, tactfully moving things on by embracing Thomasin tightly. "Do not forget you always have an invitation to stay at Chelsea. Imagine a few weeks of reading, walking in the garden, good food."

"It sounds idyllic. As soon as I get any leave, I shall write to you and fix a date."

"You must! I have so much to show you."

Thomas More handed his daughter into the carriage. "I echo her words, Mistress Marwood. You will always be welcome among us. Do not leave it too long."

"Goodnight," added William Roper, smiling kindly. "Do come, or else my wife will never stop urging me to come to court."

Thomasin laughed. "I will try."

Richard was the last one left. He held his daughter tight again, leaving his kiss upon her cheek.

"You will not let that man upset you, Father? You have told him exactly what he is, and what his fate will be."

"I could not hold back, even after these months. It has been brewing inside me; I am grateful that he gave me the opportunity." He smiled wryly. "Now, I could not speak frankly inside, and still cannot fully, but beware of Cromwell and Wolsey. This matter of the king's marriage makes them slippery as eels. The cardinal knows he has lost Henry's ear so will be seeking any allies he can in this awful business. They have tried to bribe and pressure me to back their cause with no luck, so do not let them get to you."

"I will never betray the queen, but I thank you for your warning."

"I know you will not. You are strong and honest and loyal. But they may try, and their methods are less than honourable."

Thomasin nodded.

"I will write when I reach Suffolk."

He climbed into the carriage and Thomasin watched it rattle away.

The courtyard was quiet, save for a maid tipping out a bucket of water and a cat lurking near the kitchen corridor. For a moment before returning, Thomasin paused, unwilling to run into William Hatton again. She leaned against the stone wall, warm with the heat of nearby ovens.

The patter of hurrying footsteps reached her. A cat bolted away behind some barrels and a familiar figure appeared from the service corridor, carrying a bundle in his arms. Will Carey's usual smart attire and cap were looking dishevelled.

"Will, is that you?"

He hurried over, detouring from his route. "Oh, Thomasin, it's you? Out here alone?"

"I just bid goodnight to my father; he left with Thomas More only a moment ago. What brings you here? What is this?"

In his arms, Carey was balancing blankets, towels, a basket of bread, a jar of oil and other bits and pieces. He looked around to check they were alone. "You must not share this. You promise?"

"Of course." His expression gave cause for alarm. "What is it?"

"Jane Boleyn is losing her child. She is barely ten weeks, maybe twelve, but there is no doubt now, she has lost it."

Thomasin thought back to the other night, when Jane had been glowing yet delicate and George Boleyn so attentive over her food and welfare. "I am so sorry. Is there anything I can do?"

"I have just requested hot water and wine from the kitchens. Only keep it quiet. The family do not want it known. Think how the king would react, if he suspects any such difficulties among Anne's siblings."

"Oh, I had not thought of that."

"No, Sir Thomas is insistent that it is kept secret for that cause. But I can trust you, I know."

"Poor Jane. I will pray for her, and send along some treats for her in the morning."

Carey smiled. "You are most kind. Now I must hurry back, and deliver these items. God grant that she pulls through this."

As she watched him striding across the yard and out of sight, Thomasin could not help but be struck by the thought that in spite of all his protestations, when it came to a crisis, Carey was still very much part of the Boleyn family.

Thomasin slowly climbed back up the steps into the great hall. She was not a moment too late. The party was over. Catherine was rising from her seat and gathering her ladies about her. Ellen and Gertrude were arranging her skirts. Mendoza was being helped down to his quarters, leaning heavily upon the strong arms of Henry Norris and Francis Bryan. Fisher had retired for the night and Mountjoy was making a quick survey of the hall. On one side, Charles Brandon was enjoying a final drink and conversing with Maria Willoughby and her young daughter, Catherine, a pretty, dark, obedient child of nine or ten, wearing a white dress.

Thomasin hurried over to join Catherine, trying to compose herself and not betray Will's news.

"Where have you been, Mistress Marwood?" asked Catherine. "You know better than to go wandering off at night."

"Forgive me, My Lady, I was bidding farewell to my father, who returns to the country. I did not wish to disturb you in conversation before."

"Very well." Catherine nodded. "Come, now I am tired. We shall depart for my rooms."

Thomasin saw Catherine wince in pain as she stood up. She took a moment, then pushed her spine forward and began the slow walk. Her ladies followed. Maria and her daughter joined them at the door.

"Good night, My Lady," said Brandon, bowing low.

Catherine inclined her head. "A good night to you, my friend. Always one of the loyal ones, Suffolk." Before reaching the doorway, she paused again. "Gertrude? You are dismissed from my service this evening, if you wish. Go to your husband. You have been long apart."

Gertrude stammered, open-mouthed. "Are you sure, My Lady? You will not require me?"

"I am more than amply attended. Be back before breakfast to help me dress."

Gertrude dropped a curtsey. "Thank you, My Lady, thank you so much." And she scurried away at once.

"What a thing it is," Catherine mused softly, "to desire and be desired in return."

TWENTY-ONE

The queen's chambers were cool and dark. Thomasin hurried to place more logs on the fire while Ellen lit the candles. Maria and Mary set about the process of removing the royal headdress and jewels.

Catherine called for wine and a dish of comfits. "How long can she keep this up?" she muttered in despair. "Fluttering around my husband like a moth, confusing his senses. I shall appeal to her mother to take her home to Hever."

"My Lady?" asked Thomasin, thinking of Nico's confession.

"What is it?"

"It is not Anne's mother who needs speaking with. Tonight, I discovered who lay behind the Venetian plot."

She had Catherine's full attention. The other women stopped their work and gathered round.

"You are certain?" asked Catherine. "Tell all."

Thomasin took a breath. "I know the Venetians are slippery as eels, but there is one man among them who has a semblance of honour, who has proved himself a friend to Your Majesty. His name is Nico Amato and I saw him again this evening, and spoke with him. I asked about their plot, and who lay behind it."

She looked at her captive audience: Catherine impatient, Ellen wide-eyed, Maria cynical, Mary agog.

"It was not Wolsey. Nor the initiative of the Venetians by themselves. Nor the emperor, of course, nor the Pope. It was none other than Thomas Boleyn, who asked them to move from Westminster to Windsor and put the ideas in their heads."

The ladies reacted with disappointment and surprise, rapidly transmuting into cynicism. Catherine held her counsel.

"They were to gather information for the Doge, My Lady," Thomasin continued, "but it was all to go through Boleyn — all your moves, your plans and thoughts, your correspondence. All to be used against you by that man."

At that point, Thomasin did not think she could dislike Boleyn more.

Catherine pursed her lips tight. The women around her waited. Slowly, she nodded her head. "I should have known. That man and his family will stop at nothing to destroy me. Boleyn is the very devil himself, to work against God's will in this way." She put a hand on Thomasin's arm. "You have done well. I will never forget your good service." She pulled a ring from her little finger, a band of gold set with a pearl, and held it out. "Here, take this. I want you to have it; you have earned it."

Thomasin was almost speechless. "My Lady, I cannot… It's too much."

"Please take it." Catherine would not take no for an answer, placing the ring in Thomasin's palm. "Go ahead, put it on."

Thomasin slid it over her middle finger, where it fitted perfectly. Her hand was transformed by it, as if she had suddenly become a countess or duchess. She blushed as the light caught the pearl.

A knock upon the outer door sounded, interrupting them.

Thomasin was closest to the door. She went through the parlour and into the antechamber, feeling the ring's strange weight and cold presence. It was not the servants waiting outside, but Mountjoy, looking tired.

"The queen is dressing."

"I will wait," he said wearily, stepping inside. "What is her mood this evening?"

"She is a little tired," Thomasin explained, not giving away anything about their exchange.

"She is not upset?"

"Why?"

"The court is buzzing tonight. All sorts of rumours are flying."

Thomasin thought at once of the Venetians, then of Jane Boleyn and her sorry predicament. It must be difficult to keep secrets in such a place as this.

"Oh? What rumours?"

"Do not tell the queen, but they are whispering that Anne is with child."

Thomasin's jaw dropped. "Is that possible?"

"It is not impossible, certainly, as the king assures us he is a man like any other. Don't forget he already has one bastard child, the little duke Henry, who lives at Durham House. But I had thought Anne was denying him her bed, so I do not think it is the case, yet the tongues wag."

"You do not believe it, then? It would be most injurious to the queen."

"I do not believe it. Nor what they say about his plans for the boy. It is also rumoured that the king will wed him to his daughter, the Princess Mary, in order to secure his line."

"But that cannot be. They are half-brother and sister."

Mountjoy shrugged. "Such things can happen, and often do in Europe. I give it no credence, but it shows just how desperate the king is perceived to be. His performance tonight with Anne did not help. He has retired to her chambers now, where they drink wine as the minstrels play."

Again, Thomasin thought of Jane, lying in her bed with the agony of her loss, while her sister-in-law entertained the king. Surely Anne knew what she was going through? She resolved to send Jane some wine and comfits later. "It seems to me," she pronounced, "that people have nothing better to do on a summer's evening than to spread ridiculous gossip."

"You are right, of course, but such words can still cause harm. I am glad they have not reached the queen."

"No, so far as I know, they have not, and will never do so from me."

"I am glad to hear it. I will leave you, then, assuming all is well. The king plans to ride out tomorrow, early, into the park, but he will be returning for dinner."

"Very well, I shall inform the queen."

Mountjoy got up to leave, but in the doorway he paused. The flickering candlelight caught his profile. "One other thing. One of the cooks has been taken ill. There may be nothing in it. She has no signs of the sweat, but there are one or two spots on her cheeks. I saw her myself an hour ago. She has been isolated, of course, and will be checked on in the morning. As I said, I am confident it is not the sweat, but you should be aware. Do not alarm the queen yet. With God's grace it may come to nothing."

"I pray that it is so. Goodnight, my Lord."

He looked down at her hand upon the door. "Nice ring."

Thomasin looked him in the eye. "Thank you."

Catherine was in bed by the time Thomasin returned. Propped up against double pillows, dressed in her white night cap, she was small and fierce-looking between the curtains.

"I heard Mountjoy's voice," she said. "What did he want?"

"He was just checking to see how you fared, but he did not wish to interrupt you," Thomasin replied. "He said the king is hunting tomorrow morning but will be back for dinner."

"Hunting with her?"

"I don't know. Just hunting, he said."

Thomasin slipped out of the bedchamber. Tonight, she and Ellen were on the truckle beds in the parlour.

"The queen noticed Anne especially tonight," Ellen said, looking up from where she was arranging their bedding. The fire was dying and a single candle remained burning on the table. "She takes this latest news hard."

"It was impossible not to notice her," Thomasin agreed. "She went out of her way to make a display of herself."

"I wish she would be more discreet."

"But that is not her purpose: she is fighting to win her position; every day, every meeting it is a game of status. I doubt she has forgotten the queen's words over their card game."

"It is not kind of her to flaunt herself before the queen so much. The palace is large enough that they might never meet unless by choice."

"But she wants to meet the queen, wants to display her power and force her to withdraw. She will never be satisfied until she takes precedence over her."

Ellen frowned, slipping off her shoes and rubbing her feet. "But she is nothing, nobody in comparison with Catherine, the daughter of a king and queen, with the blood of John of Gaunt in her veins, raised to be queen, married and anointed. What audacity is it that such a woman believes herself to be the queen's equal?"

Thomasin had a moment of insight. "She would not believe it, unless the king let her believe it. He must have made her promises; there must be a secret agreement between them, otherwise I cannot think she would behave so."

"I think you are right."

"And yet he will not openly admit it. That is why she is so on edge in public, always trying to push for his attention. He will not make his intentions public."

"And all the while he does not, the queen continues to hope, continues to assert her place."

"It is cruel."

"Cowardly," Ellen nodded.

"He doesn't want to dirty his hands with the whole business, but waits upon the Pope's pronouncement, so he can say it was divinely ordained, not of his making, but he must abide by it."

"It is despicable. And as for her father…"

Ellen blew out the candle and they burrowed down into their beds by moonlight. "The queen favoured you tonight, for your discovery."

"She did. I am overwhelmed by her gift."

"Show me."

Thomasin held out her hand across the beds and the pearl ring gleamed in the moonlight.

"It is beautiful."

"Yes, it is. And I was only doing my duty."

"But you uncovered the queen's enemy in this matter, and she will never forget that."

"Now, that is not the main matter I wished to discuss," replied Thomasin, changing the subject with mischief in her voice.

"Oh? How so? Is there more?"

"You know there is, full well. What have you been up to this evening, Ellen?"

Her cousin laughed. "How did you know? How in the world did you know? We were merely talking after the dance, in sight of all."

"And later, at the bottom of the courtyard staircase?"

Ellen sighed in defeat. "Yes, that too."

"Well, come on."

Ellen's expression softened and her round cheeks bunched into a smile. "He kissed me, he actually kissed me. I had explained my horrible situation, he knows everything and he still kissed me."

"That is wonderful, you seem very happy."

"I am. It's like a dream. I never thought this would happen. We will talk more, pass time together and see what happens."

"I am sure the king would grant you a divorce, or influence those who can, and Barnaby will not complain, or else you can cite his bastard child."

"It may have been born already. No, this is best for us all. Hugh is young, as I am still. I can bear him children."

Thomasin decided to say nothing of what her father had told her. "Do not move too fast. Make sure you are certain."

"I can't think of what might prevent it. We like each other well enough. When we are free, what more is there to say? I could be his wife. And happy. Imagine that."

Thomasin nodded. "He does seem a gentle soul, and I am sure he will never give you trouble."

"He is sweetness itself. You should have heard his kind words to me tonight. So gentle and understanding, such flattery."

"I am glad he has found his tongue!"

"Yes," laughed Ellen, "it is funny. The circumstances were just right. He had much to say."

"Then I am truly happy for you. You deserve happiness, both of you."

"When my marriage is taken care of, we will ask the king for his permission."

"You must catch him upon a happy day, when he is dancing or laughing with Anne at his side, then he will wish his joy upon you."

"I would have to leave Catherine's service."

"Maybe not at once. Gertrude is married and remains."

"Yes, I saw that," Ellen nodded. "But I could not be apart from Hugh as she is from Exeter. I shall be a country house wife, with a brood of children, and will visit court from time to time to cheer at a joust, and you will come and stay with us, as our guest."

"That sounds idyllic."

"It sounds too good to be true."

"Do not say that. Never say that. It is all within your reach."

"I hope so, I hope so," said Ellen, settling down to sleep.

Lying beside her, scenting the smoke in the air, and hearing the creak of the wooden furniture settling, Thomasin wondered whether she was ever destined to experience such happiness. Where could she find the man who combined the allure of Nico, or Rafe, with the warmth and easiness of Will Carey, or even the ready wit and playfulness of her friend Giles Waterson? Months had passed and no word had come from him. She wondered how his business in the north, and his engagement, were progressing.

When would love come calling for her?

TWENTY-TWO

Thomasin was just drifting off to sleep when the door to Catherine's chamber creaked open.

"Are you awake?" It was Mary in her white shift, peering into the darkness.

"I am, just," Thomasin replied, rubbing her eyes.

"The queen is asking for a caudle to help her sleep. She likes it with cinnamon."

Ellen was dead to the world, lying on her back and breathing heavily with her mouth open.

Thomasin groaned to herself, resigned to the task. "Very well, give me a minute."

"I'm sorry. She won't sleep without it."

Mary's head retreated and Thomasin turned out of her warm sheets, pulling on her kirtle which lay over a chair and picking up a shawl. She stuck her feet into some slippers and hoped there would be no one outside to see her.

The corridor was cold. The guards outside accepted her explanation, letting her pass without question, and she headed down in the direction of the kitchens, hoping that someone would still be awake, that the cook John Tandy would not have retired yet.

She turned into the dark passage that led down to the serving hatches, looking for the distant glow of light, but seeing nothing.

A figure stirred from barrels at the side.

"Hello? Can you help me?"

He had been lying back against the wall, propped against the wood, but now he struggled upright, swaying with drink. Thomasin recognised Rafe and recoiled.

"You, Thomasin?" he asked, stepping into her path. "What are you doing down here so late at night?" He ran a hand through his dark, dishevelled hair. She caught the stench of beer on his breath.

"I am fetching a caudle to help the queen sleep. What are you doing? Making a disgrace of yourself with this drunkenness?"

"Fetching a caudle?" he laughed. "The kitchens are closed, the fires are dead. Or are you meeting someone? That's it, isn't it?"

"No. Now excuse me, the queen is waiting." Thomasin hurried past, towards the serving hatches, but Rafe followed hard upon her heels.

"Who is it you're meeting?"

She ignored him, stepping inside the vast hall where a row of cold ovens was set into the wall and the central hearth and table were empty. A number of serving boys were sleeping on rushes, curled close around the bread oven.

"Who is it?" Rafe hissed. "Your married man?"

His words cut through her. "Go away, you're drunk. You speak out of turn."

"I've seen the way you are together, you and Will Carey. You know he has a wife, Thomasin, a wife? Where are your standards now? Sleeping with a married man?"

She turned slowly, as if rooted to the spot. "If you ever say such a disgusting thing to me again…"

"What? What will you do? I see you don't deny it, then?"

"Of course I deny it. How dare you? How dare you apply your filthy, base standards to me. I shall complain to the queen."

"That will get you nowhere. Anne is queen here now. She will hardly approve of you sleeping with her sister's husband."

"I am not! Nor is it your business." Thomasin had a swift look down the corridor to ensure they were not overheard. "The Lady Anne has no scruples about stealing the husband of a queen, a woman infinitely her superior in every way, nor about helping to break my sister's marriage, so she can have absolutely nothing to say concerning my behaviour, not that there is anything at all to comment upon!"

"You should mind your tongue; it could get you into trouble."

At once she regretted such a hasty public condemnation of Anne. There did not seem to be anyone else around, but Rafe was right, she should be more careful. It was her anger that had made her rash.

But Rafe had not finished yet. "You are very defensive about Mister Carey."

"Rightly so. Your accusation is obscene. Go away. Leave me alone."

"I have seen you, Thomasin, seen you dancing, laughing, flirting with him. What would his wife think? Wouldn't she ask Anne to appeal to Henry? To have you removed from court? Sent back to the country?"

"Leave me alone, or I shall report you."

He held out his hands in surprise. "Really? To whom?"

Then it came to her. "To the king. No doubt you will recall my family's former connection with him."

Rafe laughed. "Oh, I do. I do!"

He could not have been more repellent to her than he was in that moment. Deciding that he was not deserving of any more words from her, she turned her back and headed over to wake one of the boys, although her guts were twisting in anger and shame.

A lad of about fifteen sat up in response to her pleas.

"Please, I am sorry to wake you. The queen desires a caudle to help her sleep. Can you make one?"

"Yes, my Lady, I will have to start up a fire, but I can bring it up to her within the quarter hour."

"You are very kind. What is your name?"

"Jack, my Lady. Jack Green."

"Please make it with cinnamon, and thick, maybe with honey."

"I will, my Lady, then I will bring it up to her chamber."

"I am most grateful to you, Jack. I thank you, and will see you shortly, when you deliver it." Thomasin turned to go but Rafe was there once more, barring the door.

"Where are you going now? To Carey? To spend the night with him?"

"Get out of my way."

"You wouldn't yield to me, so why him?"

"Get out of my way!"

When he did not move, Thomasin walked round to leave through the second archway, but he hurried after her.

"Creeping about like a whore in the darkness to satisfy your desires! Does the queen know what you are up to? She won't want a little whore in her household, will she?"

His words made her feel sick. How could she have not seen what was lurking below the surface of the man?

As she turned the corner, with a clear path back to the staircase, Thomasin picked up her skirts and ran, grateful for the soundless dancing slippers. By the time she reached Catherine's chambers, her hands were shaking. She slipped inside.

"Is it you?" Mary had lit a candle as she waited.

"Yes. The caudle is being prepared as you requested. A young man named Jack will bring it up shortly. Do we have a coin to thank him with? I woke him from his sleep."

"I have a coin for him," said Mary, patting her purse. "But you look pale and shaken, are you quite well?"

"I am a little unsteady, I think."

"Go back to bed. I will wait up."

"If you're sure."

"I can't sleep anyway. Go on, lie down, you look as if you have seen a ghost."

Gratefully, Thomasin shed her shoes and skirt and crawled back into her bed. Ellen had not moved. She closed her eyes, but all she could hear was Rafe's angry, bitter words and the ugly accusations pouring from his beautiful mouth. Lips that she had kissed, spouting such obscenities. How could men be so cruel?

But then, as she tried to close her eyes, she could not stop the twinge of guilt creeping in. She had been spending time with a married man, it was true. She had not shared his bed, but she had allowed herself to think of him as a man, not just as a friend, and she knew he had feelings for her. Was it wrong, given the circumstances? His marriage was a sham, a contract in name only, but would the world see it that way? Would she be judged harshly if she allowed herself and Will to get closer? Wasn't she already being judged? In his drunkenness, was Rafe actually expressing a deeper truth, another danger she had strayed into without knowing?

Thomasin was finally drifting off to sleep when the soft tap came at the door. Behind her closed eyelids, she was aware of the sweet scents of honey, cinnamon and cream, before she lost all connection with the night, the room, the court, and slipped away into peaceful dreams.

Morning arrived, but Thomasin had not slept well. Rafe's words kept chasing around inside her head as she washed her hands and face and pinned her headdress into place.

Catherine was kneeling in her tiny chapel, hands clasped together, haloed by flickering candles. Her painful words washed over the women waiting in her chamber, heavy with their Spanish tone.

"My Lord, by your wish I have conceived six children by my husband and always held myself true unto him, loved, honoured, respected and obeyed him as a true wife should. Always a true wife. And I have done my best as queen, to reign over the people it was your will to deliver unto me. I have been patient through your trials, through suffering and loss, trusting in your will, wondering but not questioning, trusting in you always. And from you I received the greatest blessing of my daughter, whom I am raising in your true faith. I have ever been your faithful servant and I ask you, Lord, not for myself, but for the state of the realm and the future of my child: do not forget me in my old age, now my womb is dry and my hair is grey. Hold me to your love and mercy, despite…"

Her muttered monologue was interrupted by knuckles rapping on the outer door.

Thomasin jumped up to answer. Charles Brandon stood there in his riding cape.

"My Lady Marwood, good morning. I am about to depart from Greenwich and am here to take my leave of the queen."

"She is at prayer," Thomasin replied, holding the door open. "But you are welcome to come inside and wait."

"Will she be long?" Catherine's lengthy piety was legendary.

Thomasin shrugged.

"I will wait a little," he agreed, stepping into the room.

Almost at once, Catherine emerged, having heard voices. "Ah, Charles, I had thought you might be the king."

Brandon went forward to kiss her hand. "You must forgive me on that account, and also that I am to depart from Greenwich this morning. I am here to bid you farewell."

"Oh, you are leaving us? One of my oldest friends, and my brother?"

"I fear I must do so. My Mary is unwell and I must go to her at Lambeth."

"Unwell? Her old malady?"

"The physicians are unsure. She is suffering from new pain in her back and left side."

"Dr Butts is at Westminster; Dr Elyot is in London too, at his own house. Make sure they attend her on my instruction."

"Thank you, My Lady."

"I will have some of my special tincture made up, the one I always use on my joints and aches. See that she uses it, and apply to the Westminster kitchens for whatever diet the doctors recommend."

"You are too kind."

"I have no sister in this county but her. We were girls together; she was my constant companion after I was widowed. I will not forget her now. Wait, one moment."

She disappeared back into her little chapel and returned clutching a small tablet, made of two jointed pieces of wood, opening like a book to reveal a painted inside, picked out in gold.

"Give her this from me. It is the Virgin and St Anne; it has brought me comfort in times of trial."

"Are you sure? I would not like to deprive you of something so precious."

She pressed it into his hands. "Certain. She has need of it. Take it, please, I insist."

"Very well, then I shall. You are more than generous, as ever; Mary is most fortunate in your love."

"And I in hers. Write to me, to tell me how she fares."

"I will." He paused, as if there was something else. The room looked to him, expectant. "I should say, as you will know soon enough. Two things."

Catherine steeled herself. "Go ahead. Tell me."

"I am always your friend, first and foremost."

"I know, tell me."

Brandon stroked his square beard. "The king has received a letter from Bishop Foxe. He wrote from Dover, two days back, after crossing the sea. He has been in Rome with the Pope."

Catherine's nod was brief, impatient. "Does he indicate his news?"

"Not yet, merely that he will fully inform the king upon his return. He is expected at Greenwich any day."

"Then we shall await him with calm and conviction of our right."

"And one other thing. There has been a case of smallpox among the women in the laundry."

"Smallpox?"

Thomasin thought at once of Mistress Arnold, with her neat cap, folding the dry clothes.

"One confirmed and one suspected. Hopefully contained there, but it is probably wise to wait in your rooms until all is clear. Some others…" He broke off. "The Lady Anne and her household are moving to the rooms above the stables, to be apart from the infection."

"Above the stables?" replied Catherine wryly, smiling at the animalistic connotations. "I thank you for your warning, and we will remain here and pray for those afflicted."

Brandon nodded. "Then I will bid you a farewell. I hope the time passes quickly before we see each other again."

"And Mary is restored to health. As soon as she is well, and all is safe, I will visit you in Southwark."

"We will look forward to it. A good day, a good day to you all, ladies."

TWENTY-THREE

About midday, the sounds of horns came lilting through the distant greenness of the park. Thomasin and Ellen had been sewing, while Mary read to them from a book of saints' lives.

In one swift movement, they reached the window and stared outside, but the park was on the other side, and they could only see gardeners trimming the bushes in the friary below.

"So the king went hunting after all," said Ellen, "after we have been stuck inside all these hours."

"Perhaps he does not know, if he went early," Thomasin suggested. "Do you think we will have to move again, due to this smallpox?"

"I don't know," said Ellen, "but my servant in Buxton had it as a child and survived, although her face was deeply pitted."

"Oh, poor thing. Did she ever marry?"

Ellen shook her head. "It would be a terrible shame, would it not, if a certain Lady at court was to be infected in a similar way?"

Thomasin turned away to conceal her smile. "Now, now, we must not wish ill upon anyone, or else we risk bringing it back upon ourselves."

Catherine emerged from her chapel, followed by Maria, where she had been praying again. "Was that the hounds? Are they back?"

"I believe so, My Lady," Thomasin replied, "although I have not seen them."

"No doubt we shall hear soon enough. But you must be prepared to pack up my effects quickly, if it transpires that we must depart again. When shall we be free of all this illness?"

Before long, the outer door swung open without warning, as only the king would dare. Henry strode through, into Catherine's inner chamber. He was still dressed in his riding jacket and boots, but was wringing his hands and working his lips so that his agitation was apparent. Wolsey and William Compton hurried in after him, apparently having failed in their efforts to appease his mind. In an instant, the queen's quiet space changed mood. The very air seemed to crackle. Thomasin at once felt the tension she was certain had also seized all the others present.

"You have heard this news? The pox has hit us now? Four in the laundry and two in the kitchens? Did you know?"

Catherine curtseyed, always mindful of protocol. "We heard of a case in the laundry, after you departed, and have not moved from these chambers since, waiting to hear your will. I hope we did right."

Henry ignored her question but began to pace up and down, gripping at his sleeves. "It has come for me, it seems to follow me, determined to claim me as it did my brother. What kind of punishment is this? How have I deserved this in God's eyes?"

"Come now," said Wolsey, lifting his hands in supplication. "This is no more a punishment from God than the roses failing to bloom. It is an illness we see every summer. There are always bound to be cases nearby, it is so common."

"But my brother," Henry urged. "He died, remember, of the sweat. He was mortal, as am I."

"And we have learned the lessons of that tragedy. Sensible steps have been taken to prevent infection. Those who are ill are being removed and the areas of their employment thoroughly washed down. All their clothing and effects have been burned."

"You have seen my horoscope? Drawn up by Elyot, by Butts and a dozen different astrologers. I was born under the sign of Cancer, so I am governed by the sign of the moon, making me particularly at risk when it comes to smallpox! And I do not have my book of cures with me; it remains at Westminster. I must send for ingredients."

"We are lucky," attempted Compton, clumsily, "that it broke out in the laundry and kitchen, where it could be contained."

Henry glared at him, as if he was an idiot. "Do you not wear clothes washed by the laundry, eat food prepared in the kitchens?"

"But, My Lord, you know what I mean. At least they have not been moving among us."

"Compton is right," said Wolsey. "That is a blessing alone."

Henry's temper exploded. "Blessing? Blessing?" He lurched forward as if to cuff Wolsey's ear, but the cardinal stepped back and Henry did not pursue him. "How can there be any blessing in this situation? It is a sign of God's displeasure in me."

"No, My Lord, it is not," said Catherine, gently.

"It is nothing less. I have displeased God in this marriage. He has given me no sons and now he plagues me, chases me about with these diseases."

"You must depart at once, come back to Hampton with me," urged Wolsey. "We can shut the gates and be safe. We can summon an apothecary."

"There is no certainty of safety, and do not dare to tell me what I must do! Do you remember who your king is? Or do you presume to aspire to that title too?"

"Of course not, my apologies, My Lord."

Catherine tried to approach her husband, although he was still pacing across the floor as if his feet were afire. "My Lord, if God wanted to claim you, He would simply do so. If He is displeased, He would have done so long before now. God does not play games of chase with kings. Why don't you come, sit down and drink some wine? We can discuss our next steps."

But Henry shook his head, enraged.

"We could pray together. That will give you comfort."

"It will not!" he roared. "What should I pray? For Him to take away the plague that He inflicted? Or for the son that He denied us? Do you not think He is mocking me with this? Laughing at me? Why should I pray to Him?"

"Henry!"

Catherine was visibly shocked by his words. Thomasin and the others, also, felt their danger, verging almost on blasphemy.

"Come, My Lord," attempted Compton, "you are unsettled. We should leave the ladies to their peace; they cannot resolve this problem for you, come."

"Oh, can't they?" asked Henry, his tone savage as he turned towards his wife. "Perhaps they can? Admit that our marriage is a false one and set me free from this torment. Then I shall be at peace."

"Come now," said Compton. "The queen's position has no bearing upon the sweat or the pox."

"How can you be so sure?"

"Because this is superstition, not science, My Lord. God would not forsake you thus."

"Did he not forsake Arthur? Where is he now? Where is my brother? He lies buried at Worcester, don't you recall?"

Catherine's hands were trembling, but she refused to be cowed. "My Lord, I am your true wife in the eyes of God, and will always be so. He united us and set us on the path He chose. You were anointed in His name, as your brother never was. This illness is a trial, nothing more. You have escaped infection until now and will do so again. Focus your mind. Remain calm. Plan your next movements."

For a moment, it seemed that her sensible words had stilled his tempest. But the waves were still rising in Henry.

"What if I die now? To whom should I leave my kingdom? To a girl of twelve? We would be plunged back into civil war. The country would fall. Whomever took her to wife would rule England; a French prince? The emperor? A Spaniard? Do you understand?"

"My Lord!" Wolsey raised his voice above Henry's escalating tones. "You must stay calm. Such an outburst weakens your constitution at a time when you most need it to be strong!"

Henry immediately fell quiet.

"Now, open all the windows in here," said Wolsey, taking charge. "There have been no instances of the sweat recorded in Greenwich, just these pox cases, which have been isolated now. If you flee, it may be into greater danger."

Henry was nodding. "I will retire. Send the orders for the hall and corridors to be cleaned. I will dine in my room." With that, he strode outside without a word, not looking back.

The day passed and slipped quietly into night. By the morning, Catherine was restless, leaving her prayers to sit by the window and stare at the passing clouds. It was midday when the next knock came upon the door.

Ellen showed Wolsey in. Catherine rose uneasily, scarcely able to conceal the distrust in her eyes. The cardinal took a long time to kneel and even more time to rise, reminding them he was not a young man, nor a well one. His long, thick garments pooled red ominously on the floor before the queen.

"You bring news?"

"Good news, My Lady. There have been no new cases of the pox today. Still none of the sweat."

The women breathed a collective sigh of relief.

"It is probably wisest to remain within as much as you can, and avoid public areas. Your kitchen will supply your meals, as the pox outbreak came from the main kitchen, not your personal one, but it has been advised that you may exercise safely in the grounds, so long as you keep good distance."

Catherine nodded. "These are good tidings. We shall remain separate for another full day, to ensure the safety of all, and emerge only if no new cases are reported. But we shall take up your suggestion to walk in the grounds."

"If there is anything else I may do to be of service, My Lady, do speak. Baron Mountjoy keeps to his chamber still, on account of having visited the laundry yesterday morning, but he is still quite well. You should receive no other visitors beside myself. Or the king. All supplies will be left outside your door; the servants will knock and retreat. You should wait for the count of a hundred before retrieving them."

"Very well. It seems you have taken care to think of everything; I thank you."

Wolsey nodded. "And might I add, My Lady, that the king fares much better than when he last visited here."

"That is good to know. Again, I thank you."

He bowed low. "Then I will take my leave."

They waited as he hovered uncomfortably, then drew backwards, still bent double, in a gesture of exaggerated respect.

As he was departing in a swathe of red robes, an idea struck Thomasin and she followed him through the door.

"My Lord Cardinal?"

He turned sharply, examining her closely. "Who are you?"

"Thomasin Marwood, gentlewoman to the queen."

"And what is your business?"

"Please, my Lord, forgive my intrusion. I had hoped to ask a kindness of you."

Wolsey made a snorting noise. His eyes narrowed, and he seemed about to unleash scorn upon her head. Thomasin was surprised at the change in him, but she recalled talk of his origins as the son of a butcher from Ipswich, and tried a different approach.

"My Lord, I am only a humble girl from Suffolk, new to the ways of court and lacking influential friends. All I have achieved, I have done so using my own wits, in a dangerous world. I had hoped to speak with you about a friend of mine, a man of wit, in need of friends."

He eyed her again.

"He only seeks work, the proper employment of his talents. Nico Amato is a native Venetian who wishes to do service at the English court, to some great man. Of course you were the first who came to my mind, although I am sure a man such as yourself is already amply provided with assistants. But should you ever require a secretary or clerk, a man to translate and write letters, or undergo missions to Rome, Nico would prove himself most loyal and able."

"I have been well provided for foreign tongues by Master Cromwell, who is proficient in French, Dutch and Italian," Wolsey considered. "Yet he is increasingly occupied with legal matters and has little time for the humbler jobs of translation. What is the man's name again?"

"Nico Amato. He is with the Venetian party at present."

"I will bear him in mind." He cast his eyes up and down over Thomasin, making her feel uncomfortable under his gaze. "He is fortunate to have a friend in you."

"Mister Carey?"

Thomasin shaded her eyes from the sun. It was definitely Will Carey, disappearing behind the rose bushes ahead.

They were walking through the gardens, separated into pairs, save for little Catherine Willoughby, who was chasing a new puppy off down the path. Thomasin and Ellen were last, having dawdled about the flowers, enjoying the sunshine, with Ellen enthusing about her next meeting with Hugh Truegood.

"Was that not Will Carey?" Thomasin asked, bemused, when he didn't appear on the other side of the rose walk.

"I thought so, but I didn't see clearly. Perhaps he didn't see you, or else he has been told to keep his distance."

"But he could wave, at least."

"Not if he did not see you. Go on, hasten after him, just for a minute. No one will mind."

Thomasin shot a look ahead to Catherine, who was walking with Maria.

"Go, go," said Ellen, "I will cover for you. I'll say you're ill." Then, when she saw Thomasin's face, she corrected herself. "No, not at the moment, I won't. I'll say you were chasing a butterfly. Go on."

"Mister Carey? Is it you?"

But Will Carey did not turn to face Thomasin, his broad back clothed in grey velvet, with a cap set with a pearl on his head. Little light curls were escaping at the back, round his neck and ears.

"Will, it's me."

The roses bobbed between them as he took a right, deeper into the maze of flowers.

Bewildered, Thomasin chased after him. His mind must be occupied with something very profound if he had not heard her.

"Will?" Finally, he stopped and turned, but the reluctance in him made her heart stop.

"Did you not hear me? What is it?"

His face was troubled, he could not hide it. He tried to avoid meeting her eyes. "Thomasin, you must return to the queen."

"Why? What's the matter? Are you unwell?"

"No, it's not that," he said helplessly. "Well, it is a little warm, but it's not that. You must go back to the queen at once."

"I will not. Not until you tell me what has happened."

"The pox, you know what we have been advised."

But Thomasin wouldn't accept his excuse. "It seems more than the pox. Why so unfriendly?"

He looked away. "I must go, the king requires me."

"I thought we were friends. What is this?"

He stared down at his hands.

"Are we not? Have I deserved this, somehow? I know not what it may be." Frustration began to rise in her chest.

"I cannot say. Only that in the present time it is safer for us to be apart. Believe me, it is not of my choosing. Never."

"Only because of the smallpox? Do you fear it so much?"

"Partly, well, no." He looked around him with some anxiety, then took a step closer to her and held her with his gaze. "It is unfair that I do not tell you. But what a mess this is."

Thomasin's fears were mounting. "Please, tell me, you're worrying me."

"I was warned to keep my distance from you, by a member of Boleyn's household. I was told that it was not seemly for us to spend time together."

"What nonsense. Spending time together is not seemly?"

"Not for a married man and an unwed woman, I am told."

Thomasin's anger flared up. "Like the king and Anne Boleyn, you mean."

Carey shrugged.

"And who was it, who told you this? Someone I know? Not a certain Mister Danvers?"

His eyes confirmed her suspicion. "I … I can't say directly. I was warned that I could be damaging your reputation, your prospects, and may even prevent you from making a good marriage."

"As if anyone here cares about my marriage! Not after what they did to my sister. And how are you damaging me? By being my friend?"

He caught her eyes again. "Is that all we are, truly, Thomasin? Mere friends?"

"There has never been any impropriety between us."

"No," he said, "there has not." And softly, quickly, he stepped forwards and surprised her with his lips upon hers. Just briefly, but soft, warm and promising. "And now?"

She stared back at him, speechless at the sudden move, trying to process her feelings. It was a pleasant kiss, and not unwelcome, she thought. But was this what she wanted? Was he?

"Thomasin? You see?"

She wasn't sure she did; her emotions were in turmoil. She reached for answers but none came.

Carey saw her confusion. "I apologise. It is something I have wanted to do for a long time, but I understand your predicament. I am married, in name only, but still married. Oh, Thomasin, was it not welcome? I had thought…"

She could only stare back at him, while her feelings swirled about her, refusing to settle.

Carey stepped away. "I am sorry. I made a mistake."

"No, I don't think that. I just, I don't know. I am confused."

"Do you have feelings for me beyond friendship?"

"I may do. I need time."

"I should not have…"

"Yes, you should. It brought this out. I need to think."

"I can write to the Pope and request a divorce. If the king is granted one, why should I not be? Mary and I have not lived as man and wife in the real sense."

"You have not?"

"The match was consummated, to make it legal, but then Mary went straight to the king's bed. He did not wish to repeat another bastard at court."

"Your children?"

Carey shook his head. "In name. It is supposed but can never be proven, and I have raised and loved them as my own. I hope I may count upon your discretion?"

"Of course."

"At the moment I can offer you little. Mary would keep Pleshey, and I have only one other small house in Devon. If we divorce, I might lose my position at court and have to rely upon my mother's money. I was told to withdraw for your own sake, and I can see why. But it is for the Boleyns too; they do not want any weakness, any lessening of their faction. If I divorced Mary, it would reflect poorly on Anne and her chances."

Just as poor Jane's miscarriage would, Thomasin thought. "Is that what you wanted to do? Withdraw from me?"

He turned to her again with wide eyes. "By God, Thomasin, no."

Some impulse seized her again, whether it was her own feelings, or his passion, or the sunshine and roses, and she leaned in to kiss him a second time. He put his arms about her and pulled her in close, crushing his mouth down upon hers with unexpected fervour.

When they broke apart, Thomasin spotted a movement. In the moment, they had forgotten themselves and the presence of others. There, at the end of the long walk, George Boleyn stood looking at them, pausing while he exercised his dogs. Now he turned away and continued his path.

"Well, that's that," said Carey. "It will no longer be a secret. I must deal with whatever the Boleyns say or do, but I shall keep your name out of it. I will speak to George, make him understand."

"I hope he does not judge you too harshly, after the leniency he affords his sisters."

"Very apt." He nodded. "Now, go, please, back to the queen. I will find a way to speak with you soon, but do not be troubled."

Thomasin watched him hurry away, then walked back through the line of nodding blooms.

Ellen was waiting impatiently. "There you are! I was almost coming to look for you."

The queen and her other ladies were nowhere in sight. "Where is everyone?"

"That's the thing. Bishop Foxe has returned. Henry is receiving him in his chambers. We had a tip off and the queen has hurried there, come on!"

TWENTY-FOUR

Thomasin's heart beat hard, drumming in her chest. Her breath came short as she hurried through the palace, following Ellen along corridors and up the staircase. A crowd had already gathered in the watching chamber that led through to Henry's private apartments. People were jostling for precedence, each trying to inch closer to the doors ahead, trying to catch a few of the words being spoken within.

All fear of the pox seemed to have been set aside in the face of news from Rome. Pushing through, Thomasin saw William Compton sitting on a bench, with Henry Norris and Francis Bryan deep in conversation at the side. Thomas Wyatt and Thomas Grey were also waiting, nodding as Henry Courtenay was lecturing them on diplomatic affairs. Further along, Charles Collins and Hugh Truegood had taken a more light-hearted approach, playing cards at one of the trestles, and Truegood looked up to smile as Ellen approached.

"He has been here a half hour already," explained Truegood, beckoning them over. "Straight from the road with dust on his boots. But the king will admit no one."

"Not even the queen?" asked Ellen.

"I saw her pass through, certainly, but I think he may have refused her."

Thomasin and Ellen exchanged glances.

"It's a sad day," said Collins, shaking his head in sympathy with Catherine.

At far door, William Hatton was idling about, fiddling with the gold aglcts at his wrists, then raking his fingers through his blond hair. He looked them up and down, no doubt recalling

279

his recent conversation with Thomasin's father. "*You* can't go in *there*."

But at that point, Maria appeared on the other side and beckoned them through. The guards stood aside. Thomasin did not try to conceal her smile, but kept her eyes ahead, as if Hatton did not exist.

In the antechamber, Catherine was seated upon one of two chairs with carved legs. The depths of her fury could be read in her expression. Maria, Gertrude and Mary waited nervously, and Mountjoy stood behind them, but the doors to the king's private chambers were shut fast. Catherine waved for them to stand behind her. By way of warning, Maria pressed her fingers against her lips. Catherine was listening as best she could.

Thomasin took her place, her heart aching for Catherine. To be denied entry to her husband's chamber was bad enough, as she had witnessed that night at Windsor. But to be denied publicly, in such a matter as this, was beyond endurance. Catherine truly had the patience of a saint, she thought.

Presently, Bishop Mendoza came limping into the chamber, also vetted by the guards. At once Catherine indicated for him to sit beside her on the other chair, in front of Thomasin. He did so in complete silence, easing his old bones down in relief, shifting about to find his comfortable spot. He had the scent of smoke and salted fish about him.

It must have been about half an hour, if not more, that they waited in the agonising still of the anteroom. No one came in, and no one left the king's apartments, but the doors remained solidly closed. The guards had received clear instructions.

Thomasin allowed her mind to return to Will Carey. She had not expected the kiss in the rose garden, but nor had she anticipated the warning he had been given about her. It must have been Rafe who warned him off, although Will had not directly confirmed it. Coming, as it did, just shortly after her unpleasant run-in with him the other night, and his words about meeting a married man, it was simply too much of a coincidence not to have been him. But what were his motives? Surely not jealousy? Or a genuine desire to protect her reputation? Bitterness, perhaps?

And she had kissed Will, that second time. She hardly knew what had come over her, except in that moment, it had been what she'd wanted to do. Now she scarcely knew where it left them, but while she was hardly overcome with desire as she had been with Rafe, it had been pleasant and she suspected that, given the chance, she might do it again. She would not let herself dwell, at the moment, on what it might mean.

Come to think of it, Thomasin had seen no sign of Rafe in the watching chamber, nor any of the Boleyn faction. She wondered whether George Boleyn had caught up with Will, and what had passed between them. Or might be doing so, right now.

The doors finally cracked open, catching them by surprise.

A long shaft of light from the king's room spilled out in a measured line at their feet. A figure stepped into it, in a long coat with a fur collar and square cap. Thomasin recoiled at the sight of Thomas Cromwell, aware now of his persistent efforts to make use of her father.

Cromwell could not avoid bowing to Catherine, but then he went on his way. The doors remained open, allowing Catherine the opportunity to enter as quickly as she could rise.

Inside the king's private parlour, Henry was seated by the hearth, while Wolsey stood behind him. Opposite them, the man in the cloak and boots had to be Bishop Foxe. A second man stood beside him, also in travelling clothes. Both looked drained. Thomasin suspected the king had subjected them to a relentless round of questions. Also inside, to her surprise, were Thomas and George Boleyn.

"My Lord." Catherine bowed low and waited. Her ladies followed suit.

"News travels almost as fast as the pox in this court," Henry retorted. "So you would know my business?"

"I would know my business, My Lord, nothing more."

Henry chewed his lip. There was no arguing with that.

"Bishop Foxe, Bishop Gardiner, I welcome you," Catherine addressed the travellers. "I trust your mission was fruitful."

"It was indeed," said Henry, taking control of the situation before they had the chance to answer. "Although the Pope has not yet ruled directly either way in the question of our marriage, he has agreed that the case needs investigation as a matter of urgency. He has appointed two cardinals to try the case at a Legatine court in England, as soon as possible. I am confident they will find in my favour, no doubt within the year."

Catherine remained silent.

"You will be afforded every respect, Madam, due to your rank as Dowager Princess of Wales, widow of my late brother."

"Only if the court finds it to be so," Catherine said quickly. "Until it is pronounced thus, I am still God's anointed queen in this realm, and will be afforded that status. It is for the Pope to demote me, not my husband."

Henry looked at her starkly, as if about to speak, but Wolsey put a warning hand upon his shoulder.

"And what of our daughter," continued Catherine, "begotten in true matrimony, as we both believed at the time, joined and blessed as we were in the sight of God? Will her status remain? And all respect due unto her?"

"Mary will be afforded what her position deserves." It was a cold reply.

"Our daughter, My Lord? Upon whom you doted?"

"Our only child, with no living sons to show for nearly twenty years."

"I have given you sons, you know that. Remember our little Henry, who lived but six weeks."

The king winced and turned away.

"Let me send for Mary to join me, in my household," Catherine said. "She has been months at Ludlow, and now the threat is over, and the colder months are passed, let her come to Greenwich with us."

There was a long pause while they waited, before realising the king did not intend to answer.

"My Lady," said Wolsey, more gently, "of the two cardinals appointed to try your case, I am the first and the second will be Lorenzo Campeggio of Milan, Cardinal Protector of England. He departs from Rome at once and will be with us in weeks. The court will be held at Blackfriars. You should seek advocates to present your case, should you wish to do so. The alternative is that you retire into the religious establishment of your choice, which shall be fully endowed by the king."

Catherine could not bring herself to reply, so odious was his suggestion. She made a shallow curtsey and rose to depart.

"There is no doubt," said Henry softly, turning to Wolsey as Catherine left. "This is God's path and we must fight to defend it, for the good of the realm. Consult all the lawyers in the land. Get Marwood back to collate the results. I shall be married to Anne by this time next year. And, God willing, we may even have a son on the way."

As she was passing through the doors, Thomasin heard them speak her father's name, and a chill passed through her.

All the way back to her chambers, Catherine held her emotions in. Once the doors were closed behind her, she allowed the dignified façade to droop.

"Present my case? Present my case? As if I have to fight for my right to be queen, I, who am God's anointed? How long can this torture be endured? And I must fight, fight against that little Boleyn whore who has nothing but her age as an advantage. I have seen how cheaply she behaves, conducting herself with airs and graces, demanding attention, displaying herself in public. The king's late mother, our beloved Queen Elizabeth, God rest her soul, would never have countenanced behaviour like it. Her court was a place of dignity and breeding. This little whore does not even have good looks! She is like a ragged crow, dressed up in French robes. I must fight against her, to keep my husband! It is outrageous."

Thomasin had never heard Catherine speak so savagely before, but the situation was unprecedented. Nor had she heard her refer to the late queen, Henry's mother, Elizabeth of York.

"And that Wolsey!" continued Catherine. "I can barely speak from fury. The way he dared address me with his information. He is a butcher's son, no less, raised in a hovel, promoted above his rank and qualities by my husband's generosity, nay, his foolishness. He, who has corresponded with me as queen for fifteen years, wished me well during my confinements, celebrated my successes, reassured me about my husband's health; now he is to judge my marriage? Judge it? The religious establishment of my choice?"

"I will need another pet dog," said Maria, eyes glinting wickedly, "so I can name it Wolsey. It can be a companion to my little terrier Gardiner, who has been treated for worms. I was sorry to see his sad face return from Rome. A pox on both of them!"

"I remember this Campeggio," nodded Catherine, searching her memory. "I thought his name was familiar. He was here, in England, some ten years ago, under the former Pope, Leo. Yes, yes, he is no friend to Wolsey, if I recall. There was some trickery back then, when Wolsey undermined him as legate and took credit for his arrangements, claiming the peace treaty of London was all his own work. Campeggio was most put out, but he had good grace about it. He was always respectful to me. I shall write to him, and put my case. After that, I will require Archbishop Warham and Bishop Tunstall to speak for me. If my husband wants to make this into a battle, he will be matched against a strong army. He has clearly forgotten that it was whilst I was regent, and him absent in France, that the Scots were defeated at Flodden."

"That's the spirit, My Lady," encouraged Maria.

"There is a long way to go," replied Catherine, "but I believe I am following God's true path, and I shall fight to defend it every step of the way. My husband is being misled, and it is my duty to save him."

That evening, they ventured back to the hall for dinner. The mood was different, though. Thomasin sensed it at once as they approached. Henry was buoyant, defiant, determined to interpret Foxe's message as a victory. He had apparently not been expecting Catherine to make an appearance, and had invited the Boleyn faction to occupy the top table with him. Thomas was placed to his right, and George to his left. Anne had deserted the safety of the stables, pulling a chair right up to him, so their arms were touching. Their heads were bent close together as he whispered in her ear.

Catherine froze. It felt like walking into the lion's den.

The chatter in the hall ceased abruptly, as all faces turned to see what would happen next.

Thomasin's eyes were drawn to Anne in her long green gown, seated in the carved chair, usurping Catherine's designated position, as if she was queen herself. Her dark eyes flashed and blazed when she spotted Catherine, and she drew back from Henry at once. And in that moment, Thomasin spotted the glint of something red about her neck, hanging from a gold chain, and recognised the Venetian ballas ruby that the queen had returned to Vernier.

"My Lady," she whispered to Catherine, who was close enough to hear. "See what the Boleyn woman wears about her neck."

There was a pause as Catherine observed the scene, then she took a deep breath. With the whole hall watching, she began to make a beeline for the table ahead like an arrow released from a bow.

Thomasin noticed Henry shift in his seat, unnerved by the energy and power in Catherine's walk. It was as if all her aches and pains had suddenly melted away.

Catherine stopped short of the dais. She addressed herself directly to Anne, in a firm, clear voice for the entire hall to hear. "Mistress Anne. You appear to have taken my seat. I am sure it must be by mistake, as everyone knows it is the seat reserved for the queen. The queen is now here, come to dine. You will vacate it at once."

"Anne was here by my invitation," began Henry, but Catherine ignored him and turned to Thomas Boleyn.

"Sir Thomas, you are aware of the severity of this breach. Remove your daughter from the chair of the queen of England and aunt of the emperor."

Boleyn twitched. As a former foreign ambassador, he had no wish to incur the wrath of Emperor Charles Hapsburg. Nor, it seemed, did the king. Not yet, at least. Not until the Legatine court gave him a firm decision to act upon.

Henry did not look at Anne, but he turned his head and gave Boleyn a short nod, as if to suggest he should withdraw.

But Catherine had not finished. "I would also add, Sir Thomas, that the ruby your daughter wears is a fitting gift from the Venetians for your service."

Her words surprised Boleyn. He turned pale. Anne did not flinch, perhaps unaware of Catherine's meaning.

Henry frowned. "What is this? What do you mean?"

Boleyn tried to rise to leave, but Henry stayed him with his hand. "What is this talk of the Venetians?" He looked fiercely across the hall. Thomasin followed his gaze and saw Vernier and his group at the far end, looking like rats caught in a trap. Nico did not appear to be among them.

"Did you not know?" asked Catherine in mock surprise. "Sir Thomas has made an unexpected alliance with the Venetians, and his daughter is wearing the rewards. That ruby was given to me at Windsor this spring, along with many other gifts, and more to my ladies, in the hope that they would correspond with the ambassadors and reveal secrets about my movements. Secrets that were to be shared with Sir Thomas, so that he might use them to further his cause. Fortunately, it was so clumsily done that we were aware of it at once. I returned the ruby to Signore Vernier and I see it has found a new owner."

A murmur ran around the hall. Eyes turned towards the colourful group in the corner.

"Is that not true, Signore?" Catherine called to him.

Vernier held up his hands in surrender.

But if Catherine had been hoping to win her husband's support against Boleyn, she was mistaken. Henry was on his feet, glowering.

"This is unnecessary, Madam. We were about to enjoy a peaceful dinner with good company. You would do better not to attempt to discredit my friends."

"But, My Lord, do you not see the actions could have been treasonous? National secrets might have been passed on."

"Who are you to lecture me on treason, Madam? Since you have disrupted my dinner, I shall remove to my chamber and dine in peace. It seems you will find any way to try and part me from those I love."

He rose and indicated for his company to follow him.

Stunned by his response, Catherine retreated into a statuesque silence as they passed her by. At this moment, she understood she had truly lost her husband. She waited for the hall to erupt in noise, but there was nothing. Not a movement. The king's public rejection of his wife had shocked those watching.

It was painful to stand there so rejected. Thomasin felt the burn of shame, not too dissimilar from the suffering she had endured at Cecilia's failed wedding. All those feelings rushed back to her. To be the subject of gossip and ridicule was almost more than she could bear.

George Boleyn was the last of the king's party to leave. As he stalked past them, he paused beside Thomasin, and she prepared herself for harsh words regarding her kiss with Will Carey.

"I wished to thank you," he said softly, "for the wine and comfits you sent to my wife. It was kindly done."

Thomasin met his eyes in surprise, but then he was gone.

The room was waiting. It was down to Catherine to deliver the final act.

Conscious of her position, Catherine walked forward, mounted the dais and took her seat in the chair that Anne had vacated. She cast her eyes around the room, catching the glances of friends, determined not to be defeated. "Let us eat. Bring in the next course!"

And, unexpectedly, a single pair of hands began to clap in approval, then another, until the hall was applauding the queen.

Taking her seat, Thomasin fought back the unexpected emotion that threatened to spill into tears, and one look at Catherine showed her the queen was trying to do the same.

TWENTY-FIVE

The sun was setting behind the hill, bathing the palace gardens in evening light. A charmed, golden light that caught the red brick and set it afire, lit the grassy paths and delved deep into the hearts of the flowers. Catherine had granted them an hour for exercise, while she wrote to her daughter, miles away in Ludlow. Gertrude had flown away to see her husband, Exeter, Mary was dozing, and Maria was walking with her little daughter. Three days had passed since the confrontation in the hall and Catherine had since chosen to dine in her rooms.

Ellen and Thomasin linked arms as they walked through the archway into the main park. Midsummer was only a few weeks away. The days were getting longer, the sun rose earlier and earlier, and it felt pleasantly warm upon their skin.

"It is truly a beautiful palace," said Ellen, looking back at the chimneys and windows of Greenwich Palace, bright and abundant. Strings of smoke rose up into the clear blue sky. "I prefer it to Windsor and Hampton. There is more space here, too, and more privacy. And it's so beautiful. I understand why it's a favourite."

Thomasin's eyes were among the roses as Ellen chattered on.

"I can scarcely believe so much time has passed already. Summer is upon us. I know the king and queen used to go on progress, but I wonder if fears of illness, or their current breach will stop them. I would like to see more parts of the country. I'd like to go wherever Hugh is, though. I don't want us to be parted at this delicate stage, don't you think? Thomasin?"

"Sorry. Yes. No, I agree."

"What's the matter with you?"

"I'm tired, I think. Just tired."

"Those truckle beds are not comfortable. It's always Maria who gets to share the queen's bed, with all that space and those cushions. I'd like to try it for one night."

"Maria is her oldest friend. They've been friends for longer than I have been alive!"

Ellen shrugged. "Just one night, although I probably couldn't sleep through Catherine's snores!"

They giggled, a little guiltily.

Ahead, the path led two ways, one back towards the walled garden and the other towards the tilt yard. Ellen chose for them, heading back to the arena where they had witnessed the men riding at the ring.

It was quiet now, the wooden stands just empty rows awaiting an audience. The ground had been freshly sanded, but was still pitted with more recent horse hooves. At the far end, the tilting ring still hung from its frame, swaying slightly in the breeze. Three young men had gathered round it, one mounted with a lance, but no armour, as they discussed tactics. Thomasin recognised Hugh Truegood at once, if by nothing but Ellen's reaction. Charles Collins was also there, mounted on the horse, and in the shade on the other side of the ring, stood William Hatton.

Thomasin stopped, just as Ellen was pulling forwards. Truegood had seen her and was already bidding his friends goodbye. The sun was bright in his auburn hair.

Thomasin unlaced their arms. "Go, don't worry. But I cannot stomach Hatton, so I'll go back to the roses. I will see you back at the queen's apartments. Go."

Ellen did not need to be told twice, but hurried forwards. Thomasin waited to see her meet Truegood, beaming smiles, then turned back to the garden, alone.

It was not far back to Paradise. The scents reached her before she entered the flowery paths, somehow more intense in the evening light, having been gently warmed throughout the day. Thomasin plunged into the central circle walk, trailing her fingertips against the clusters of petals; white, pink and yellow. It was a perfume that spoke of luxury, daubed at the jawbone, stuffed into a pomander or distilled into water, for handwashing in a crystal basin. The rose seemed to her a symbol of the height of the summer, of abundance, hope and long days. She was drawn to a particular variety, a sort of pinkish-apricot colour, but streaked in darker orange, whose petals clustered closely to make a really dense, tight flower. Stretching up slightly, she bent the stem down to brush against her nose, cheeks and lips. The scent was exquisite.

"Meeting someone?"

The unexpected voice, so close, startled her. Looking up, Thomasin was horrified to see Rafe Danvers a few yards away, apparently quite alone. His head of dark curls was visible above the tall bushes.

She turned away at once, recalling his harsh accusations and intending to leave.

"Please, wait. I want to apologise."

He appeared around the side in his habitual black, but with white collar and cuffs, embroidered in the fashionable blackwork style. He had her for a few moments, but she resolved to give him nothing.

"I behaved badly towards you the other night. I can scarcely recall what I said, but I know that I had far too much to drink and I am sure I spoke unforgivably. It would have been entirely due to my own shortcomings, of jealousy or frustration, I am sure. None of it was deserved by you, or justified in the slightest. I offer my sincerest apologies."

His words gave her pause. Never had she heard Rafe so sincere before. But she could not help questioning his motives; always there was another master with him, a higher purpose, or a lower one.

"And now I am certain I have lost your good opinion entirely."

"You do not think that was lost last autumn?"

He held up his hands. "Fair enough. But I truly am sorry and regret those words."

Thomasin paused a little longer, her heart beating faster, wondering whether this was the time to leave, or to linger a little more, and wait. His proximity, with the rose petals between his fingers, made her feel uneasy, unsettled, but not entirely in a bad way.

"Do you remember the night we met last autumn, in the gardens at Westminster?" He spoke coyly, eyes cast down into the heart of a rose.

Of course she did. She was straight back there, in the scented night, under the moonlight and his enticing smile. "When there was a fire?"

"Caused by Francis Bryan."

"And you gave me a rose."

He nodded.

"I kept that rose under my pillow until it faded."

"Did you?" He came towards her hopefully, and she felt the same pull in her gut, the urge prompted by his physical beauty as the sun caught him full in the face. His eyes, usually dark, blazed chestnut as he squinted against the light.

For a moment, she wanted him. The feeling rose up within her unbidden, like a visceral reaction to his presence. Despite all she had learned about him since, his loyalty to the Boleyns, his coldness, his temper and cruelty, there was still that spark of lust between them, threatening to drag her in.

But Thomasin was not the same girl she had been last autumn. She would master those feelings because he did not deserve them.

"It does not change the way you treated me the other night. Your words and tone were unforgiveable, although you say it was the drink. Did you then not speak to William Carey, and warn him not to be my friend? To keep away from me? In some misguided way of protecting me, or was it something else?"

"I did speak with him, yes. It was kindly meant."

"As your words the other night were? It is not kindly to meddle in my business. You had no right to do so, and you cannot use the excuse of drunkenness this time."

Rafe was thoughtful for a moment. "I was thinking of the harm done to your sister."

Thomasin shook her head. "I don't believe that for a moment. What harm were you protecting me from?"

"The damage to your reputation."

"Was there any need for that? There were no questions, no rumours, no doubts about my conduct. The queen is more than satisfied with me; why should you be less so, when you have no right to be?"

"I could see the danger, if you could not. Carey was being reckless."

"How so? By speaking with me? Dancing? I recall that you took far greater liberties with my person with absolutely no care for my reputation, only for your own satisfaction."

"That is not true! Carey is too close to the Boleyns."

Thomasin frowned. "From what I can see, he is not at all close to them."

"He is married to Anne's sister. No matter how free he might think himself, those legal ties remain. He will stand or fall with the Boleyns. Do you want to unite your fortunes with a married man in their circle?"

"I am not looking to unite my fortunes with anyone! We were merely friends. None of this was your business."

"No? Are you not my business at all? Nor want to be?"

She found she could not answer these questions. Something reluctant deep within her did not want to close that door. Just in case. Not while he stood there, glowering in the sunshine.

"You do not have the right to meddle in my life, nor to speak to me that way. Now I have said all I wish to, and must return to the queen."

"So soon? Can we not speak further?"

"I have said my piece."

Thomasin was determined to turn her back upon him. It was the best way to take control of her feelings, and let her rational mind control the waves of emotion. Now she had to put distance between herself and Rafe, to deny the physical charge pulling them together, and go and devote herself to Catherine, perhaps even to pray. She strode away through the roses, back towards the path.

Rafe refused to accept this and hurried after her. "Go away, leave me be!"

Ahead, in the distance, she could see the turning to the tiltyard. Beyond it, Hugh Truegood and Ellen were dallying by the fountain.

A kitchen hand was walking along the path, carrying a pannier of wood, while others were leading out the king's dogs for exercise.

As she hastened towards the path, Thomasin saw the figure with the wood slow to a halt, pause and then drop to his knees. The basket crashed beside him, spilling the logs out onto the grass, while the figure unfolded and lay upon his side. The sight was shocking, stilling her in her tracks. The dog keepers hurried over and gathered round.

Thomasin was about to hurry forward, to be of assistance, but Rafe was at her side. He held her back by the arm.

"No, wait. We don't know what this is."

Instead, he ran forward, halting a short distance from the crowd. One man was kneeling, talking rapidly, while the others began to back away. Thomasin strained, but was unable to hear their words. After a minute, Rafe also was backing away, heading towards her, his face registering alarm.

"What is it?"

He put his arm about her shoulder and began to lead her in the opposite direction. "Be quick, we will go round the long walk. It is the sweat."

"What? No."

"Yes, there is no question. That sudden collapse is typical. It is the sweat. Soon it will be all through the palace."

"But I should not return to the queen. Oh, Ellen!" She tried to turn round and see the spot where Ellen and Hugh had just been, but they must have moved on.

"You have not been close enough for contact. You cannot be considered a risk."

"No. But you have."

For a moment they looked into each other's eyes.

Rafe shook his head. "You will be well, all will be well. You must go and tell the queen. I will go straight to the king. No doubt they will move at once, to some other palace. Wait."

She had begun to turn away.

"Wait," he said again. "If we do not see each other again, or have the chance to say goodbye, I am sorry for it all. I wish things had been different. God be with you."

"May God be with you too," she replied automatically, allowing his words to sink in.

"Go, go to the queen, hurry! Lives are at stake!"

Thomasin's hands were shaking as she ran through the corridor and up the stairs. People stepped aside to stare at her in surprise, but she could give them no clue, nothing, until Catherine had been informed. The guards admitted her without hesitation. The first chamber held Maria and little Catherine, playing chess.

"The queen?" panted Thomasin. "Where is she?"

Maria rose to her feet. "What is it? She is at prayer. What has happened?"

Thomasin stood back against the wall as Maria started towards her. "Stay, perhaps you should not. I don't know. There is a case of the sweat. A man collapsed before me in the park, a kitchen hand. I was nowhere near, but within sight. My companion," she added, remembering Rafe, "he went to look. But still, he was not close. Not close enough. He has gone to the king."

Maria's face had turned white. "You should wait here. I will tell the queen."

Thomasin suddenly felt the tension of the moment. Her body was exhausted, her mind a fog, and she leaned back against the door.

Little Catherine Willoughby started carefully packing up the chess pieces, understanding that the game would not be resumed. "So," she said, pertly, "it has caught up with us. All that running and you can't outrun it."

Thomasin was not in the mood to answer, but the girl was right. If the sweat came for you, it would take you, no matter what. She pictured Rafe, entering Henry's chamber, breaking the very news she had just given, followed by the king's reaction. Judging by his emotional outburst the other evening, he would not take the news well.

She listened. There was silence within.

After a while, Catherine came and stood in the doorway. She was moving stiffly and slowly, as if trying to stave off great pain.

"This is true? You saw the man fall?"

"I was in the rose garden and he fell on the path, so I was a good distance away."

"It is a definite case?"

"That's what the others said. My companion went to look, but he was further than I am from you now. He believed it to be so. He is informing the king as we speak."

Catherine nodded. "And Ellen?"

"She was at the far side of the gardens."

"So far," said Catherine, "you are the only one of my ladies to be in proximity to the case. And there is a breeze, is there not?"

"A slight breeze."

"It may carry the infection. You should not enter further. No doubt we will be leaving shortly for a safer location. My ladies will need to pack up my effects. Mistress Marwood, you must retire for now. Please leave."

Uncertain, with her hands still shaking, Thomasin stepped out of the chamber. The long corridor stretched before her, with its doors leading to chambers, stores, steps and other places she had yet to explore. Where was she to go? Where would be safe? Should she be trying to protect others, in case she carried the illness?

At once she focused on her body. She did not feel unwell, but now she thought of it, her stomach was churning and her head pounding, and an almost overwhelming tiredness came over her. She needed to sit down. There was an antechamber where the guards sometimes slept when they were taking it in turns to be on shift at night. It was round the corner, down a side corridor, tucked away in an older part of the palace. Luckily, the door was unlocked; the place was tiny and cold, but empty. There were barrels of supplies, including wood and coal, and some glasses and plates stacked on a plain cupboard. Thomasin lay down on one of the truckle beds.

Darkness was falling outside the window. No one would be leaving at this hour. Dawn would see the carriages loaded up, the gold and jewel-adorned riders galloping away. By then, all would be decided, and the fallen man's fate known.

At first, Thomasin resisted the urge to close her eyes. She lay awake, waiting for news, for footsteps down the corridor. As darkness fell, she strained to hear voices, or horse hooves, but nothing reached her. Eventually, sleep overcame her.

TWENTY-SIX

It was late when Thomasin awoke. The light was bright and full, ripened by the hours. She was used to rising with the dawn on these long summer days and helping Catherine dress, then waiting patiently whilst she prayed. Yet her senses told her that she had slept far past her usual hour, perhaps even as late as midday and clearly, no one had searched for her. Or at least, they had not found her.

When Thomasin tried to rise, she felt heavy. With effort, she pulled herself to her feet and straightened her dress. Her hair badly needed a brush, but fortunately she had been wearing a simple headdress, easy and quick to replace. Her fingers fumbled to set it into position, where it would at least cover the worst of her tangles. She must look a mess, but with the sweat such a fear, surely no one would notice a crumpled dress?

She pushed open the door gingerly. It was stiffer than she remembered. The corridor outside was still and quiet, so that not even an echoed voice or step reached her.

Suddenly, fear seized Thomasin. A presentiment of disaster. What if the sweat had spread through the palace at night, claiming lives? What if the king and queen lay dead, or dying? And Ellen too, and Will, and Rafe?

Thomasin's mouth was terribly dry. Little sunshine filtered through the latticed window, but it felt like a hot day. A very hot day. She must find a drink somewhere, but was it safer to go to the kitchens or the queen's chamber? Would she even be admitted?

After that long, deep sleep, she felt a little unsteady. Putting out her hand, she balanced against the wall for support and inched forwards. The corridor was impossibly long; she did not remember it being this drawn out, and each time she thought she had reached the end, there was yet more of it. And in all that time, no one passed the end. Not one soul. The butterflies in the pit of her stomach were beating their wings hard.

Finally, her hand slid along the wall and round the corner. Thomasin looked right towards the queen's apartments and left, to the stairs. It was deserted. Her head began to swim, brimming with questions she could not formulate as she leaned against the cold stone, trying to get her bearings. It felt as if she remained there a long time, eyes fixed upon the pattern of interlocking stones. Time passed, but was it minutes or hours? A terrible realisation slowly dawned upon her.

Then, suddenly, the footsteps were close behind, echoing like thunder so that she almost jumped out of her skin.

"Here she is!" cried a voice. "I have found her."

But Thomasin could not recognise the voice or face of her saviour, as her knees went from under her. Her last conscious act was to put out her hands to protect herself as she fell.

When Thomasin woke again, it was dark. She was lying in bed, with covers pulled up to her chin. She could see a glow of fire in the hearth but was shaking uncontrollably, shivering with cold. The room was shifting, too. Walls and corners absorbed all the darkness.

A figure passed in front of the fire, briefly blocking out the light. A woman, perhaps, with wide skirts.

"Are you awake?"

"Cold, so cold."

"It will pass."

Thomasin closed her eyes.

The next time she came round, it was dark again, dark as pitch because the fire had died. Thomasin lay still on her back, held in terror by what she was experiencing, but also by not knowing where she was, or who was tending her. Were they still present? Her ears keened in the darkness, reaching for any little sound. Was that the soft breath of another sleeper?

Her throat was dry, so dry, and her mouth felt as if it had been rinsed out with sand. She coughed, spluttered.

At once there was movement.

"Are you thirsty?"

Thomasin croaked out a yes. Gentle hands raised her head and she felt the rim of a vessel placed against her lips. Liquid ran over them like a blessing. It was sweet, perhaps a weak cordial made from boiled water and summer fruits. Most of it spilled down her chin but she swallowed what she could, gratefully.

"It's Ellen, don't worry. You must rest."

Thomasin realised she was no longer cold. Instead she was hot and sweating, stifling. She struggled to push off her covers and felt Ellen's hands assist her.

"This is the final phase. You are strong. You can do this."

It was light, but early. Behind the thick curtains gleamed a soft early morning, brightening the dark room. For a while, Thomasin lay there, settled into the truckle's mattress which had reformed its shape around her. Her limbs were stiff, as if she had not moved in a long time. How was she feeling? Neither hot nor cold. Not dizzy, nor unwell. Thirsty, yes, but the room was not spinning.

She was in the queen's antechamber; the very room she had slept in for the past few weeks, but it looked different. The other beds had been stacked away. All the usual objects — the clothing, books, plates, shoes, headdresses and the little artefacts like the hairbrushes, the box of ribbons, pots of salve and comfits — were missing. The room was practically bare.

Except, on the furthest side of the room, as far from Thomasin as possible, a second bed was occupied. The sleeper had rolled onto their side, so their back was facing the room, and their breath came out in the rhythms of deep slumber.

And the sensation of not being alone washed over Thomasin. It had been the sweat, no question about that. But now she felt calm, at peace. Surely, surely, thanks to the grace of God, she was coming through it. She closed her eyes again.

"Here, I have a little broth for you."

Ellen was sitting on a stool beside her with a bowl and spoon.

"It is chicken and cream, very good for your strength. The kitchens have made it specially."

Thomasin lifted her head a little, then managed to prop herself up on one elbow. A momentary dizziness swiftly passed.

It was sweet and nourishing, thickened with almond milk, and contained a spice like cinnamon or saffron. With the second spoonful and the third, Thomasin discovered that she was extremely hungry. "Thank you," was the first word she breathed to her cousin.

"Don't speak unless you feel well enough." Ellen held out the spoon again.

"What day is it?"

"It is the eve of the feast of St Boniface."

Thomasin could not think.

"The fourth of June," added Ellen. "But it matters not." She held out the spoon again and waited while Thomasin gratefully finished the soup.

Ellen put down the bowl.

"The queen?" The door to Catherine's inner chamber and chapel was tightly shut.

"She packed up and left that same morning following the first case. She and Henry have returned to Hampton Court with Wolsey. All the others, Maria and her daughter, Mary and Gertrude, went too. These rooms were already empty by the time you were found. They were gone by eight. I pray that God will spare them."

"And we are left behind? And you?"

"I offered to stay. I was in the park, the same as you, when the first case was known. I passed the man on the path. Luckily I have not yet succumbed."

"And all this time, you have nursed me back to health."

"We are cousins, more like sisters. You would have done the same for me."

Thomasin took her hand. "I can't thank you enough. You stayed by me when everyone left; you cared for me, watched over me, at great danger to yourself. You risked your life for me." Her fragile voice cracked as the tears broke through her defences.

"You have got over the worst of it."

"You did not suffer? You have had no symptoms?"

"I have been tired, and there was one day when my head ached so that I thought I was coming down with it too, but blessedly, I have been spared. I had none of the sweating or the thirst I observed in you."

"God is merciful indeed."

"When you are strong enough, we will go back to Eastwell. Your father is sending his carriage."

Eastwell. She was returning to Eastwell. The thought of her Suffolk home was almost overwhelming. The house with its well-loved rooms, the shady avenue, the nut walk. "Really? Back to Eastwell?"

"Yes, we are both going. They are admitting no one new at Hampton at present, until the outbreak abates. The queen will summon us to join her when it is safe to do so. Probably in the autumn, when infection rates die down."

Eastwell. Father and Mother and Cecilia and the little ones. It was all she longed for, now. But they were not the only ones she cared for. "Everyone else has left? Where is Hugh?"

"He has gone to his estate in Kent for now, to wait until this passes. Afterwards, we are both invited to visit. Who else?" Ellen mused. "The Boleyns have all gone to Hever, leaving right after the king, and your friend Rafe went with them. All save for George Boleyn and his wife Jane, who are at New Hall, in Essex."

Thomasin felt there were others, but her brain was a fog.

"The Venetians have left for home," Ellen continued. "They rode for Dover, to seek a boat across the channel. They are probably halfway across France by now. That sly weasel Vernier tried to come and see the queen before departing, hoping for some final truce with her, or any gleam of hope to take back to the Doge, but she turned him away at the door. Oh, all except that one you liked, what was his name? He went to Hampton with Wolsey, I think. I saw them from the corridor window. He saw me looking and tried to speak with me, but I could not hear him, nor him me. I had the feeling he was asking about you, though."

"Nico."

"Was that his name? Handsome man, with those golden eyes."

"Nico Amato. He went to Hampton?"

"And he looked well, and rode behind Cromwell. I wonder at his change in service."

"And Will Carey?"

"He left last. He asked after you constantly, left instructions and paid the kitchen staff to give you their best fare. He was last to leave and asked to be remembered to you, saying he would see you again soon. He left a letter, for when you are well enough."

"Where has he gone? To Pleshey?"

"I believe so. To the estate where his wife is."

"Did Rafe say nothing?"

"Nothing that I am aware of. I'm sorry."

Thomasin turned her face away. "The world has moved on and left us behind."

Eastwell. The haven lay waiting. That was where she would grow strong again, in the tang and mulch of the Suffolk air.

The following day, Thomasin sat in the window seat overlooking the orchard, wrapped in a woollen shawl. In spite of the palace emptying, the friary was still occupied, and in the silence left by the absent court, the regular bells and chanting voices were again audible.

Will's letter was sealed with red wax. She thought of him pressing down on the paper with his ring, leaving the strange little mark. What was that device? A branch, an arrow? She would have to ask him when they next met. The words were written in a neat, slanting hand:

Dear Thomasin,

I pray to God that you will recover sufficiently to be able to read this for yourself. If not, and this letter falls into the hands of a well-meaning friend, I ask them, nay, beg them, to respect my wishes and cast it into the fire unread.

Thomasin, I cannot leave with you in such a condition, without trying to confess something of my feelings. Again, I ardently pray for the opportunity to speak these words to you in person, in the weeks to come, when you are restored to health. I am going to Pleshey, where your letters can find me, and will watch every day for news about your recovery.

"I must write, as soon as possible," Thomasin said to Ellen, who sat darning a stocking. "And reassure him I am well, thanks to your care." She read on:

Thomasin, I cannot say all I wish to in a letter, but I am fearful that it may be my only chance. So I will say what is in my heart and trust to God and his mercy, that he will permit our reunion to come to pass. I speak the truth when I say that you are in my heart and I cannot dislodge you. Since our first acquaintance, I have admired you, but when I came to know you better, I found you to be more than I had hoped for in a woman, in the situation I find myself in. At the moment, I am bound, as you know. But it may not be forever. I have no right to ask you to wait whilst I untie this Gordian knot, immense as it is, but I can only offer my continuing, unwavering devotion and love. If the king can riddle himself out of a marriage, so will I. I wonder then, if you would consent to be mine?

Yours, Will.

Thomasin folded the paper in her lap. His words cut her to the heart, so simple and earnest they were in their declaration. Part of her wanted to leap up in response, and cry out the answer that the letter deserved. But another side of her remained anchored, rooted in uncertainty, her feelings tepid and foggy. Underneath it all, despite his charm and warmth, she did not feel that deep visceral desire that Rafe's physical presence evoked in her. She knew it did not mean that her feelings for Will were any less; in fact, they might be more lasting and stable for being less intense, less based in desire. They might spend a gentle life together of security, affection and admiration. But there was that core of her, still, that she could not deny. Deep inside, she longed for that thrill of attraction, the anticipation and excitement of passion.

What had possessed her to kiss Will that day in the garden? Quite simply, she had wanted to. An impulse had seized her to take the risk, and see how it felt. And she did not regret it. Could it be that over time, passion might grow between them, and supply that need of hers?

There was nothing to be done, now. She was in no position to make any sort of decision, but had to rest and get stronger. When she was safely back at Eastwell, and recovered from her illness, she would think about putting pen to paper and writing Will a few lines of reassurance.

Two days later, Thomasin and Ellen descended the staircase to the queen's apartments for the last time. Greenwich was silent around them, with just a skeleton staff remaining in the kitchens, laundry and stables, to care for the place until it was safe to return. Thomasin had bathed and changed into one of the shifts and dresses that Gertrude had left behind in her haste. The gown she had worn during her illness needed to be burned, and it was fortunate that she and Gertrude were of a similar size and height.

Yet Thomasin had lost weight in the last week. The pink and grey folds of fabric hung off her hips and the bodice was loose about her breasts, but it would be passable until she reached home. Her long, dark hair was washed clean and hung down from the back of the plain headdress, seeming to have grown longer during her ordeal.

They took a detour round the back of the building, so they might see the roses. The sunny weather had brought them out in even more of a blaze, with their plentiful heads merging into a sea of colour. There was the place where Thomasin had spoken with Will, and there, with Rafe. She saw the spot on the path where the man had fallen, and the way down to the orchards and tiltyard. Above them on the hill, the red-brick hunting lodge watched over it all. A couple of deer appeared boldly against the skyline, surprised at the quiet, before bolting away. There was not another living soul in sight.

Ellen sighed. "It's a shame there is no one here to see this beauty. The roses will begin to turn soon. It will be midsummer, and then the days will begin to shorten."

Thomasin agreed. "It feels strange to be leaving like this. As if the world is continuing elsewhere and we have stepped out of it. It's all just carrying on as before, but we are no longer a part of it."

"Do you mind so much?"

"I don't know. It's been our entire world these past nine months. When you're here, when you're in it, it's the only life you know; it's all absorbing, so intense. But now the palace is so quiet, I remember there is life elsewhere. Not the same, but a different kind of life."

"It's only for a short while. Fear not, the queen will summon us again when she can. She will not want to lose our service."

"I hope not." Thomasin looked down at her finger, where Catherine's pearl ring felt loose.

"No, we can expect to hear from her. She said as much before she left. But for now we can enjoy a summer in the countryside, away from the heat and the dangers."

"And proper beds," added Thomasin.

"And not having to rise at dawn or be on alert all through the night."

"Long walks in my favourite gardens. And my family. All that talk, last autumn, about free will. Hatton and More, I remember most; this new idea, this new learning, where we are creatures that take charge of our own destiny…"

"It sounds dangerous."

Thomasin nodded. "It's what led Cecilia into trouble. But when something like this happens, I mean the sweating sickness, we realise we are powerless against God's will. Are we simply living out His plan, waiting for the day He claims us?"

"Goodness, cousin, I don't know," said Ellen. "That is a very deep question."

"But what is the answer? Does that mean that we submit ourselves and accept His will, or do we try and forge our own paths? I do not know. I can see both are right and both are wrong. Did you make the choice to stay behind and nurse me, or did God send you to me, to save my life?"

Ellen shrugged. "You've got the whole journey to think about that. All that matters now is that we are both alive, well and safe. Come on, it's time."

The familiar coach was waiting outside the stable block. Thomasin's heart gave a leap to see the arms painted on the side, of the intersecting star and moon. Four fresh horses stood waiting for the journey to begin, their eyes blinkered against the sun. Their few possessions had been loaded up into a chest strapped to the back.

Thomasin turned and looked back up to the palace. Rows of dead-eyed windows stared back, and cold chimneys where the fires sustaining life had once pumped out smoke. This was goodbye.

The coachman jumped down to assist them. At once she recognised Reynolds, who had been with the Marwoods for as long as she could remember.

"Will you embark, my Lady?"

She took the hand he offered and stepped into the carriage. "It is good to see you, Reynolds."

"And good to see you in health, my Lady. We will have you home in no time."

He handed in Ellen, who took the seat beside her cousin. The carriage door clicked shut. Greenwich Palace was nothing but a picture, framed by the window. Then they felt the horses stir and the carriage rolled forwards, driving them away from court. They passed through the park, up the sloping hill and out through the gates, onto the open road.

TWENTY-SEVEN

Amid the darkness, a tiny light kindled. It was little more than an acorn, then it grew to the size of a thumb, before suddenly multiplying and leaping across the pyramid of twigs. Dry leaves caught hold, rolling and curling with bright edges, and the scent of woodsmoke was released into the air.

Thomasin breathed in deeply. This was the scent of home. Sweet air rolled in from the Suffolk fields, catching the tree blossoms, drawing up the roses. And this acrid tang of smoke in the woods was just as she remembered. At the edge of the clearing, they'd lit the bonfire to celebrate the eve of the feast day of St John the Baptist, to burn bright through the hours of darkness. All day long they'd been busy, making preparations to mark the height of summer, and the longest day of the year. Together with Ellen and her sisters, Thomasin had scoured the grounds to find the best green branches, and armfuls of wildflowers to decorate the inside of the hall. The daylight hours would stretch until almost ten of the clock, and there would be feasting and dancing. Neighbouring families from the Essex-Suffolk border had been invited and would be arriving shortly.

"Look, it's a fine blaze now! Step back. Don't get too close, in case the wind blows it towards you."

At Thomasin's side, her father Richard held out the palms of his hands to be warmed by the heat. He looked tired, she had noted when she returned, but he assured her that he would not be attending court again soon, nor could he offer the help that Cromwell desired from him in relation to Catherine and Henry's marriage. Thomasin wasn't sure that Cromwell would relinquish his support that readily, not from a man so experienced in law, but she hoped that it was so.

She tugged back from her face the long, dark hair that she was wearing loose. One advantage of being back at home was the freedom in her dress. She no longer needed to be laced, knotted and trussed up in all the formal garments, stockings and headdresses required at court. Never would she have been permitted into Catherine's chambers in this old, rust-coloured kirtle and worn shoes, with bare legs under her skirts and her hair tumbling about her face.

Colour had returned to Thomasin's cheeks. She was as rosy as an apple again, just as Catherine had said when they first met. It had taken almost two weeks since her illness, before she began to feel fully returned to herself. Most of her first days at home had been spent sleeping, while her mother gently tended to her, then she had felt strong enough to venture out into the grounds, picking nuts, reading in the walled garden or walking with her father and his dogs. The sun had caught her skin, warming it to a rich gold and bringing out the usual crop of little freckles across her nose.

From the fire they had lit on the rise, she could see back across the gentle downward sweep of green land that led to Eastwell Hall. It lay before her in all its long-desired beauty, rediscovered again in these heady summer days. Never had there been a better time to return home, with the fields rich in colour and nature at its fullest. There was the long lawn, criss-crossed with the dimples of footsteps and bright with daisies and clover. Down one side stretched the nut walk, shaded on one side by the stone wall, and planted with two rows of gnarled trees that met overhead. Beyond the wall, she could just see the sloping rooves of the stables and kennels, the outhouses clustered together, and then the uneven canopy of the orchard. Further along, the walled garden with its intense scents of flowers and herbs was her favourite place to sit, with the walk leading down to the pond, the six-year-old Digby's pride and joy, where he sank as many wooden boats as he sailed.

Then there was the house. Red brick in the old style, its long windows and stone archways bathed in light. Upstairs, there was the prominent roofline of the long picture gallery, hung with the faces of Marwood ancestors. Down below, in the kitchens, the cook and servants would be turning the spit, kneading dough and chopping herbs.

The boy Mark would be drawing water from the courtyard well and sweeping away the straw. Scented pastilles would be strewn on the flames in the rooms where hearths and braziers burned. In the hall, bright with flowers, her mother would be watching as the trestle tables were dressed in white linen, with silver plates and dipping bowls. Barrels would be brought up from the cellar, rolled into position, their taps loosened, ready for the wine and ale to flow.

In the bedrooms, scented with cedar and lavender, her sister Cecilia would be preening her perfect gold curls, lacing herself into her best dress, in an icy shade of jade green or cornflower blue. In the nursery, her youngest sister Susannah was being laid down to sleep in her cot bed, tucked under blankets. It had been the greatest surprise, when Thomasin returned, to see little Susannah toddling towards her, who had been a babe in arms upon her departure last autumn.

"Thomasin!"

She turned to see who was calling her name, shading her eyes against the still-bright sun. Over the crest of the hill came three figures, wading through the long grass, their arms full of flowers.

"Here you are," cried Ellen at the front. "We followed the smoke."

The country life was suiting Ellen, who was looking rosy and full in the figure. She had a cream-coloured flower tucked behind her ear and another in the front of her bodice, and like Thomasin, she wore her hair loose.

At her side came Thomasin's next two sisters: thirteen-year-old Lettice, who worshipped her cousin, watching her with dark, adoring eyes; and the six-year-old Alice, up past her bedtime, clutching the hand of her favourite poppet, which was dressed in threadbare lace.

"Yes, over here!" Thomasin waved. "Come and see the fire."

The girls clustered round as the heat spread to them.

"Will they be able to see it for miles?" asked Alice.

"Miles and miles," Thomasin replied, "and they will drive all the demons and bad spirits away."

"Are there very many?"

"Not here, no," said Richard, joining in. "Because we made such a big fire last year. This one will last all through the year to come."

"Most of them are at court," said Thomasin, wryly.

"Oh, I had a letter from Hugh arrive this afternoon," recalled Ellen. "He and his mother are well, remaining on their estate, safe from harm. But he wrote with news from Charles Collins, who went to Hampton Court with the king. It seems that Wolsey has the sweat, so both the king and queen have already moved on, and are travelling in the country, staying at religious houses and praying for their salvation."

"Wolsey has it?" Thomasin received the news with surprise. "Even God's own cardinals cannot escape, it seems."

"Poor Catherine," said Ellen, "forever chasing after peace and security. We will pray for them, especially for her during her trials."

"Is that the queen who you served?" asked Lettice. "I hope she is not unwell."

"With God's grace she will be well," replied Thomasin.

"I wish that I could see her, a real queen."

"Perhaps one day you will."

"And another thing," continued Ellen, pointedly, "all the others at Hampton are well."

Thomasin understood Ellen was reassuring her about Nico.

"And your mother says to come inside and wash, and prepare yourself for the guests."

Thomasin laughed. "I will come with my hair smelling of smoke and my kirtle stained with grass. Mother can make the best of me that she can, but I will never be another Cecilia."

"Well," smiled Richard, "we can be thankful for that. One per family is quite enough."

Two hours later, and the hall was filled with guests taking their place for the next dance. There were so many Suffolk faces Thomasin had not seen in such a long time; local landowners with their wives and children, with whom she had witnessed weddings and funerals, the baptism of babies and the harvest celebrations during her youth. The local Waits from Bury had agreed to play for the evening, with their lutes, pipes and homemade instruments, making a very different sound from the European minstrels employed by the king.

"Is it good to be home?"

Cecilia and Thomasin were surveying the floor.

"I cannot tell you how much, yes. And all is as I remember it."

Cecilia nodded, her eyes fixed on the dancers. "Did you dance much?"

"Occasionally, when there was dancing, but the sweat meant we did not always have company."

"Who did you partner?"

"Mostly Venetians. The ambassadors came to Windsor. Sometimes William Carey or another of the king's gentlemen."

"And her? She was there?"

Thomasin knew that Cecilia referred to Anne Boleyn, who had drawn them into her circle before weaving intrigue about them both. "She was there, yes. But I saw little of her and when I did, she was not kind. Remember I was in Queen Catherine's household, not hers."

"Are you going to dance?" Her sister turned to her brightly, with blue questioning eyes.

"I may, if I am asked, although I am not sure how long I would last."

There were few promising young men in the room. Most were of an age with their father, or else were married, and Digby's tutor definitely did not dance.

"Will you dance with me?"

Thomasin was surprised, but quickly smiled at the request. "I will, if you will promise to be gentle with me."

They took the floor in line with the other couples. Despite her questions, Thomasin noted that her sister's sharp edges had softened during her absence. She seemed more open, more willing to connect.

"Did you enjoy yourself at court?" she asked as they stood face to face, waiting for the first chords.

"I don't know if enjoy is the exact word. It was hard work. We had very little time to ourselves, always up early and assisting until late at night. It was tiring."

"No time for love affairs, then?"

Thomasin smiled, unwilling to confide yet about her friendship with Will. "Barely time for anything else. Occasionally we were permitted an hour to walk in the gardens. But only if we were very good."

"And what were the palaces like?"

Thomasin realised Cecilia felt she had missed out, being home in the countryside whilst her sister embarked upon adventures at court.

"Much the same," she downplayed, "old and cold, as you will recall. We thought that winter at Windsor would never end."

They curtseyed and linked hands, turning about in a circle, then back the other way. Then the group began to promenade, first up then down the room, to the clapping hands of the onlookers. Thomasin thought how no one at court would have dared clap along in that manner, unless the king forgot himself enough to initiate it.

"Did anyone speak of me?"

Thomasin paused before she replied. What was the answer her sister wished to hear? That the rumours of last autumn were still alive, or that she had been completely forgotten?

"Only to enquire after your health. There was no talk of what happened, you can rest assured."

Cecilia nodded but made no reply. Suddenly Thomasin realised what she really wanted to know, but dared not ask.

"I did see him, once or twice. He was in the king's company, but I made sure our paths crossed as little as possible. The queen was cold to him in her manner, so he kept away." She did not mention the conversation between Hatton and their father. "Do you think you would ever like to return?"

Cecilia lifted her arm so that her sister might walk underneath. "I might. When the time is right."

The group then formed a large circle and the tempo of the song changed to a lively beat as they stepped to the side. Some were singing along, others almost galloping until they were pulled around the circle, and ended up collapsing in laughter.

"I dare you to dance like that back at court," laughed Ellen, looking on.

With a flush of heat, July arrived. In the fields around Eastwell, the crops grew tall and sheep nibbled lazily at grass. The sun beamed down on the pond where Digby sailed his boats, filling it with lily pads like floating islands, and the odd treasure of a spiky lily. It warmed the hard little apples and pears growing in rows in the orchard, so that they swelled and began to soften, ready for the table.

Day after day, the heat began to climb, so that the best times were the fresh early hours and the cool evenings. Accustomed to the habit and the light, Thomasin would often wake at dawn and lie listening to the birds in the park, calling, cooing and saluting the sun. On the third or fourth day of the month, she stretched and yawned, as a blackbird summoned his mate in the bushes outside, thinking how glad she was not to have to rise and tie the queen's laces or kneel behind her in the chapel.

She must have dozed again, for the next thing she was aware of was a knocking at the door and Ellen calling her name.

"What is it?" She propped herself up on one elbow and squinted into the room.

"Can I come in?"

"Yes, yes."

Ellen was wearing a simple smock and cap, her sleeves rolled up where she had been playing with the children or helping in the kitchens. She had developed a friendship with the family's old cook, and was often scurrying about seeking herbs or begging to knead bread. Just yesterday, she and Lady Elizabeth had bottled up the first crop of strawberries.

Today, though, Ellen's face was serious.

"Letters for us, from Gertrude."

Thomasin was awake at once.

"Two came together. They must have been held up, I think."

"Come, come, open them."

Ellen sat on the edge of Thomasin's bed and cracked the seals. She quickly read the first line of each then chose one. "Yes, this is the first. It is dated two weeks back, though." She scanned it quickly. "I will give you the gist, then we can both take our time to read them fully. So, the queen and all her ladies are well. They are currently staying in an abbey in the country. The king is well, but no news of Wolsey. Oh, Thomasin, Anne Boleyn and her father have the sweat!"

She looked up in surprise, then quickly returned. "They both have it, and are ill at their home at Hever in Kent, but the king has sent his physician to do what he can for them. My goodness, what if she is taken by the illness? What a change there would be then. All the others there are well. Oh, there is something more. Oh, Charles Collins has died." Her breath caught. "We knew he had it, from Hugh's last letter, but Gertrude writes that they heard at court this morning that he worsened and then died, just after John the Baptist's day. Almost two weeks since. Oh, poor Charles."

She put down the letter. "There is only more about the abbey and the queen. Oh, that is sad news."

"It is very sad," agreed Thomasin, thinking of the young man's happy manners and easy smile. "He was a man who gave no trouble, a gentleman, quiet but sincere."

"I must write to Hugh. I wonder if he knows. He must, I think, but he will be greatly saddened. They had become good friends these past months."

"Where was he, when he passed?"

"Hold on." Ellen consulted the letter again, then read aloud. "Charles had remained at Hampton when the king moved away, as he was already showing signs of illness, and we heard by letter this morning that God has called him to His side."

"It is hard to understand," said Thomasin, "why some succumb and others survive. I am eternally grateful to you, and to God, for having pulled through my illness, but it is a mystery."

"And Anne?" said Ellen. "I should read the second letter and see what Gertrude has to say next. It was written only three days ago, so most recent news." Her eyes ran down the page. As Thomasin watched, her expression seemed to change.

"What is it? What? You must tell me."

"Anne has recovered. She has risen from her bed and is much stronger. Her father, though, is still weak but appears to be past the worst. And, you will never believe it, Wolsey is also coming through it. So all seems well there, although I just cannot fathom why it should be so. Gertrude writes that they are to move on to a priory tomorrow and that the queen has been in good spirits, although she received the news about Anne in silence."

Ellen looked up. "I don't doubt it. Poor Catherine, it must have felt as if God was answering her prayers. How easily it might have gone the other way, had it been Anne not Charles who was taken. It certainly is beyond my understanding. She writes more about Catherine; she is always at prayer and has endowed a new shrine to Our Lady, and she has been off her food a little and troubled by headaches. She speaks of returning to Windsor after the summer and hopes that Cardinal Campeggio will prove amenable to her cause. Now she breaks off, because they are to pack up the queen's belongings, ready for departure."

Thomasin's mind had wandered as Ellen's voice wafted over her. Through the open window came the scents of the summer's morning, of freedom and life continuing. Her thoughts began to slip away to happier hours, dancing and laughter, music and feasting, roses and kisses; but then there was the Suffolk greenness and peace, the wandering sheep, the calls of swallows and swifts meeting in the air, the simple pleasures of milk fresh from the farm and eggs still warm from the hen's feathers.

Ellen's gasp drew her back. Her eyes were wide, her hand clasped over her mouth. She shook her head as she looked from the page up to her cousin. "No, no, it can't be."

Tears began to well up, threatening to spill over her fingers.

Thomasin sat up and reached to embrace her. "What, is it Hugh?"

Ellen shook her head wildly. All she could do was hand over the letter. Thomasin took it and sped down to the last paragraph:

I return, just before we depart, to add the news that has just arrived. We are all most shocked to hear firstly of the death of William Compton, one of the king's dearest and oldest friends, which he has taken very hard. Almost immediately after this, we received news by a second messenger from Essex, that Sir William Carey, husband to Mary Boleyn, has sickened and died in the space of a single day. God have mercy on their souls and raise them to the light. I am sorry to be the bearer of such bad tidings. God bless you all and keep you safe,
Gertrude, Marchioness of Exeter.

Thomasin shook her head and read the words a second time. "It can't be. There must be some mistake. Perhaps the messengers were confused by the similarities in their names?"

"Thomasin," said Ellen, gently, "the second messenger came from Essex, while the first was from Hampton. I am so sorry. He is gone."

"No, no, I will not believe it."

The kiss, the letter, his eyes, their future.

"He is gone; we must believe it."

Ellen wrapped her arms around her cousin and held her until the pair of them were shaking with sobs.

Outside, a blackbird called to its mate.

EPILOGUE

The candles flickered inside the little church of St Mary. Thomasin had been coming here to worship with her family ever since she could remember, and the chantry tombs held effigies of her ancestors, carved in stone, flanked by their moon and star coat of arms. With Ellen at her side, she passed down the central aisle, stopping to kneel before the statue of Our Lady. It was a face she had looked upon weekly as a child, sometimes daily. The Virgin was painted brightly, her robes blue, her hair golden under the white kerchief. She held a carved, wooden child in her arms, looking down at the congregation with a beatific smile. At her feet, people from the village had lit candles and left gifts of eggs, flowers, beads, colourful stones or whatever they prized or could spare.

Yesterday, a parcel had arrived at Eastwell. Thomasin had been reading to Lettice and Alice in the quiet of their mother's chamber when they heard the gallop of a rider approach. It was Lady Elizabeth herself who brought the gift up to her daughter, wrapped in cloth and tied in string. The accompanying letter, in an anonymous hand, simply stated that Mister Carey had wished for Thomasin Marwood to have it.

She'd opened it gingerly, uncertain of what she might find. Her mother insisted that the cloth be burned at once, in case of infection.

Within lay a round gold frame, barely bigger than her palm, painted with a fine-tipped brush. Its sitter was instantly recognisable, with his wavy brown hair and warm eyes, the mildness about the mouth and gentle expression. Thomasin had felt the tears well up again as Will stared up from her hands, captured in paint, a shadow of the real man. He had constantly been in her thoughts, along with the tortuous questions of what might have been. She turned the miniature over, seeking a signature, but there was nothing. It must have been painted by the artist he had spoken of at court, or the artist's sister, by whom Will had been so impressed. Try as she might, Thomasin could not remember the woman's name. It was something foreign. She gently laid the image in the chest beside her bed, among folds of linen. She had not realised how much Will had meant to her until now.

One question still troubled her. Was this God's will? Or was it mere accident, a question of chance that she, Anne and Wolsey had survived the sweat, whilst Collins, Compton and Will had not? And why? Why them? It almost felt like a judgement upon the lascivious Compton, whom she would not mourn, but Collins and Will had been good men. There were no answers she could find today, not beyond her own determination to keep fighting to live. Today, she was here to light the way for a dear friend's soul.

The statue smiled down at her. Thomasin selected one of the squat, cream candles and ignited its wick against the flame of another. It caught at once, blazing brightly upwards, spreading warmth across her hands. She knelt and placed it in a space at the feet of the Virgin. Into the gloom, she whispered words of love, regret, remembrance and hope for eternal peace, while the carved stone ears listened and the painted eyes bestowed their mercy.

Thomasin rose slowly to her feet.

"Goodbye, Will. God bless you."

The church door behind her opened. Her candle flickered a little in the draught, then flared up bright and tall again. Thomasin turned. Cecilia and Ellen stood waiting, with the green sloping land behind them, and the scent of cut grass.

Taking one final look up at the statue, Thomasin turned towards the summer's day and walked out to join them.

A NOTE TO THE READER

Dear Reader,

Welcome to the world of the Marwood family. Thank you for reading the second instalment of Thomasin's story; I hope you enjoyed it. You may have come to *Troubled Queen* after reading the first book in the series, *Dangerous Lady*, following her debut at court, or started with this one, in which case I hope my snippets of backstory allowed you to understand the origins of Thomasin's unfolding relationships.

The second book in a series has its own challenges. The exciting tasks of introducing characters and establishing their world had already been done, so I now had to do something with them. Fortunately, the actual history is so well documented, that there was plenty going on. So much so that I had to hone my focus and select a limited number of characters, in order to pursue their stories fully.

The narratorial gaze has also shifted a little. With Thomasin becoming a member of Catherine of Aragon's household, her sympathies currently lie firmly with the queen, pushing Anne on the outside, as the "other" woman. This doesn't mean I am pro-Catherine or anti-Anne, it's just where Thomasin is at this point in her journey. Later books will show shifts in her allegiances and perspectives, as she navigates the treacherous waters of the Tudor court. I also chose to centralise Ellen for this book, as an ally for Thomasin, whilst pushing Cecilia into the background, in order for her to recover from her recent ordeal. But fear not, Cecilia will return, stronger than ever and determined to make her mark.

There are three driving forces behind this book's plot. Firstly, I aimed to follow Thomasin's learning curve, in which she negotiates relationships and learns about love and life. Secondly, there is the continuing marital struggle of Henry VIII, Catherine and Anne, which I wanted to explore in all its stages and complexities.

By 1528, Henry had already decided his marriage was over and had secretly proposed to Anne. Yet Catherine was still queen, and almost two decades of court ritual had embedded her position. I wanted to show the human struggle involved, when it came to the gradual separation of two people who had been married for so long, and had once been in love. Feelings do not switch off overnight, and old habits die hard. Catherine was determined to fight for her man, and Henry had not yet arrived at the point where he was prepared to repudiate her in public, still fearing the domestic, spiritual and international consequences of separation. I wanted to depict the court as a battleground where every dinner, every card game, every interaction, offered the opportunity to gain the upper hand and a brief glimmer of hope. It was a mixture of tiny victories and intense pain.

Thirdly, I also wanted to highlight the larger, indiscriminate danger of the sweating sickness and its impact upon Henry's psyche. The hypochondriac king was terrified of being struck down as his elder brother Arthur had been and spent much of summer 1528 fleeing from the dangers, moving between properties and remaining in the countryside. His belief in his astrological predisposition to smallpox and his personal compilation of a book of cures were very real. This was the time when the king wrote his love letters to Anne, during their separation, but letters play a significant role here for other characters too.

Anne Boleyn did contract the sweat and survive, as did her father and Wolsey. Real life historical figures William Compton and William Carey both died in June 1528. There is nothing to suggest an actual romantic connection between Carey and any other lady at court, or that he was distanced from his wife Mary, despite her earlier affair with the king. The secrets of their marriage remain so, but I have interpreted that void for the purposes of Thomasin's story, for the poignancy of her loss and the eternal question of what might have been.

The idea of the randomness of fate, and the indiscriminate nature of the illness, contrasts in this book with the humanist concept of free will, espoused by William Hatton and Thomas More in *Dangerous Lady*. The sweat's return was a brutal reminder of mortality, which no one could escape, no matter what their rank. In this second book, Henry frequently questions God's plan for him, and whether God has rejected him. Catherine tries to reassure him with her cast-iron certainty, but fails to do so in the face of the spreading illness.

Fear of the sweat also threw Henry and Catherine back into each other's company out of practicality, and their shared isolation may have encouraged a false sense of security, which was then shaken by Anne's presence at Greenwich. I see this as a critical stage in the process of Henry's decision to change his life and, later, to break with Rome. The looming threat of the sweating sickness also felt like an appropriate theme for our era of Covid, adding another layer of human connection between us and people of the past.

I am currently writing the third book in the series, *False Mistress*, continuing Thomasin's adventures and the unfolding drama at court. Towards the end of *Troubled Queen*, the seeds are sown for next phase of the royal marital drama and the anticipation of Thomasin's return to court. But what will autumn 1528 hold for her? What, and who, will she find waiting? An increasingly desperate Catherine will stop at nothing to keep her husband, hatching a plan that will put the Marwood family right in the eye of the storm.

Reviews do matter to writers and I would appreciate a review on **Amazon** or **Goodreads**. Often, we're writing in isolation, working in something of a vacuum, living most intensely in our heads, sending manuscripts into the ether. It's lovely to receive feedback and contact from readers, to know our work is being enjoyed and see the ways we can improve when planning our next part of the story. You can contact me **on Twitter** (@PrufrocksPeach. I am a T. S. Eliot fan) via **my author page on Facebook** (Amy Licence Author), or **via my website**.

Kind regards,

Amy Licence

www.amylicence.weebly.com

Sapere Books is an exciting new publisher of brilliant fiction and popular history.

To find out more about our latest releases and our monthly bargain books visit our website: **saperebooks.com**

Made in the USA
Columbia, SC
09 October 2024

44038322R00180